I0542359

TAKEN IN THE NIGHT

The Promise Me Series, Book 3

By

Tara Fox Hall

Tara Fox Hall

Published by
Melange Books, LLC
White Bear Lake, MN 55110
www.melange-books.com

Taken in the Night Copyright © 2013 by Tara Fox Hall

ISBN: 978-1-61235-543-6 Print

Names, characters, and incidents depicted in this book are products of the author's imagination or are used fictitiously. Any resemblance to actual events, locales, organizations, or persons, living or dead, is entirely coincidental and beyond the intent of the author or the publisher. No part of this book may be reproduced or transmitted in any form or by any means, electronic or mechanical, including photocopying, recording, or by any information storage and retrieval system, without permission in writing from the publisher.
Published in the United States of America.

Cover Art by Caroline Andrus

Taken in the Night
Tara Fox Hall

When Theo disappears, Sar is left bereft, the uncertain guardian of Theo's newly born werecougar daughter, Elle. As months pass, clues emerge about Theo's disappearance, yet the twisting trail ends repeatedly without answer. In her grief, Sar turns to Danial and hesitantly begins to build a life with him and Elle.

About the Author

Tara Fox Hall's writing credits include nonfiction, horror, suspense, action-adventure, erotica, and contemporary and historical paranormal romance. She is the author of the paranormal action-adventure *Lash* series and the vampire romantic suspense *Promise Me* series. Tara divides her free time unequally between writing novels and short stories, chainsawing firewood, caring for stray animals, sewing cat and dog beds for donation to animal shelters, and target practice.

Chapter One

Danial's dark brown eyes stared down into mine. I was hyperconscious of his body as it lay on mine; the weight of him, the coolness of his skin, the way we fit together so well.

"Relax, Sar," he whispered, nuzzling my neck with his soft lips. "Let me in."

"I'm trying," I said irritably.

I'd been trying for the last twenty minutes. Yet I remained tense and as pliable as a board.

Danial sighed and rose. He went to the bedroom door and opened it. "Theo, you may as well come in. It's not working."

Theo quickly entered the bedroom and sat next to me on Danial's bed. "Sar, what is it?" he said, giving me a concerned look.

"She's too nervous," Danial said, leaning against the wall and looking at me. "Just like she's been every time we've tried this."

Theo glanced at him, and then back to me as if he didn't know what to say.

I sighed. "I'm sorry. I'm doing my best."

I didn't add I had every reason to be nervous in the presence of a vampire. I'd nearly been exsanguinated on this very bed a little over two months ago by Danial's brother, Devlin. While I'd been saved in time by Theo and a sorcerer half-demon friend of mine, Terian, I still bore two scars on my throat from Devlin's fangs. I wanted them gone. The easiest way was for Danial to bite me in the same exact spot just as deeply, and then use some of his saliva to heal me. That would ensure complete removal. The trouble was the pain would be substantial.

"I haven't even been able to touch you with my fangs, Sar," Danial said, breaking the silence. "You'll never be able to relax enough for me to heal those scars."

"She has every reason to be leery," Theo said defensively. "Just be quiet a minute."

Danial shrugged.

Theo leaned in and hugged me. "Don't worry. You don't have to rush."

I leaned my head on his shoulder. "Thanks."

"He's right," Danial said softly. "Take your time."

I glanced up at him, studying him for a moment.

Danial's hair was back to a little below shoulder length, falling in silky curtains down the sides of his face. It was almost straight with just a hint of a wave in it. His body was tall and lean, with a powerful chest. His face was so sculptured to be almost beautiful, yet the arrogance and sexuality that radiated from him was all male. His skin shone like a pearl, lustrous, which meant he'd fed before Theo and I had arrived. He was dressed in one of his old-fashioned shirts, the red one made of heavy cotton, and some dark jeans. The one he'd promised to wear for me some night when we'd been together.

"You didn't have to dress up," I said meaningfully. "It's only me."

Danial narrowed his eyes and glared back at me. Yet his lips curved into a faint smile, pleased I'd mentioned the shirt.

We had history to put it lightly. Danial had been my lover, and, at one time, we'd been oathed, a.k.a., what vampires called married. It hadn't lasted long, only about twenty-four hours. I'd miscarried our child when I hadn't known I was pregnant and then left him for a while to think things over. When I'd returned, I'd found a rival wearing my clothes in his bed. I'd broken up with him for good then. To make matters worse, I'd fallen in love with his best friend, Theo, shortly after.

"Do you want to come back in a couple days?" Theo gave me a smile.

I gazed back at him, his blue eyes like an overcast day in fall. His strong features had just a hint of feline grace to them. Theo was not beautiful like Danial. He was traditionally handsome with a touch of ruggedness in the cast of his face. While he was almost as tall as Danial, he was far more muscular. He worked out hard almost every other day to be that strong and ensure he could handle whatever or whomever might come looking for trouble with either Danial or with me. He was and, had been, Danial's bodyguard and head of security, as well as Danial's best friend when I first met Danial. He was also a werecougar and had been since he was nineteen. He was still those things only now he was my lover instead of Danial.

Despite how much Theo and I were in love, our coming together had happened entirely by chance. Terian had dosed me with a potion to find out if I liked him. I hadn't, and he'd been okay, if not exactly happy. Later the same night, Theo and I had inadvertently reactivated the potion, revealing his feelings for me and mine for him, feelings we had kept hidden until then, especially from each other. That night, we'd shared a dream of being together, one where we had no limits, guilt, or consequences. In short, in the dream we had done all the things we wanted to do with each other. It had driven Theo half mad, and I'd felt so guilty we'd stayed apart for months afterwards. Then Terian admitted plying me with his spell. He mentioned any dreams I'd had later that night could've been shared by anyone of whom I dreamed. I called Theo, and he'd come to my house. We'd been together ever since.

"Sarelle, do you want to try another day?" Theo spoke again.

"Sorry," I said quickly. "That would be fine."

Theo's phone rang. He flicked it open, his eyes still on me. "Hold on a minute," he said, standing up. "I'll be right back, Sar."

That meant, "Don't do anything with him while I'm gone."

"Okay," I answered.

Theo went out, curiously closing the bedroom door behind him. Wondering why he had, I pushed myself up to a sitting position.

"Sar, you know why this isn't working," Danial said.

"I know," I said heavily. "Because he's right outside the room. I heard you and Angelica having sex that night—"

"You would have to bring up that," he muttered darkly.

"—and I don't want him to hear me moaning, even if we aren't being intimate," I finished.

"Are you worried he'll hear you or that we might go too far?" Danial said seductively.

"Stop it," I said. "There's nothing sexy about this."

"I'm sorry." Danial came over to the bed. He put his arms around me, and I let him, leaning into his shoulder. "I'm worried because you won't be moaning," he whispered anxiously. "I don't want to hurt you. I was always apprehensive about biting you after we'd been together so long that it started hurting you—"

Danial had taken enough blood from me in the months we had been together that I had become resistant to whatever substance it was that numbed pain in his saliva. His blood would still heal me. The problem was Danial had usually only bitten me during sex and used pleasure to offset the pain. I'd hardly felt it. In the best circumstances, it had heightened my arousal the way it did his.

"I know you're scared, too, because of what Devlin did to you—"

Devlin had bitten me deeply with no prep work, not that I'd wanted any from him. I'd been in agony and scared to death. He hadn't cared how much he hurt me because he was trying to kill me at the time.

"Please know I won't bite until you ask," Danial whispered gently. "You have nothing to fear from me."

"I know," I replied. "I'm scared anyway."

"Some of that is your memories of us," he said, kissing my cheek. "They come back to me unbidden when in your arms."

"Yes," I said, resting my head on his shoulder.

"Maybe I'm not the best vampire to remove your scars," he said, tilting my head up to look into my eyes.

"Who else could I trust?" I gave him a smile. "I wouldn't want anyone else to bite me, Danial."

He didn't return the smile. "You're worried about Tawny, too. About how Theo will react when he becomes a father. She is scheduled to give birth in two weeks."

Tawny and Theo had been lovers for years before I came along, getting together whenever he was in Europe. Two months ago, almost six months pregnant, she'd showed up at my door looking for him. The baby was his. She was set to deliver in a few weeks. Danial, Theo, and I were all going to be in Europe for the birth. It made me more than apprehensive.

My smile evaporated. "I'm scared, Danial. Scared he'll want her and not me."

"Your fears are groundless, Sar. He loves you the way I've never seen him love anyone else since I met him. He'll love the child to be sure, but that's as it should be. He isn't going back to her."

"I know, Danial, but I still have this fear—"

"Tell him, Sarelle. Don't keep it from him," Danial said, the old pain in his voice. "If I had shared more of my fears with you and given you a chance to ease them..." He trailed off with a sigh.

Theo came back, slightly mistrustful. "Did you make any progress?"

"No. I think we should forget it for tonight," Danial replied, rising to his feet. "Sar's not ready. If I bite her now, it will hurt her. At worst, she'll have a new scar. We can try again another time."

"Okay," Theo said. He held out a hand for me. "Ready to go?" I took it, and he pulled me to my feet.

"Thanks for trying anyway, Danial," I said.

He nodded once to me and looked away. "Have a good night."

Theo and I left, heading out to Theo's truck. We got in, and he drove us towards home.

"I'm sorry," I said, when we'd reached the road. "That was a waste of time."

Theo took my hand in his. "It's not your fault. I know you're remembering how you got the scars. Without the, um, usual distractions, it's going to be difficult to remove them. Danial understands it, too. This way is easier than surgery and much safer for you. We'll try as many times as it takes."

I lay my head back, closed my eyes, and drifted, listening to the hum of the engine.

8

"You don't have to worry about Devlin either," Theo growled. "He's remained at his estate since being dethroned. No one's seen him since."

That didn't comfort me. Just knowing he was still alive was cause for fear.

Devlin, Danial's older brother, had been turned with him over four hundred years ago. Yet Devlin had been more powerful than Danial for most of their existence. His ability to create vampires was a rarity. At least a century ago, he'd assumed control in the United State.

Since then, Danial had gone along with everything Devlin demanded until it came to me. Even then, Danial had not been powerful enough to fight his brother directly. Devlin had been the Vampire Ruler of the United States until recently. Then, Danial had taken his blood and his power with it. Devlin blamed me for his fall from influence. I'd seen it in his golden eyes that night. He was not the type to forgive or forget.

"Terian is going to stop by later, isn't he?" Theo said.

"No, he said he's too busy to do dinner anytime soon."

Terian had moved in a little south of Theo and me, and was currently living with a woman he called Sundown. He claimed he was only looking for fun, but, the way he talked about her, he was beginning to love her. I was happy for him. He'd been alone a long time. It was high time he got a break.

"Want to pick up some takeout?" Theo offered.

"Sure," I said gratefully.

* * * *

The two weeks flashed by. All too soon, the three of us were boarding the plane for Europe. I was apprehensive about the visit and not just because of Tawny. Last time I'd been to Europe, a man had accosted me in the hotel's Jacuzzi, and an unknown vampire had come to my rescue, scaring him off. Despite not being harmed, I was not eager for any more adventures. That trip had lasted only a couple of nights. This trip would last a week, far more time for mishaps to happen.

My boss hadn't been crazy about it. After I explained some of the particulars—boyfriend plus another woman, married, equaled a baby being born in another county—he told me to take the time, but to be prepared to come in extra the next week. I didn't argue. He'd been flexible about my hours when I'd needed it. I owed him a lot for letting me work part time anyway.

Danial, accompanied by Lander, one of his bodyguards, met Theo and I at the airstrip at dusk. Lander was prone to suggestive remarks.

"We'll be racing the dawn the whole way," Danial said irritably, buckling his seatbelt. "Lander, get some sleep. You'll need to be awake most of the next few days."

The plane lifted off in a few moments. As soon as we were airborne, Theo and Danial began to discuss the cases and meetings they would be handling in

9

the coming week. I tried not to listen in on the business end. It really wasn't my business anymore; it was Danial's. Yet my ears picked up enough to get an idea of the danger they faced.

One of Danial's meetings was with the CEO of a company called Gemini GmBH. The CEO suspected a rival company had murdered Gemini's COO, a close, personal friend of his. He'd hired Solutions, Inc., Danial's company, to find the murderer and deal with him—no police, no court, just justice.

I didn't know how I felt about Theo and Danial being the dispensers of said justice. In terms of Danial, it wasn't my business anymore. As for Theo, he had done this type of work when I met him. Adding to that, was his new ranking of number five in the who's who of the bodyguarding world. Theo had made it clear when we got together that this was his life, and he wasn't going to give up what he did. One of the driving reasons was his righteousness was fairness was so important to him. He'd spoken to me bitterly of more than a few past cases where justice had fallen by the wayside, undermined by the law. I was contemplating the pros and cons of private justice when I fell asleep.

I awakened when we touched down. The jolt of the wheels snapped me from my slumber. After a hurried drive to the hotel, we checked in and made our way upstairs to our suite. I quickly drew the curtains in Danial's room, he went inside, and then Theo and I crashed in the other bedroom. We were both too tired to do anything more than sleep though Theo teased me that tomorrow night he'd make it up to me.

We slept the day away, waking at the night. After dressing, Theo and Danial went out to attend their first meeting, and I stayed in and watched some TV. I wasn't about to wander around without a chaperone at night, especially because this time I wasn't wearing the proper identification on my neck, a.k.a, a mystical choker that signified a human belonged to a particular vampire.

I'd worn one while dating Danial, at his request. It had been made of gold with his symbol, a fox head charm adorned with ruby eyes. I'd brought it along at Theo's urging in case I needed to go out at night. It seemed senseless because Danial was the only one who could fasten or remove it. There was no way I was letting myself be "collared" again, not even for a gourmet dinner. Bringing it had been easier than fighting with Theo.

Danial returned at midnight, but Theo didn't. With barely a hello, Danial went back out to feed. Disgruntled, I dozed, only to be awoken by Theo's phone call at two in the morning.

"Hi, Sar. Tawny has gone into labor early. She's having a difficult time, at least that's what the doctors say. I wanted to tell you so you weren't worried."

"How long will it last? Is she close to giving birth?"

"They don't know. They think in the next few hours, maybe more. They're afraid to speed up her delivery, but they're also afraid to stop it."

10

"Okay," I replied, not knowing what else to say.

"Stay with Danial. He'll keep you safe. He's back, right?"

"He went out to feed, but I'll tell him what you said if that's what you're asking."

"What I'm telling you is not to go outside by yourself. Danial told me about the strange vampire you met last time you were here. I don't want you leaving the room unless Danial or I are with you. You don't have any marks, or a collar, or a ring now."

When he said it like that, I felt bad, as if I'd lost something. I reminded myself I'd fought to get free of all that. I couldn't have it both ways.

"Sar, tell me you'll stay in the room."

"Okay, Theo," I replied. "I'll do that."

"I love you," he said.

"I love you, Theo. Goodbye."

I sat by the phone for a while, but no one called, and Danial did not return. Grumpy, I went back to bed, dozing fitfully.

About three a.m., Theo called again.

"Sar?" he said, excited and proud.

Part of my heart broke hearing how happy he was. "I'm here, Theo," I said, trying to sound normal.

"It's a girl. She's so beautiful."

I'd thought that tone was reserved only for me. My heart broke a little more, realizing it wasn't any longer. "Is Tawny okay?" I managed.

Theo didn't reply.

An ominous feeling flooded me. "Theo, what happened?" I said, alarmed.

"Tawny's in bad shape," he said reluctantly. "My child was born cougar, not human. They don't know why, maybe something about us both not being the same type of werecat." Theo swallowed hard. "It ripped her up coming out."

Pity swept me. "Oh my God, Theo, I'm so sorry—"

"She's not stable yet, but that's not the worst," he said hesitantly. "She didn't tell him, Sar. The doctor came out with the baby and asked where the father was for Tawny's child, and both I and another man stood up. Her husband wanted to know who the hell I was. Then he saw the baby, saw my cougar markings, saw it wasn't an African lion like him." Theo paused.

"He tried to fight me. I defended myself, and now he's downstairs in the ER, waiting to heal up a knife wound."

"That's awful," I said compassionately. "What if he comes after you again?"

"He won't. He said he's done with Tawny and with the baby. Look, I'm going to stay here until she pulls through. I most likely won't be back until tomorrow afternoon, maybe tomorrow night. Please stay with Danial, and don't leave the room."

As much as I was frustrated by another day in this room, I couldn't refuse. "I will. Are you going to be okay?"

"Yes, absolutely. I never expected to feel this way," Theo said in wonder. "I love her already, though they say I can't hold her yet. She's so tiny—"

The rest of my heart broke, consumed by resentment. "I'll see you when you get back," I said quickly. "Bye."

I was crying as soon as I hung up the phone. I'd known he'd feel like this, so excited, so in love with his child. Danial had been right, it was natural. It would have been different if it were my child. I could've shared that pride with him for our child, and that sense of wonder and joy. Instead I was on the outside looking in, the jealousy and bitterness overwhelmed me.

On cue, Danial came back to the room and found me sobbing on the couch. He didn't ask what was wrong. He picked me up and carried me into his bedroom. He laid me down on the bed beside him and stroked my hair. I held him as tight as I could and tried to cry it all out. When my tears were done and I lay exhausted in his arms, a deep resentment still burned inside me.

"Danial, try again to undo the scars," I whispered.

"Why?" Danial said wearily, our heads a few inches apart on his pillow. "What makes you think tonight will be any different?"

"Do what you did the night you removed my oathing marks," I said. "That worked for them. It's worth a try." I leaned closer to him, and kissed him gently.

"Sar, you're playing a dangerous game," Danial said derisively, pulling away from me. "I won't be your instrument of reprisal. You'll blame me later for this."

"I'm sorry, Danial," I said hastily. Very ashamed, I bolted for the door.

Danial called for me to wait. Upset, I shut the door on his words and went into my bathroom. A quick glance in the mirror confirmed my eyes were still red from crying. Wonderful. I took a long shower, telling myself it would make me feel better. Yet when I emerged, my eyes were still that bright green color of new grass in spring, a telltale sign of my sobbing. Disheartened, I put on a hotel robe, ordered room service, and ate some pancakes and bacon. What the hell, I hadn't eaten all day, and I was starving.

Danial came out of his room while I was finishing eating. Still embarrassed for my behavior, I didn't look at him.

"If you want me to try now, I'll try," Danial said heavily.

I looked up at him hesitantly. "I'm sorry," I said, flushing. "I shouldn't have asked—"

"It is I who shouldn't have refused, Sar. We'll never get a better chance."

He held out his hand to me. "Come."

Danial led me into his bedroom and shut the door behind us. He embraced me and then leaned gently forward. We lay back on the bed, his hands easing us down. Immediately, I tensed.

He chuckled. "Relax, my clothes are staying on, much as I might want to remove them," he said seductively. "Work with me."

He leaned forward and kissed me. His hair brushed my cheek. His signature scent of nutmeg and cedar wafted from it. Instantly aroused, I kissed him back. He pulled me tight against him with a groan, and the dam inside me broke loose, remembering all the times he'd been like this with me, all the times I'd kissed him, wanted him, and loved him.

I wrapped my legs around him and slid my tongue into his mouth. He shuddered slightly and then pressed down with his hips, showing me what I was doing to him. I let out a gasp, pushing my hips up to meet his, rubbing against his hardness. His insistent kisses moved from my mouth to my cheek, then traveled down toward my neck. My breath came rapidly, my chest heaving. He kissed one of the scars and then sucked gently, as his hand slipped beneath my robe to cup my breast. I threw my head back with a loud eager cry, arching my back.

Danial struck fast, sinking his fangs into me. I jerked, my cry half arousal, half pain. Danial groaned, his sighs of pleasure muffled as he drank from me. Abruptly, he withdrew, holding his mouth over the wound. The pain suddenly eased, and I went limp in his arms.

He drew back from me, his eyes almost black with desire. "I've taken one. I don't want to risk doing both in one night. They're too deep."

"Thank you," I said breathily and drew him down for another kiss.

Danial pulled away from me, rolling onto his back to lie beside me.

I reached for his hand and held it gently. "Thank you."

Danial didn't reply. We stayed like that for some time, and gradually, our breathing slowed. I fell asleep, holding his hand, our bodies just touching.

When I woke up about an hour later, the dynamic had changed. Now Danial's arms were wrapped around me. I was sleeping in the hollow of his throat, his chest against mine. I reached up and stroked his face, remembering how vulnerable he'd always looked when he was asleep. I ran my fingers through his hair, feeling its softness. I curled a strand around my finger absently and then let it go. He didn't stir.

"Danial," I said with light accusation. "You aren't sleeping."

He opened his eyes. In their darkness, desire still burned. "I was enjoying your touch. I didn't want to ruin it." He moved slightly against me, repositioning his weight.

"I need to go shower," I said, beginning to rise.

"Don't go yet, Sar," Danial said beseechingly. "Stay here with me. Let me hold you, as we sleep."

Hearing how much he missed me, I didn't have the will to refuse. I looked up at him, nodded once, and settled back down into his arms. We slept that way until morning.

I left Danial sleeping soundly and went to take another shower. Theo was going to be irritated enough to have missed my mark being healed. He would be more irritated if I was covered in Danial's scent.

I showered, dressed, and then tossed the hotel robe I'd been wearing in the hotel's laundry chute. I checked out my reflection, eager to see the mark was indeed gone.

It was. A single bite mark adorned my neck now. Maybe Danial could do that one tomorrow.

I was also pleased to see I looked like my normal self again. My hair was a dark golden brown, all one length, falling in loose waves to my waist. My eyes had gone back to their normal sea green color. Yet the hardness in my eyes and my movements were at odds with my fair looks. Some of it was what I'd been through in my life—widowed at aged thirty and the hard physical work that went with country living and working in a metal fabrication shop. The rest was from all Theo's defensive training, like the correct use of firearms.

I brushed out my long hair, remembering our first big fight about that.

He couldn't understand why I practiced only sporadically with my gun. From then on, he made a point to make me practice with both the gun he'd given me, which could take out almost anything, my regular .38, and the shotgun. I'd been enthusiastic at first, but as the weeks passed and more and more time was consumed by gun practice, especially with the barrel cleaning afterward, my enthusiasm waned.

Finally, one weekend I blew my stack. "Really, I understand you needing to practice for your job, but why do I need to, at least this much?"

"You are going to practice until you can hit exactly what you're aiming at least most of the time." He glared angrily at me. "Your enemies aren't always going to think you're no threat or present themselves to you as targets."

"I know I got lucky when Devlin attacked. I understand you wanting me to be able to protect myself, but—"

"No buts, Sar. You are going to do this, like it or not," he said, folding his arms across his chest. "Now let's start again with the .38."

I relented and dutifully practiced with him every weekend. My aim did improve, too, as he'd said I would. I also felt better about myself and more capable of dealing with an attacker than I had. Even so, those benefits didn't stop me from grumbling now and again.

I wandered about the suite for an hour, restless. I could only watch so much TV or read and I wasn't hungry. Finally, I went back in and curled up next to Danial, sleep my only option left.

I awoke to Danial softly kissing me.

"Sar," he said softly, his cool lips brushing my cheek. "Wake up. It's after five p.m."

"How did you sleep?" I asked, giving him a smile.

"Wonderfully, with you beside me," he said, nuzzling me. He drew back abruptly. "Why are you still beside me?" he said in confusion. "Have you slept the day here?"

"Theo isn't back yet," I said, exasperated. "His baby was born, a girl."

"And Tawny?"

"She's in bad shape" I said. "The baby hurt her coming out because it was in its animal form."

"That should not have happened," Danial said, wide-awake and strangely upset. He rose and keyed the phone before I had both feet on the floor.

"Theo? Yes, what happened? Sar's right here, she's fine. What happened?"

Danial listened in silence for a while and then nodded. "Yes, I'll take care of her. Take your time. Most of these meetings I can go to alone anyway," he said reassuringly. "They're in the early evening, in public places. Just watch yourself."

Danial shut his phone with a click and then strode into the other room. I followed him. He went to the suite door and opened it. Lander was sitting outside in a chair, leafing through a magazine.

"Anything?" Danial asked.

"Nothing's happening," Lander replied. "All quiet."

Danial shut the door and took my hand, pulling me with him to the couch.

"Sar, what happened to Tawny should not have happened," he said earnestly. "Part of the problem is the baby seems to have developed too fast. That may be a problem because of the interspecies mating, or just a problem with this particular pregnancy."

"Danial, why are you telling me this?" I said flatly.

"Because Theo is probably going to want another child now he sees what a joy they can be," Danial replied, sad and wistful. "I don't want you to be afraid."

He was thinking of his son, dead these many years and perhaps of our child, who never even got to be celebrated before it was gone. Yet he was also leaping to conclusions.

"Danial, you are getting ahead of the game here," I said with a little irritation. "Tawny's a wreck, and she's werelion. My body is mortal. I won't heal like she can, and she's still on the verge of dying even with her regenerative power." I paused. "Theo and I haven't even talked about marriage, much less kids."

Danial got to his feet. "You're right," he said coolly. "What matters is Theo is going to stay there with her, and I need to attend a meeting. Lander will need to come with me. Are you going to be okay here by yourself?"

Fear of being left completely alone, a prisoner in this hated room, made me erupt.

"And Theo wondered why I didn't want to come," I said sarcastically. "Not only am I waiting to see if he's is going to leave me for the mother of his child, I'm also alone, with nothing to distract me from thinking about it! I'm glad I spent a week's vacation on this little trip."

Danial looked at me dubiously, and his eyes narrowed. "I understand you're upset. That is not what I asked you. Will you promise not to leave this room?"

"I promise," I replied with a sigh. "Just hurry back. I'm going stir crazy in here."

Danial hugged me, kissed me lightly, and then left. I felt a momentary twinge of guilt and then rationalized that the kiss had been to reassure me.

I made sure the door was locked and took a long bath, listening to a few CDs I'd brought on the high-class stereo system. The sound was phenomenal, although the hardware made me feel dated. It was about two cubic feet and looked like a shiny metal cube. Technology had come a long way since I'd listened to music in my youth.

I was luxuriating in the bath when a noise came from the other room. I froze, listening. If I'd have been home, I'd have guessed it was one of my cats, or maybe one of the dogs, but there weren't any pets here.

The noise came again, closer this time. Cold fear drenched all my nerve endings.

The door suddenly opened to reveal Theo.

"Sar?" he said in a tired voice.

I eased back into the water, relief making me limp. "Come in," I said, beckoning. "There's enough room. I'll let some of the water out."

Theo shed his clothes and sank into the tub. "Ahh," he groaned. "This feels so good." He looked at me apologetically. "I'm going to have to cut this short. I'm beat."

"Go ahead," I replied, rising from the water and grabbing a towel. "It's all yours."

I dried off and then climbed into bed. Theo came out in a few minutes, slid into bed and embraced me hungrily, raining kisses over my face.

"Wait," I said forcefully, pushing him away. "Stop."

"What is it?" he said, worried.

"I haven't seen you for more than a day," I replied. "You have a child now. I need to talk to you before we have sex."

His eyes narrowed a little. "You're right; we should talk. You seem to be missing one of your scars, Sar. I'd like to hear about that."

I really wanted to fight with him then. What right did he have to be angry? I'd gotten these scars because he hadn't been there with me when Devlin came for me because he'd been with Tawny, just as he had been tonight. Instead, I bit my lip and made myself answer him.

"I asked Danial to try again. It worked."

Theo stared at me. "It didn't go farther than kissing, right?"

"Was I turned on? Yes. Did we do anything, in terms of clothes coming off? No."

He sighed. "I believe you. I'm sorry I overreacted. I'm just upset."

"Will you tell me about what happened?"

"Tawny's doing better, but like I told Danial, she's pretty ripped up inside. Even if she makes it though this, she'll never have another child. Never." He paused.

"Sar, they had trouble stopping her bleeding. It was like when you were bleeding, only worse. There was so much blood, and I could do nothing. The worst was I did this to her. I caused her to suffer this way." He swallowed. "Do you know how awful it makes me feel?"

"It's not your fault," I murmured.

Theo kissed me suddenly and then rolled me over, straddling me with something akin to desperation. I kissed him back, his hard muscles bunching under my fingers as I pulled him closer to me. He moved his hips deftly and slid inside me. I let out a small cry, which he quieted with a kiss. Then he was moving within me quickly, kissing me, his strokes purposeful. I basked in his energetic attention as the familiar sensations engulfed me.

Theo's lovemaking was usually incredible, an intense ecstasy that engulfed like a tidal wave racing to its conclusion. Always, this wave receded and then shortly returned, breaking over me again and again. Some nights our recurring encounters were almost too much pleasure. Tonight, I wanted nothing more than for him to consume me utterly. To my surprise, he fell asleep in my arms only a few moments after we'd begun.

I hugged him close, comforted by his even breathing. Then guilty thoughts descended to torture me.

Danial and Theo had both been tortured by the sight of a pregnant woman suffering. Both of them had created life and not meant to. Yet I'd blamed Danial then as easily as I'd forgiven Theo a few moments ago.

I lay there a few more moments. Then, I carefully got up and slipped on a robe. There was no point lying here restively, I wasn't the least bit tired.

Danial returned from his meeting as I came out of the bedroom.

"Lander said Theo came back."

"Yes, he's sleeping," I said awkwardly, trying to put aside my guilty thoughts.

"Get him up if you can," Danial said wearily, sitting on the couch. "I should sleep soon and need to know if he's going to be around or if he's going back to the hospital."

I went back in the bedroom, and roused Theo, who was none too happy to have had only a few minutes sleep. He put on a robe, staggered out to Danial and filled him in on Tawny's condition.

"You have your child, Theo. That's what matters," Danial replied, putting his hand on Theo's shoulder.

"By the way, Danial," Theo said anxiously, "I'll need your help."

"With what?" Danial said cautiously.

"Getting Elle home."

Both Danial's mouth and mine dropped open.

Danial glanced at me and then back to Theo. "I thought Tawny wanted the child?" he said cautiously.

"You named her Elle after me?" I asked in wonder.

"Yes," Theo said, giving me a warm look. "It was the first thing that came to mind."

I was so floored I couldn't reply.

Theo turned back to Danial. "Tawny does want the child, but I'm afraid to leave her here. I love her already, Danial, I'm desperately afraid something will happen to her. Tawny's still critical, and she's not up to taking care of Elle. I know with Sar and me, she'll be safe."

I moved to the nearby chair and sank into it, my legs suddenly weak. Theo wanted to bring his child home with us to live. Everything would change if he did that. I'd feared this almost as much as I'd feared him falling in love with Tawny again. Yet with Tawny so bad, what other choice was there?

"Theo, how long will it be until she changes form?" Danial stared at him.

"I don't know," Theo said, shrugging. "This is the first time I've heard of a were-baby being born in animal form to a were-mother in human form. The doctor who delivered Elle said he'd never seen this before either. Tawny never had an ultrasound, so no one knew. They weren't prepared."

"We could maybe ship her in on a commercial flight in baggage—" Danial began.

"I'm not putting her alone in some plane's baggage hold—" Theo retorted.

"There is no way we are going to be able to sneak a cougar cub onto an aircraft, even one of my chartered ones," Danial said, exasperated. "Even then, customs, the airport, and a slew of other authorities are going to want to know where she came from! She'll need real shots, in addition to forged papers. Why didn't you mention you wanted her to come back with us?"

"I didn't plan on taking her home," Theo replied, desperate. "You know that, but I can't leave Elle here. I can't stay here with her for a few years, hoping she'll change form. I've got to bring her back to the United States. The doctor at the hospital is a friend of Tawny's husband. He's covering the bases with the hospital and taking care of the paperwork, making sure she's got a birth certificate and the normal human baby shots. For a price, he said he could forge some other documents for me showing she was orphaned in the wild and is destined for a zoo. I've paid for him to give her animal shots already."

"He's Tawny's husband's friend. Why would he help you or the baby?" I said, confused.

"Despite the circumstances, he wants what's best for the baby and knows it is not to stay here with a critical mother and a stepfather that already doesn't want her," Theo replied angrily. "I can't believe you two could think I'd let that happen with how things stand now."

Danial met his gaze and then looked away, rubbing his hands over his face. "Okay, Theo," he said in capitulation. "Let me make a few calls." He snapped open his phone and began pacing, dialing as he moved. Then he spoke once more to Theo, without turning around. "Meanwhile, I need you tomorrow night. We will leave at dusk."

Theo nodded. "Fine. I'm going to get some sleep." He headed back towards the bedroom.

I sat there with my head in my hands awhile, thinking. Finally, I went to bed, too. What was the point in staying up?

I crawled in next to Theo, who was asleep. An hour later, lulled by his slow deep breathing, I slept.

* * * *

I woke at dusk to find Danial and Theo had already left for their meeting. Irritated, I resolved never again to go on a trip overseas with them again, no matter what the reason.

I couldn't handle pancakes again, so I ordered some fettuccine. After devouring the entire plate, I showered and got dressed, resolving to go for a walk to the lobby. I peeked outside the door hesitantly. Lander was there, still in his chair, looking bored.

He noticed me at once. "What is it, Sar?" he said, trying not to look at me.

"Lander, just look at me, why don't you?" I said, frustrated. "No one cares what you did or said in Danial's kitchen half a year ago."

My words pricked his pride. His head came up, and he looked me square in the eye. "Fine, Sar, what do you want?" he said flatly.

"Better," I said approvingly. "I want you to escort me downstairs. I want to work out, sit in the lobby, or just walk the hallways. I've been in this room for three days and nights."

"Danial instructed me not to let you leave the room, even with me," Lander said apologetically. "Theo said the same thing. Sorry."

I swore and went back inside. "Some fucking vacation."

I paced for a while, fuming. I tried to calm myself, rationalizing Theo had thought he'd be around, not holding Tawny's hand in a hospital. Thinking about that, I wondered if at this moment he was sitting by her bedside holding her hand. That image gave me a slow burn, after all she had done to ruin us.

I took a deep breath and let it out. There was no point in getting angry, at least not while there was no one here to yell at. Resigned, I opened my book and lost myself in its pages.

About an hour later, at approximately eleven, the phone rang. I picked it up, hoping it was for me.

"Hello?"

"Sar, it's me." It was Danial, sounding uncertain.

"What?" I said, apprehensive. "Is something wrong?"

"No. Theo and I did a little recon. We're planning on hitting the guy tomorrow night. It should be relatively easy," Danial replied, relieved.

I grimaced. I didn't want to know about hits. When we were together, Danial had promised to give up this kind of work. Yet he'd gone back readily enough to it when I left him. That meant Theo was involved with it, too.

"Sar?"

"Okay," I said, reaching for words that weren't disapproving. "That's good for you."

"Theo went back to the hospital, but he feels bad you've been stuck here in the hotel for days." Danial paused. "Have you eaten yet?"

"Yes, I got room service."

"Then would you want to go out with me tonight?" Danial said hesitantly. "We could do something fun."

He didn't have to ask me twice. I didn't care where we were going, so long as I got out of this room. "Yes," I said very quickly. "What should I wear? How long do I have?"

"Something you can dance in, of course," Danial said, relaxed and suddenly happy. "Casual dress is fine. I'll be there in about twenty minutes."

Hanging up, I shed my jeans and old shirt, went quickly to my suitcase, and tried to decide what to wear. There was only one thing suitable—the red dress. I picked it up, smoothing it out. It was a Lycra cotton blend, perfect for traveling and conforming flatteringly to my shape. It also happened to be the dress I'd worn for Danial when we'd went out dancing back when we were dating. I'd brought it in case I'd needed to get dressed up and also as payback for Danial for wearing that red shirt of his when he was trying to heal my scars at his house.

I slipped it over my head and smoothed it down over my hips. It still looked good on me.

Taking out a small box from my suitcase, I opened it to reveal the fox head choker and the earrings that matched it. Though my conscience told me it was wrong, I dumped the box out onto the sink and put on the fox head earrings. Their ruby eyes winked at me the way they had all those months ago on Christmas Eve, the night I'd given myself to Danial. Why not wear them? They were the nicest earrings I owned. When else would I get the chance?

The choker I left on the edge of the sink, the gold shining in the overhead bathroom light, the ruby eyes of the fox sparkling.

Studying my reflection, I decided to fluff up my hair. I put my hands in the roots—the way a good witch friend of mine had showed me to—and pulled lightly, slowly, all the way back and through, murmuring a few words under my breath. My hair fluffed up, as if I'd just washed it, some of the curl returning to the bottom.

I studied myself in the mirror. Pretty sweet. I still owed Tatiana big time for showing me that little trick. As I was congratulating myself on my appearance, it occurred to me with something like shock I'd never fluffed up my hair for Theo.

I also never wore the sexier things for him either, like bustiers or garters, because he preferred me naked. Theo was loving and sexy, but he wasn't seductive. Danial was, and his seductiveness brought out my own. I enjoyed flirting with him, knowing he still desired me, but was that fair to Danial? He didn't have someone to burn off all the lust we generated together. I had Theo.

I was again ashamed. What exactly was I trying to prove, dressing like this? I should take off the dress and wear something else. Danial didn't need a reminder of what he'd lost…

There was a knock at the door.

Shit. I wasn't going to have a chance to change the dress now. I did remove the earrings quickly, leaving them on the sink, before I hurried to the door.

To my shock, it was not Lander standing there, Danial, or even Theo. It was the vampire I'd met by the side of a Swiss hotel Jacuzzi almost seven months ago, the courteous one who had saved me from a jerk who'd crossed the line between annoying and dangerous.

He was facing away from me, pondering some artwork across the hall from the doorway. It was a different hotel, a different city, even a different country, but it was him, without a doubt. I had maybe a few seconds before he turned around and saw me.

Why hadn't Lander said something? Where was Lander?

The man turned around with a quick motion and saw me. Recognition dawned in his eyes immediately.

"Good evening, Lady," he said, his blue eyes locking on mine.

Chapter Two

I stared at the vampire. He stared back, curious, clearly trying to remember where he'd seen me before.

"You," he said, after a moment with a trace of surprise. "You were the Lady I met that night in Switzerland, by the Jacuzzi—"

"Yes," I said quietly. "My thanks again for your assistance. My name is Sarelle."

"I'm Samuel." He reached for my hand and kissed it, his eyes holding mine. "I'm looking for Racklan," he said, dropping my hand gently. "Is he here?"

"I thought you were him," I said smoothly. "I am waiting for him to return."

"I'll escort you downstairs to the lobby," Samuel offered, extending his elbow elegantly. "You will be safe with me. I promise you, we will not leave the hotel, Sarelle. You should not be alone, even in your hotel room. These are dangerous times."

"I had a guard—" I began.

"Who has left you alone for at least the last five minutes," Samuel interrupted darkly. "Much can happen in five minutes, Lady. Need I say more, or may we leave?"

"Thank you," I said nervously, not knowing how to refuse his offer. I took a step forward.

"Aren't you forgetting something?" he said, a hard question in his tone.

"Yes," I stammered, more than a little panicked. "Thank you. Excuse me for a moment, please."

I retreated into the bathroom and grabbed the choker, holding it to my throat with trembling fingers. I'd almost died to get it off. Now I might be dead if I couldn't get it to stay on.

I'd never attempted putting it on myself. Still, I had to try. I put the choker around my neck and brought the ends together. Nothing happened.

"Shit!" I swore vehemently

"Sarelle?" Samuel called. "Is everything alright in there?"

"I'll be right out," I called back.

I held the choker tightly around my neck, bringing the ends together again, and envisioned the ends reaching for one another, wrapping around each other, fastening to complete the circle. Closing my eyes, I shouted mentally PLEASE GOD, LET THIS WORK!

There was a soft sliding sound of metal on metal. Fingers shaking, I took away my hands, then looked into the mirror. My shoulders slumped with relief.

There was another knock at the door. "Sarelle?"

I grabbed the earrings and my purse, bolting for the door. I hurriedly put them on, then opened the door. "Sorry about that. I'd lost one of my earrings under the bed."

"That sometime happens," Samuel said, nodding, a faint grin on his face.

Heat reddened my cheeks. I didn't reply.

Samuel beamed at me. "Your blush becomes you. You look lovely, my dear," he said, again offering me his arm. "Shall we go?"

I locked the door behind me, took his arm, and we rode the elevator down. Samuel was silent. I contemplated what small talk to make with him, remembered his silence by the Jacuzzi that night, and decided not to speak. I had enough to think about anyway, like where in the hell was Lander?

The hotel elevator reached the lobby floor, and we disembarked. To my abject relief, Danial had just come through the double doors and was striding towards us. He noticed me in the next second, pausing as his eyes took in the dress, the choker and the earrings. Desire flared briefly. When he saw my escort, his eyes narrowed as he moved quickly to intercept us.

"Racklan," Samuel said, dropping my arm and holding out his hand. "I'm Samuel. I know you must have heard of me, now you've become Ruler in the States."

"I am glad to see you, Samuel," Danial said smoothly, taking hold of my arm to draw me to his side and slightly behind him. "Sarelle told me what you did for her that night. I'm grateful, and I have long wanted to thank you."

I had to be looking at the Ruler of France, if not of Europe. I held my breath and squeezed Danial's arm with a death grip.

"It's no more than you would have done for any oathed female you saw in your travels, Lord," Samuel said with a slight nod of appreciation. "I merely did what is expected of a gentleman."

Danial held out his hand. "Please call me Danial or Racklan if you must, Samuel. That is formal enough. It's good to finally meet you."

They shook hands and then stood apart from one another, sizing each other up while still appearing sociable.

"Danial, I'm here about the Jonas murder you're working on," Samuel said next, switching topics without preamble. "It is in my interest that the killer be caught and punished. So I'm here to offer what help you need while you're here, one Ruler to another."

Danial's face registered surprise and then quickly smoothed into a casual smile as he regained his composure. "I thank you, but it has been handled already. Justice was done this very night by my own hand."

"Then I thank you," Samuel said, offering him a business card. "Still, call me if you need any help while you are in my territory."

Danial took the card, pocketed it, and offered Samuel one of his own business cards.

Samuel took it. "Are you off dancing?"

"Yes," Danial said, smiling politely. "Sarelle loves to dance and so do I."

"If you have time then, please try a place called Hyde. I own it, and, if you show the card I gave you, they'll make sure you have a great time."

"Thanks," Danial said with a smile, "We'll stop by later tonight."

Samuel turned to go and then turned back, his light blue eyes locked on Danial. "Racklan, please excuse my forwardness and understand it is out of concern. Your Sarelle should not be without her choker. I understand taking it off to feed from her, but she could be in danger, especially if you leave her unattended."

"I left her guarded," Danial replied evenly. He turned to me. "Lander left you alone?"

"I'm not sure," I said worriedly. "He wasn't at the door."

"Then I thank you for watching over Sarelle for me yet again," Danial said cordially to Samuel. "I will address the matter of the guard."

"There are a lot of newer vampires who would not pause at her scar, especially as she seems to be missing the other one," Samuel continued, as if Danial hadn't spoken.

Samuel clearly wanted to know why I was missing my right scar, one he had seen with his own eyes less than a year ago. I shifted uneasily.

"It was my fault, Samuel," Danial replied easily. "In my exuberance to get going tonight, I forgot to help her put it back on, after our loveplay. As for her oathing marks, that it not your business, though I appreciate your candor. Be assured Sarelle will wear her choker from now on anywhere outside the bedroom."

"She managed to put it on herself tonight," Samuel said curiously, smiling. "Adieu." He gave my hand a final kiss and left, striding out the lobby doors onto the street.

My knees went weak with relief, as I held onto Danial.

"Come, Sar," Danial said gently, escorting me outside to the waiting limo. "Let's get out of here."

When we were sitting inside, I leaned into him. He put his arm around me, even as he dialed his cell phone with the other hand.

"Lander," he said sharply. "Where are you? Get your ass up and go guard my room. Don't leave your post again, not for any reason." He hung up abruptly, then hugged me hard. "I should've brought Ivan. He's had more experience."

"I'm fine," I said, regaining my composure. "What does Samuel rule?"

"Europe," Danial said with a sigh. "He's one of the oldest and most influential vampires around. I hope I played my cards right."

"You sounded fine," I assured him.

"Why did you leave the room with him?" he abruptly demanded.

"What was I supposed to do?" I said angrily. "If he'd wanted to bite me before, he could have. I was worried when Lander wasn't there."

"He'll be sleeping in the room in front of the door for the rest of the trip," Danial said grumpily. "Theo can discipline him later." He lay back on the seat. "I must have looked like an absolute idiot."

"You and me both," I retorted. "Thank God the choker worked for me."

"How did you manage that?" Danial said curiously, sitting up and examining the back of my choker. "I thought you'd wired it together under your hair."

"That's what Samuel thought, too, probably, but I got it to fasten by imagining it weaving itself together, binding the two sides into one."

"You should not have had the power to make it fasten by yourself, just as you should not be able to remove it," Danial said. "I'll want to try something with you later on."

"Sure," I agreed. "Now where are we going?"

"Hyde." Soon the limo stopped. "We're here," Danial said, offering me his hand.

I didn't take it. "Isn't it dangerous? Shouldn't we go somewhere else—?"

"Sar, we have to make an appearance here tonight so he has no reason to take offense. He is Ruler of Europe, and it is customary when one Ruler enters the territory of another to let him know. It is not a surprise he wanted to meet me now I have become a member of the ruling class." He sighed. "Besides, this was our planned destination anyway."

Reluctantly, I gave Danial my hand and followed him to the head of the line. We showed the bouncer the card. He didn't even ask us for the admission charge. He just opened the gate and let us inside.

The place was huge. There was a central bar area at least a few thousand square feet. Two staging areas for bands in different rooms were off either side, each with a live band playing. Danial and I gravitated towards the softer music, and, again, he showed the hostess at the door our card. We were quickly escorted to a private table overlooking the dance floor and the stage. Thirty seconds later, a server came to ask us what we wanted. I ordered a glass of Shiraz, and Danial declined. Yet when the server returned in a few minutes with a glass of Shiraz for me, she had a pretty woman in tow, dressed in a simple black party dress. The server put the glass of wine in front of me, and the woman sat down next to Danial.

I sipped my wine. Whatever brand it was, it was excellent—very full-bodied, with currants and berries, and an exceptional finish. I sat back, savoring it, as I watched Danial. All his attention was focused on the woman.

"Why are you here?" he said to her. The words were a question, but his voice implied he already knew the answer.

"You know why, sir," she replied, neither sarcastic nor light.

"What is your name?" he said, bloodlust and interest in his tone.

"You don't need to know—" she began in that same respectful, yet firm tone.

"I will know beforehand, and you will tell me," Danial said arrogantly. "Now."

"Jeannette," she said, meeting his eyes. She offered him her open hand. "As much as you need."

By the way she said it so casually, this was her job. Samuel or one of his men had sent her to us so Danial would not have to bother hunting tonight. It was thoughtful, yet creepy, at least to me.

Danial was grateful, but also wary. "Are you safe?" he asked. "I sense you were bitten recently. I'm sure you know there are still some diseases that can affect me, if an infected vampire bit you within the last twenty four hours."

"Any health information you would like to see is on file here," Jeannette said. "The manager can show you any paperwork you require. We are checked after each donation that involves physical contact." She smiled prettily. "And for you, my Lord, I was checked twice."

Danial pulled her to her feet and backed her against the nearest wall, his palms flattened on either side of her. Without preamble, he bit deeply into her throat. Instantly, her head went back against the wall, her eyes closing as he moved against her, swallowing Her arms pulling him closer. She writhed against him as he held her to the wall, swallowing her down. Ten minutes later he stopped and stepped back from her. Jeannette was barely conscious. He hadn't healed her wound, and the bite was weeping blood steadily.

Two men appeared from a service door nearby and supported her. One immediately bandaged the bite, pressing down to stop the bleeding. "We'll take

27

care of her, sir," they said to Danial. They helped her walk to the service door nearby, the door shutting behind them without a sound.

Danial sat back down. His pale skin shone in the darkness, almost radiant. He looked over at me, his expression teasing and just a touch seductive. "Did you enjoy watching?"

I'd been so riveted I'd forgotten to breathe and was practically writhing in my seat for wanting him. My eyes had to be dark forest green with lust. I cleared my throat. "Why didn't she feel pain? She acted like the women in the movies act, when they're bitten."

"She's ultra-sensitive to whatever it is that relieves pain in my saliva," Danial murmured softly. "So much so my bite gives her intense pleasure and no pain. Some women are like that."

"Ah," I said, trying to keep the envy out of my words.

"But we didn't come here to talk about donors," Danial whispered, standing and offering me his hand. "Dance with me, Sar."

I took it, a tremor going through my hand when I touched him.

We went down the stairs to the stage with the softer music and began to slow dance. There were no songs I recognized, but the melody was happy, light, and easy to move to. It helped Danial knew what he was doing on a dance floor. I was still breathing harder than I should've been, and I kept my eyes lowered so he wouldn't see my desire.

"You seem ill at ease," Danial asked inquiringly. "Is it being alone with me?"

It was imagining being alone with him, not with people surrounding us, but somewhere else, quiet and dark. Quickly, I asked him a question that had nothing to do with my feelings for him. "Where was Lander tonight? Why wasn't he outside the door? He could've warned me—"

"It's my fault," he said grudgingly. "I'd told him he could have the night off, knowing I'd be with you to keep you safe. He wasn't supposed to leave until I'd arrived." Danial paused, though we kept moving to the music. "I didn't expect Samuel to come looking for me."

"How old is he? More importantly, can we trust him?"

"He's easily as old as I am, most likely almost double my age. He's strong because of that. Devlin's blood gave me more power than I had, but Samuel is still more powerful than I am." He leaned in closer. "It is good you brought the choker with you."

"It was Theo's idea." I felt suddenly guilty, wondering if he was still in the hospital. Then I thought of him sitting by Tawny's bedside and angrily put them both out of my mind.

"I think it's true what Samuel says, because if he wanted something from us, he could take it," Danial answered. "He wouldn't need to ask. I trust that he wants the justice he spoke of, but that is as far as we'll trust him. I wouldn't call on him if we needed help." Danial paused. "You won't be coming on any more trips with Theo and me," he continued firmly. "Not outside my territory. I will not allow it, no matter the reason."

I protested, even though secretly, I was relieved. "You have no power over me to tell me where I can and can't go."

"It's too dangerous, Sar. I forbid it," Danial said arrogantly.

I pushed him away and looked up angrily into his eyes. "Who are *you* to forbid me—?"

Danial blinked once, his arrogance vanishing, his lips parting slightly.

He'd seen the desire in my eyes. I looked down again immediately.

Danial took one hand and tilted my head up to look at him. "I'm a man who loves you." Then he leaned in fast, pressing his soft lips hard to mine, his one hand running down my back to pull my lower body against him while the other went around my shoulders and crushed me against his chest.

I knew it was wrong, but I wanted him so badly in that moment. If we had been alone, I would've given myself to him. I wanted him, all of him, his body sliding against mine, inside mine, to scream out his name, as I drowned in pleasure of his making. Most of all, I wanted to hear his cry of release as he climaxed, to know I was the one who had given that pleasure to him.

I put all that wanting into the kiss and gave it to Danial, my tongue caressing his. He clutched me to him tighter, devouring me, his breaths coming fast.

"Get a room, you two," someone said sarcastically. Laughter followed.

I flushed redder than my dress, breaking the kiss. Danial turned in anger with red-tinted eyes, but the person had already passed by, lost in the crowd. The song had ended, and we were alone on the dance floor.

The moment had been broken.

Still flushing, I took Danial's hand and led him back to our seats. I sat down heavily in my chair, and Danial sprawled in his own, leaning back as he studied me.

"This is another reason why it's not a good idea for you to come with us, Sar," Danial said. "It's one thing if we say hello now and again, but when we spend any amount of time together—"

"I know," I said, looking over at him. "I get it. You're right, Danial. I'm sorry."

Alarm flashed across his face. "Come to me. Now." He beckoned to me.

Afraid, I scrambled up and went to him. He pulled me down to sit in his lap, grazing me gently with his fangs. "Trust me," he whispered and said louder, "Just a little bite, Love?"

"Later," I managed, trying to sound sexy and still cover my terror. "You know I'm shy in public."

"I hope you've been having a good time," a courteous voice said.

I looked up, startled. Samuel was back, sitting in my chair. I hadn't even heard him approach. I leaned in closer to Danial.

"We've had a great time," Danial said, inclining his head. "I appreciate Jeannette, and Sar thanks you for the wine."

I parted my lips to say I did have a voice of my own, then decided to keep quiet. Danial knew what he was doing. This was not the time to open my big mouth, not to Samuel.

"I saw you two on the dance floor," Samuel chuckled, his tone indicating he had seen the steamy kiss. "How long have you been together?"

"Almost nine months now," Danial lied smoothly.

If we had stayed together, that's how long it would've been. I squeezed Danial's hand, touched he knew that.

"I see how much she wants you, Danial," Samuel said. He looked expectantly at me.

Danial nudged me. I realized with a rush of panic I was supposed to say something.

"I've wanted him since I first saw him," I said softly, hoping it was the kind of thing Samuel expected me to utter.

Samuel nodded. "You love him very much?"

Again, Danial nudged me.

"I will never stop loving him," I replied. "He is part of me." I looked up at Danial, letting everything I usually hid inside show itself in my face. His face softened, and he kissed my lips once more.

Samuel nodded again. "Cherish her, Danial. You will not find someone else like her easily again, if ever. Not in today's age where tradition means so little."

"I understand that all too well," Danial said, his whisper tormented.

Samuel stood then, and we both turned our heads to look at him.

"I'm off to handle some business in Spain, but I wish you both the best. My thanks again to you for your help in the Jonas murder. If you are ever in town, Danial, you have a standing invitation here, for both entertainment and nourishment. It's the least two such as we can do for one another."

Danial thanked him, and Samuel walked away.

I grabbed for my wine and drained the glass.

"Shh," Danial said, hugging me. "He's gone. Once I can't feel his presence any longer, we'll leave."

"Danial, I—" I started.

He lifted me to my feet and then stood. "If you can walk now, we should go back to the hotel. I can't take any more tonight," Danial said heavily.

We walked out of the club, got in the limo, and rode back to the hotel in silence. When we arrived, Lander was back at his post. Danial didn't say a word, just went into his room and shut the door. I took off my dress and stuffed it into my suitcase. I put the earrings in there as well. The choker I left on, remembering Danial's promise to Samuel. Then I took a long shower, washing away the scent of Danial and of my own feelings for him. If only my emotions could be washed away so easily...

I dressed in a nightgown and robe and then removed all traces of makeup. Finally, I couldn't put it off any longer. I went and knocked at Danial's door. "Danial?"

"Sar, I can't see you right now." Danial's voice was full of sadness mixed with bitterness and longing.

"You said there was something you wanted to try. Besides, I'd like the choker off."

"You heard Samuel. We spent considerable effort convincing him you're off limits. Until we leave, you should wear it."

I imagined Theo coming home and finding me wearing it. He'd go ballistic. "You said there was something you wanted to try," I said, persistent.

There was only silence, though I repeated myself several times. After a while, I went away. I slept briefly on the sofa, wanting to hear the phone if Theo called.

Danial awakened me near dawn by touching me on the shoulder. "Did Theo call?" he said apprehensively.

"No," I said, my worried tone echoing his. "Can you try his cell?"

Danial dialed quickly. Relief flooded through me when Theo picked up almost immediately.

"Are you coming back before dawn?" Danial asked. He listened for a while. "There is someone else here who needs to speak to you," and handed me the phone.

"Sar," Theo said. "How was your night? Did you go out and have fun?"

"I'll tell you all about it when you get here," I replied, stalling. "Will you be a while yet?"

"I should be there soon," Theo said. "Tawny is stable now, and she's awake."

"That's good," I said, trying to mean it.

"I'll see you then," Theo said and hung up.

I turned off the phone and handed it back to Danial. "Thanks."

"Sar, come here," Danial said, sitting down on the couch. "Now, try to take the choker off."

"I can't," I said, sitting down next to him. "You know that, Danial."

Months ago, I'd tried to take off the choker myself. The more I pulled on

31

it, the more it had seemed to tighten around my neck.

"Don't pull on it. Do what you did when you put it on and think about the strand ends coming undone."

I did as he asked. Nothing happened.

"Concentrate, Sar," Danial said patiently.

I concentrated, willing the stands to unlock, imagined them pulling apart. With a sliding sound and a metal clink, the choker fell off into my lap. I looked immediately at Danial, my eyes wide. His were shocked as well.

"How is it possible?" I said, reaching out to pick up the necklace.

"I don't know," Danial said, thinking hard by his expression. "Try to put it on again."

I tried, and again, the ends slid together, meshing quickly. I tried to take it off again, and this time it unclasped much faster. This was good. If I needed to wear the choker, I could, and I could take it off when I wanted to.

"It must be my blood, Sar. The blood I gave you two nights ago," Danial said thoughtfully. "That is the only thing it could be, but it was only a few drops—"

"Your blood is more powerful now," I reasoned. "How much does it take to turn someone?"

"I have never heard of this happening before," Danial said quietly, taking my hand. "You should not be able to work the choker in any case, not even if I turned you. Devlin's blood was old, and it made me more powerful. I seemed to have passed some of that power onto you. I can't say whether it will be a permanent change or not, but I'm guessing not—"

"So long as I'm not turning," I said uneasily.

"I'd have to take a lot more of your blood for that to happen," Danial assured me. He hugged me tightly. "This doesn't mean you are turning, don't worry—"

The door opened suddenly, and Theo entered. As before, he looked haggard, which quickly shifted to suspicion. "Am I interrupting?" he said flatly.

"We've had a bad night, so don't start," I said coolly. "A Vampire Ruler's been on our asses all night, and we had to playact."

"So long as that's all it was," Theo said, yawning. "Danial, everything has been arranged." He sat down in a nearby chair. "Elle is ready to go, and her paperwork has been completed, saying she came from a private breeder in Germany, and is headed to a wildlife refuge in the Northeast. We can pick her up anytime, if you handled the plane."

"Yes, it's arranged. Bring her here tomorrow," Danial said, rising.

Theo hugged Danial quickly. "Thank you."

"I can finish everything I need to do here by the night after next," Danial said, returning the hug and then stepping back. "We can leave later that night."

He headed toward his room.

Theo called out "I thought you had another meeting on Friday?"

"Like she said, it's been a bad night," Danial said heavily, not turning around. "I already canceled the meeting on Friday earlier tonight. We'll do it by conference call." Danial shut the door of his bedroom behind him.

Theo gave me a suspicious look. He grabbed my hand and pulled me into our room. He sat me on the bed none too gently and sat beside me.

"Spill it, Sar."

"Why don't you shower, and then I'll—"

Theo pushed me back on the bed and leaned over me, pinning my shoulders to the mattress. "Now, Sar," he growled at me. "Tell me right now."

I told him the whole story, downplaying the kissing part, but repeating the words I'd said to Samuel about my feelings for Danial. Theo was angry about what had happened, but not with either of us. He was angry with Samuel for putting us in a position where we'd had to act as though we were a couple to keep me safe.

As he showered, I got into bed and dozed, thinking about Elle. There had been so much relief in Theo's voice when he'd told Danial the plans were settled, so much love for Elle. I decided then to do my best to love Theo's child, even though it was Tawny's child and not mine. That wasn't Elle's fault. Besides, she did have part of me, my name.

A half hour later, Theo crawled in beside me, his hair still damp. He pulled me into his arms. "Danial is right," he said, kissing my cheek. "You are not going to be coming with us again."

"I agree." Being around Danial was constant stimulation, temptation, and sensation. It was easier when we didn't see each other. "So, tell me your plan for when we get your daughter home."

Theo seemed to be trying to find the right words.

"Theo," I said gently. "I'm just asking for pointers on what she'll need, so we can think of what to pick up on our way home."

"This is my last job for Danial," he tentatively said.

"What?" I exclaimed.

"I'm going to tell him on the way home. I'm quitting the business. It's too dangerous. I should have quit when I met you, when we found each other." His eyes were boring into me, deadly serious. "I have too much to live for to keep risking my life. I'm were, but I'm not indestructible. It didn't matter when I was alone, when I only had to worry about myself. I want to be around to see Elle grow up, to spend my life with you."

"What about being fifth?" I asked.

"I'm going to sign a paper, relinquishing my ranking completely," he replied. "I'll post it to the internet when we get home. No one should care. I'm not in the top four, and I've only been ranked six months. You won't have to worry about me anymore."

There were tears in my eyes now. I blinked them back.

Theo took a deep breath. "Tawny died tonight, Sar."

"What? How?" I pulled back from him.

"She had a heart attack, at least that's what they think. Having the baby was too much for her. There was something wrong with how big Elle grew inside her, and they still have no explanation for why she wasn't in human form. Tawny's doctor has called a bunch of his colleagues who routinely deliver babies of wereanimals, and no one has heard of this before."

"I'm sorry, Theo," I lied, hugging him. I wasn't sorry; I was hugely relieved to know she was dead.

"I don't want you to worry, Sarelle," Theo continued. "I have enough money to float us for a few years easily. I'm thinking about being a carpenter. I've also thought about working for Danial or someone else just training other people for security, but it would be a nine-to-five kind of job, no more nights or weekends. No more killing. No more blood."

That would be so much safer, for all of us. I took a long deep breath.

"Sar, you're supposed to say something," Theo said impatiently. "What do you think?"

"I am happy you've decided to quit. I worried about you every night when you were working and I was home alone. I worried when I saw blood on your clothes. I know you can take care of yourself, but I didn't want to lose you."

Theo knew what I'd meant to say and hadn't. I'd lost my husband almost two years ago in an accident, and the shock had messed me up for a year afterward. He kissed me tentatively, then drew back from me.

"Are you sure you want this? That you want this with me?"

"Yes," I assured, giving him a big smile. "I told you that. I want a life with you, Theo."

He kissed me, then quickly rolled on top of me, his hard body moving against mine insistently. "Show me," he said, with a touch of a leer in his eager smile.

* * * *

The next night, Theo woke me. "Come with me to the hospital, Sar. I want you to meet Elle. Hurry."

"Okay," I said, apprehensive. We quickly got dressed and left. Danial was nowhere to be seen, though Lander was back guarding the door.

Theo and I grabbed a cab to the hospital, and we walked to the newborn area of the maternity ward. Theo took me to a private room and checked in with a security guard outside. I wasn't surprised; I knew Theo. It wasn't too out of the ordinary he was already protecting Elle, even if no one knew she was even here or she was his child to protect.

I walked through the door and into a regular room. It was carpeted and had a window high up so the stars of the night sky were visible. There was a rocking chair, a playpen, and a crate, along with toys here and there. Some of them had been torn apart, and stuffing was scattered in tufts around the room.

Theo went to the crate and opened it. It was huge, the size I'd had when I had crate trained my German shepherd dogs. A little growl came from the crate, and Theo growled back. Then there was quick movement inside, and a little furry head poked out. I moved and immediately she scooted back in. Theo kneeled down, and I did the same, staying back. He made some more noises, something like growls, but also like the sounds my cats made when they wanted something. Was he asking her to come out?

There were noises from the crate, but no head peeked back out again. Finally, Theo made a purring/growling sound, and Elle scooted quickly out into his arms. He held her, as she peeked through his arms at me.

"Theo, she's beautiful," I said, overcome. Elle was the same buff color Theo was, but she had darker speckles on her sides. Her eyes were blue, not golden yellow yet, and she did not have the white patches he had in his cougar form on her face.

Theo closed the crate door softly, so Elle couldn't retreat inside. I stayed motionless, not wanting to scare her. Soon enough, Elle decided she was more curious about me than she was scared, and she came toward me hesitantly, the black tip of her tail twitching.

She sniffed and then licked me. I petted her, and she let out a tiny purr. She crawled up on my lap and plopped herself down. She was very heavy, and I picked her up a little as she was hurting my legs. I sat back down cross-legged and petted her some more. She lolled there in my lap, pricking me with her claws, which I gently stopped her from doing. I stroked her head, and she rolled into my hand, purring in that soft tiny sound.

I fell in love with her, right there. She was so beautiful, so perfect in every way. She bit me gently right then, as if to prove me wrong about her.

I removed my finger from her mouth, telling her firmly "No."

She stopped immediately and looked at me. Then she erupted in a flurry of movement, running around the room, grabbing toys and shaking them. She hid one moment, and pounced forth the next to grab another toy and shake it, growling. I watched her, smiling. Theo came over to me and sat behind me, pulling me into his arms. We watched her playing, growling at toys and rolling over, swatting them. After a while, she came back over to Theo and me and lay down in my lap. Within minutes, she was asleep.

I stroked her gently as she slept. There weren't any words for the emotions I was feeling. They were too big, too powerful, and too deep.

"Come on," Theo whispered. "We need to go."

"How are we going to do this?" I asked him, not moving.

"The toys, especially the trashed ones, we can throw out. We need to put her in the crate and transport it to the hotel." Theo flipped open his phone and made a call to a limo service.

I wasn't eager to ride in another limo, but it was true a cab would not have enough room.

"They'll be here in about ten minutes," Theo said, disconnecting.

He put Elle, still sleeping, in the crate and began to gather up the toys. He tossed most of them in the garbage, but I put others into a plastic bag I found in the closet. I shouldered that, and he hefted the crate outside as I held the door for him.

"Sar," Theo said, turning to me. "Go to the desk and get her paperwork. They are expecting you. I'll wait here with her."

I left him near the elevator and went to the desk. By some miracle, everything was in order, and I signed for Elle's paperwork, which they handed to me. I got back to the elevator as it was opening, and Theo, Elle, and I rode down together.

We got to the curb as the limo pulled up. Theo loaded the crate, and we got in. By now, Elle had woken and was screaming her head off. Theo growled at her, and she quieted, looking through the bars at us. I worried she was essentially in a cage, but we were in the middle of a city. If she got loose, she'd be lost and possibly killed. She might be were, but she was tiny.

We made it back to the hotel without incident. Theo and I got the crate up to our suite. He did most of the work. Lander was again standing guard. He opened the door for us and shut it behind us, not saying a word.

Theo put the crate down and let out Elle. She ran to me this time, and I picked her up. She had to weigh at least twenty pounds. She wasn't big, but she was dense.

She purred for me, and I hugged her. I looked up to see Theo watching me with joy on his face when he saw me holding her. I gave him a smile, and he gave me one back.

"Danial's out," he said, "but he should be back shortly. His meeting should be over by now."

"What do we feed her?" I said.

"She's supposed to have milk, but I've been able to feed her mashed up chicken," Theo said. "She doesn't have teeth yet. They are just coming in."

I didn't know what to do. Order chicken from room service and tear it up for her? What if she got sick? What if I hurt her? She was so small, so fragile...

Theo saw the panic on my face. He came over to me and hugged me. "Sar, do the best you can. I'm winging this myself."

36

I threw out an idea. "What we need is a high quality wet cat food, something made almost entirely of meat and ground up. Is there a pet store nearby?"

Theo nodded. "I'll go get some right now. I should have thought of that myself." He kissed me and left immediately.

I got some water for her, put it in one of the oversize coffee cups in the room, and offered her a drink. Elle was dubious at first, tapping the surface of the water with her paw, dunking her nose in it, and sneezing. Eventually she found the right angle to hold her head and drank some water.

Seeing that, I had another thought. I borrowed Lander's phone and called Theo. I cursed myself for not bringing my own, but I hadn't thought I'd need it.

Theo picked up on the first ring. "Lander? What's wrong?"

"It's Sar. When you get the food, get a litter box too, the biggest one they have, and some litter. We need two dishes, too, dog sized."

"Anything else?"

"A litter scoop," I said, kicking myself for forgetting. "A big one."

"Okay, Sar. I'll be back soon."

I hung up and returned the phone to Lander. He took it, glaring at me. I thought about telling him it wasn't my fault he gotten in trouble, but decided his petulance wasn't worth fighting about.

I played with Elle for the next twenty minutes. She liked to chase me and for me to chase her. She was clearly more than a cougar. She understood "no" already, and I was working on "come." I hoped fervently that would translate into her being able to be litter box trained. I knew regular great cats could not be.

Danial arrived back about eight p.m. He came in the door as I was beneath the end table playing with Elle, so I didn't see him.

"Sar, what are you doing?"

He startled me so much I bonked my head and then cursed loudly. I rolled out from underneath the table, and Elle came to lay on me, purring. Danial came over and kneeled down next to us.

"She's Theo's, all right," Danial said with a kind of admiration. He reached out to touch her, and she scooted back into her crate, peeking out at him with her blue eyes. His face fell.

I touched him on the arm as we got to our feet. "Don't worry," I said, chuckling. "She was shy with me, too, at first."

I had him sit with me on the couch. After a few minutes, Elle again came out to investigate. She bounded up onto the couch with me and extended her head toward him, sniffing. He kept still. Slowly, she walked over onto his lap and lay down. He offered his hand to her, and she sniffed it. Then he petted her, and she purred. I watched him with her, the joy on his face as he stroked her.

"She's beautiful," he said, besotted.

Elle sprawled on his lap, as if saying it was right we all adored her because, after all, she was wonderful.

"Where is Theo?" Danial said finally, still petting Elle.

"He's getting her some food and supplies. He'll be back soon. How did your meeting go?"

"Fine. After tomorrow's we can leave," he said coolly.

By his tone, he didn't want to talk about it, or else just didn't want to talk to me, period. My happy mood glaciated, and we sat in silence, Danial still petting Elle until she fell asleep on his lap.

Theo came back about an hour later with two huge bags. I helped him unpack them, set up the litter box, and quickly put Elle in it. She got right back out, as expected. I resolved to watch her closely until she did something.

Theo had gotten two cases of cat food too, some whole foods brand with pure ingredients. I opened two cans and gave them to her. She ate them both in a few minutes and looked around for more.

"Should we give her more?" Theo asked, looking at me.

Danial looked at me.

"Why are you both looking at me?" I said crossly, walking over to Elle. "You could easily tell if she's had enough."

I picked her up and felt her belly. It was hard and full. "That's enough for now," I said. "I don't want her to get sick. Maybe in another four hours or so."

Elle struggled down from my arms suddenly and began looking around the room.

"What is she looking for?" Danial said curiously.

I walked quickly to her and scooped her up just in time to plop her in the litter box. "Right here," I said encouragingly.

Elle did her business and then covered it up. When she got out, I scooped out the mess and flushed it down the toilet. After, she went back in her crate and curled up to sleep. I shut the door and then sat down on the couch. I was already exhausted from caring for her, and she wouldn't sleep for long. This is what living with a newborn would mean...

"Theo, I need to go out to feed, and Lander needs another break," Danial said, interrupting me. "Can you stay here with Sar?"

"Yes," Theo said. "I can go with you tomorrow night to the last meeting too, now Elle is safe here."

Danial left quickly.

I wondered if he really needed to feed. He'd taken a lot of blood last night from Jeannette. More likely, he'd left because of Elle, specifically, seeing me with Elle. Theo and I had a family now, even though Elle was not my daughter. That Danial was hurt saddened me, and I curled up on the couch, dejected.

Theo ordered room service for us. I got a hamburger, a soda, and some fries, and he got a large steak. We ate, sharing some pieces with Elle. We had to chew them up a little before we gave then to her, but she liked them. Seeing her eat made me feel a little better for some reason, and I latched onto the feeling.

After, Theo changed form, so he could truly play with her. He chased her around the room, and she knocked over the lamp and a vase trying to get away. He picked her up in his mouth and carried her. Then he lay down, and she gnawed on his tail and bit his ears. He swiped at her, his paw knocking her to the ground, but his claws were sheathed. She struggled to get up and hissed at him. He hissed back at her and then the game started all over again.

Watching them, I understood now why he'd been so tired coming back every night. He had been tired from playing with Elle, not from worrying over Tawny. Guilt flooded me again, for all the times I'd begrudged him his time away from me. I fell asleep still watching them.

We fed Elle again right before dawn, and she ate two cans this time. After, I took her to the litter box and she again did her business. I took care of it and then put her in her crate. I wanted to let her sleep with us, but knew I'd worry. What if she chewed a light cord or something? Besides, she should be used to being in the crate since Theo had had to leave her alone, right?

That proved to be true. Elle curled right up in a ball and went to sleep.

Theo and I went in to bed, not bothering to turn on the light, pull the shades, or do more than drop our clothes by the side of the bed. I was very tired and so was he, but we were parents now and that was to be expected.

"You like her, Sar, don't you?" Theo said hesitantly, as we got into bed.

Again, the guilt came crashing down on me. Why had I been such a bitch? "I love her," I said, sighing. "She's wonderful, Theo. I'm dead tired, but I'm happy."

He smiled in relief. It brought home to me how worried he had been I wasn't going to like her, that I'd tell him I didn't want to be Elle's mom. She needed: a mother, one who would love her, protect her, and teach her everything she needed to know.

He kissed me suddenly, stretching the length of his body to press against mine. I responded, rolling over and straddling him. He groaned, his hands caressing my body as I ran my fingers through his chest hair, watching the blue of his eyes darken as he looked at me. I rubbed my hips against him and kissed his neck. Instantly, he rolled me over, pressing himself to me. I opened my legs for him, and he moved so he lay between them. Theo drew back to look at me beneath him, savoring the sight.

"Sar, I love you. It scares me sometimes how close we came to not being together."

"Don't think about it," I said, kissing him. "We are together, Theo. The past is past, and it can't be changed. We have a future, you, me, and Elle."

Theo went still at my words. Suddenly he bore down, thrusting hard into me, and I gasped. He held me to him and kept thrusting, kissing me, as he ran his hands over my face and chest, stroking me. I was as eager for him as he was for me, meeting his thrusts with my own. The urgency in his movements increased, as the feeling built between us. I felt him jerk inside me with a loud roar. I came then, crying out wordlessly, clutching his body to mine. We held each other tightly as we finished. Then he rolled over on his side, taking my face in his hands.

"Sar, marry me?" he said suddenly.

My breath caught in my throat. I stayed motionless for a full minute, gazing into his hopeful grey-blue eyes.

I'd wondered when Theo was going to ask. Despite his talk several months ago that we weren't ready, it had been obvious he had been thinking about it. It was in the way he watched me, the way he'd held me. So what the hell was I waiting for? I had a man who loved me, and he was going to give up his dangerous life to be with me. I already loved his daughter. How much better did things need to get for me before I decided I was ready?

"Yes," I said. "Yes, I'll marry you."

Theo hugged me tightly. "I'll make you happy, Sarelle. I swear I will," he said tenderly. "Now…again?"

I was tired, completely exhausted. Yet I didn't want the night to end. "Say it once more," I whispered. "Please."

"Again," Theo said arduously, slipping my hand down to touch his stiffening member.

I bit my lip at his misunderstanding me. "Of course," I said, kissing him.

* * * *

I was sore when I got up the next night. Make that I could barely walk. Theo was still sleeping. We'd only gotten about a few hours of sleep. He had gone on all night until I was nearly numb. We'd made it a night to remember, which was what mattered most to me.

I got up and went to check on Elle. She had made a mess in her crate, so I cleaned her up, cleaned it out, and then gave her some food. This time after eating, she went to the litter box on her own. I was grateful for that. She was picking up what I wanted of her so fast. I cleaned up after her when she was done and played with her a little. I needed to shower, but I was too content sitting here, contemplating my upcoming nuptials.

I'd said yes. I was getting married to Theo.

I thought about calling my mother and telling her, but I wanted to wait until I got back to the states. Then I thought about Danial in the next room and dreaded telling him. This would hurt him deeply, no matter that he'd be happy for us…

On cue again, Danial came out of his room and saw me sitting with Elle. He watched us for a while, silent and unmoving.

Finally, I said, "Theo's still sleeping."

"I think he probably should be, Sar. He was up most of the night making love to you," Danial said sardonically. "Ah, the energy of the young."

I cringed at his tone, but felt worse knowing how he must have felt to hear us all night. I couldn't bring myself to tell him the reason why. "I'm sorry we kept you awake."

He sighed and came over to sit beside me. "Don't be. I want you to be happy. Theo has been unhappy most of his life. I can't begrudge him being happy now, even knowing you are his and not mine."

He looked at me as if he wanted to say something more, but instead he got up and went back to his room.

I played with Elle for a little while until she slept again. Then I showered quickly and packed up everything. We'd be leaving as soon as they got back from the last meeting tonight.

Theo got up about eight p.m. We called down for room service, had breakfast, and then he showered, leaving quickly afterwards, his hair still wet.

With one eye on Elle, who seemed content destroying a rubber toy, I used Danial's laptop, logging on to the Internet to discover everything I could about baby cougars. I'd read only a paragraph when I heard Theo's angry voice outside the hotel room door.

They'd been gone only an hour, not the three I'd anticipated. Something was very wrong. I closed the computer and hurried toward their angry voices.

"Something's not right," Danial argued, closing the door behind them.

"Danial, let it go!" Theo said loudly. "So they didn't want us to find this missing person. What does it matter?"

"The client, Peterson, contacted us two weeks ago. This is the only meeting that was crucial, the one we had to be here for at this particular time. They said it was dire and they'd pay extra if we would be here at this time. The rest of the meetings I had this week could have waited for another month. Now we're here, on time, and they tell us not to bother?"

"Peterson said they think the guy, Frank Feren, left Europe, right?" Theo replied. "That's what he told us, anyway. Maybe they think they can find him themselves. Peterson only wants him found because he stole that software program, anyway."

"That's odd, too. He wouldn't say what the software did."

"It's proprietary, Danial. We hear that all the time."

"This company makes weapons, specifically guns for use in special situations," Danial retorted. "You know they're thinking of making guns for handling people like us."

"That's only something they are starting to do. Fenris, the company that makes our weapons, has a much bigger share of that business, and they do it much better. They recently sent me a new gun, a prototype, to try out and give my opinion on. It's supposed to make a larger hole, with more stopping power—"

"We should leave at once," Danial was waiting at the door. "I'll make the call to the airport."

Theo turned to me, suddenly uneasy. "Danial's right, Sar. We shouldn't take any chances, especially with you or Elle. Can you be ready to go in a half hour?"

"We are both ready now," I said worriedly, gathering up Elle and putting her in her crate. "I think we should leave right now."

Danial went into his room and got his bag. Theo grabbed our bags, handed them to Lander, and hefted Elle's crate. We went to the elevator and down to the lobby, where Lander and Danial went to check us out of the room, leaving Theo, Elle and I to stand near the front doors.

To my shock, Samuel appeared beside me suddenly. "Sarelle, you and Danial are leaving?" he said, disappointed.

"Yes," I said, reaching my fingers up to touch my choker involuntarily. Samuel reached for my other hand and took it, giving it a chaste kiss.

"You must come back soon," Samuel said charmingly. "I enjoyed seeing you and Danial dance. Perhaps I and my current Lady could join you for an evening next time."

I cast a look at Theo, even as I nodded. "That would be nice."

"Love tends to elude those in power," Samuel said wistfully, his eyes still on me. "Not that Devlin didn't exacerbate Danial's misery this past century—"

"Step back," Theo growled. "Only one man touches this lady, Sir."

"I'm glad to see your guard is more attentive tonight," Samuel chuckled, dropping my hand and moving back a step. "It's hard to find good help among the inferior races."

My eyes remained locked with Samuel's, yet I felt the rage pouring off Theo. Please, God, let him keep quiet. If he did anything more, he'd betray the lie of Danial and I. Then I'd be fair game, to say nothing of Elle.

Samuel turned to Theo suddenly. When his kind blue eyes fell on Theo, they went frosty and chill as the North Sea. "Who are you?" he said gratingly, offering his hand to Theo.

"I'm Danial's chief of security, Theo," Theo said, taking his hand.

"You must have a last name?" Samuel said sarcastically.

"It's McGarran," Theo said without blinking, his blue eyes cold.

I stopped breathing for a moment, but managed not to gasp.

"Are you taking good care of your master's lover?" Samuel said darkly in double meaning. "I assume that's your job, keeping her safe from other men—"

Oh, shit.

"I try my best," Theo said, his smile not reaching his eyes, which were livid. "So far I've had no complaints, Sir, from—"

"I'm sorry, but we must be going," I interrupted. "The night is waning, and we have a long way to travel. Lord, I thank you again for all your hospitality, on behalf of Danial and myself."

"You're most welcome, Lady," Samuel said mildly and then turned to meet Danial returning with Lander. "Adieu, Racklan. It was good to meet you."

"And you," Danial replied pleasantly. "Farewell. Come, Sar."

He led me away to the waiting limo. Theo got Elle's crate in first, and then we embarked. Theo growled to himself the whole way, holding my hand so tight he almost bruised me.

As we walked from the limo to the waiting aircraft, shots rang out. Theo immediately dropped the crate and fell to the ground, covering me with his body. Lander, who'd been last, threw himself down on Danial. Poor Elle in her crate began to yowl. Theo drew out his specially made weapon from his back and fired over me. Someone screamed, and then more bullets thwacked the pavement by our bodies, making large smoking craters.

The men firing at us had guns like ours.

Chapter Three

Theo yelled to Lander "We have to make a break for it. We're sitting ducks out here!" He turned to me frantically. "Stay down. If I don't make it, take care of Elle. I love you."

Then he stood up and bolted, roaring as he shifted, his clothes falling in shreds on the ground as he ran off on all fours. Shots fired, but they missed him. Lander and Danial returned fire, their bodies flattened to the ground. Then a loud cougar scream of rage rang out as Theo tore into someone.

"Everyone's got a gun but me," I gasped, crawling toward Elle.

Elle's crate was hit. She squirmed though the still smoking hole, trying to get free, screaming. I grabbed her and pulled her down as another round thwacked into the crate, just missing her. In her panic, she clawed me up, writhing hard. Hissing in pain, I grabbed her hard by the back of the neck to hold her still. She tried to bite me. I twisted the back of her neck hard. She was still against me, her tiny heart beating fast.

There were human screams, and Theo roaring and screaming in rage, though I couldn't see anyone. Lander and Danial had also disappeared.

Silence descended. I lay still, too afraid to move. Arms were suddenly around me, lifting me.

"C'mon. Where is—?" It was Theo, naked. He lifted me to my feet, saw I had Elle, and gripped us both, dragging us with him. "We've got to go!"

We ran as fast as possible back to the limo as Danial ran up with Lander. The driver was dead, a regular gunshot wound in his temple. Theo pulled him out of the driver's seat and got in while Danial, Elle, Lander, and I got in back.

"We're stuck here another night," Theo muttered, looking in the rearview mirror at Danial. "I saw a bed and breakfast on the way here—"

"No," Danial replied. "Back to the hotel. We need as many people around us as possible—"

A gunshot rocked the limo, as the left rear window blew apart. I screamed. "Go!" Danial yelled.

Theo drove back to our hotel, and we decamped from the limo, running inside. Everyone in the lobby freaked out, seeing us running to the elevators with guns at the ready. Theo's nakedness didn't help. We cleared a path quickly through the normally crowded lobby as everyone ran to get away from us. We got upstairs in another few minutes and back to our rooms, which hadn't been cleaned yet. I sat with Elle on the bed, holding her tightly and crying. She licked my tears away.

Theo came in the room a second later. "You're safe, Sar," he said, kissing me. "We all are. Calm down and breathe."

Danial came in, his gun still in his hand, looking murderous. "I'm going after them tonight, Theo. Will you stay here with Sar?"

"I'm going with you," Theo said, the anger in his tone a living thing. "You go alone, you'll end up dead."

"Come on then," Danial said impatiently. "I'm only going to have a few hours as it is before dawn."

"Don't go, either of you," I yelled at them. "We were all almost killed. I don't want to lose anyone else."

Danial looked at me and then looked at Theo, as if telling him to handle me. Theo took me by the shoulders, composed yet angry.

"Sar, if we let this slide, we might as well hang bulls-eyes on our heads. Peterson is making weapons designed to kill weres and maybe vampires, too. They didn't call us here to do a job for them. They wanted to see how their prototypes would hold up against the real things. We were here to use as practice. This is straight intel right from one of the shooters tonight."

I had suspected that, but to hear it said aloud was horrifying. Deep rage built inside me. "Give me a weapon," I said in fury. "I'll go, too."

"No way, Sar," Theo said immediately. "You're staying here, where you're safe."

"Why the hell did I practice so hard with you all that time?" I yelled at him. "Give me a gun and let me go with you. I want my pound of flesh."

Danial turned and left, calling over his shoulder "Five minutes, Theo."

Theo hugged me to him. "I wouldn't let you go in any case, even if I had to go alone."

"I want to go," I said loudly. Elle cried in my arms, my resentment scaring her.

"You need to stay here with Elle. You need to protect her."

I looked at the scared little cub lying in my arms and hugged her to me. He was right.

Theo handed me his gun and two extra full clips. "Take these. This is one of the guns used against us tonight. It should stop anyone, and it's got most of the silencer left."

I picked up the weapon. It was similar enough to mine that I could guess where the safety and the clip release were. "Okay."

"Stay here. Don't leave this room," Theo said. He threw on some clothes and grabbed an extra gun from his duffel bag. He'd had the foresight to grab it from the ground when we were running back to the limo. He put about ten full clips in his pockets and then came back to me to kneel beside the bed.

"Sar, I'm coming back to you, I swear it," Theo said, looking into my eyes. "I love you, and I'm going to marry you."

He kissed me once, a long lingering kiss. Then he picked up Elle and cradled her in his arms. "I love you, too," he said to her, as she purred back at him and licked his nose.

He handed her back to me and left. The hotel room door slammed, and all was quiet.

* * * *

The minutes seemed to last as long as hours. I didn't know what to do. Elle began crying because she was hungry, and I had nothing to feed her. I was afraid to call room service, not knowing if Danial had registered us with the hotel again. If Peterson and his men had found us on the tarmac between our limo and the plane, they'd find us here, too. We'd be safer if no one knew we were here.

I finally gave Elle some water, as I had nothing else to give her. She made a mess in a corner of the room, and I cleaned it up with towels, crying, because she didn't have even her box to use. She'd been trying so hard for me.

Another hour passed, making the urge to eat more than an annoyance. I debated looking for a vending machine, but, while it might have been possible in a motel, it wasn't in a four-star hotel. There was nothing but coffee packets in the tiny bathroom. I drank some water, and tried to ignore my hunger.

Finally, I lay down. Elle slept beside me, and I had the gun in my hand, safety off.

I was uneasy about that, but I didn't want to wake up to a nasty surprise and not be able to fire. Naturally, when I woke up, my hand tightened on the gun, and I fired.

Looking at the smoking hole in the interior wall and the blown apart dresser in Danial's room, I was supremely thankful the gun was silenced and I'd not fired out into the corridor instead. We didn't need to face police, on top of everything else. I clicked the safety on, calling myself an idiot for not thinking it through. I might have hurt Elle or myself with what I'd done. I had to protect us both, until Theo and Danial—

A noise came from the adjoining room. I eased out from under Elle and

46

crept toward the door. The noise came again, a scuffling sound. I peeked out the door. Danial was there lying just inside the door, moving with effort, covered in blood. I kept hold of the gun and moved out to him. He saw me, but didn't speak, his eyes pain-filled. I moved around him to the door, closing and locking it. After I wedged a chair under the handle for good measure, I put down the gun and pulled Danial into my arms.

His eyes were closed, his body motionless and limp. He looked like he had been dipped in blood. It coated him nearly from head to toe, even in his hair. There were big holes in his clothes: one in his arm, two in his right leg, and four in his torso. The skin underneath was healed. Some of the blood covering him was his own; the rest had likely come from the several persons he'd had to kill to heal that much damage. The gun he'd taken with him was gone. He looked exhausted. That was too bad, because I needed him.

"Danial," I said softly. He didn't stir.

"Danial!" I yelled in his ear.

"Sar?" he said weakly, opening his eyes. "I so glad I made it back to you."

"God damn you both, I told you not to go!" I screamed, almost hysterical.

"Where is Theo?" Danial said weakly.

My blood ran cold. "Where is Lander?" I said, sounding dead, devoid of life.

"He's dead. He didn't have any real experience in this kind of work, and took a round in the heart a few seconds into the fight."

I remembered Lander glaring at me when I borrowed his phone and being embarrassed by Suri when he'd flirted with me. I blinked back tears. I hadn't liked him, but he was dead now and wherever his spirit was, he was never going to be angry, or laugh, or run through a sunlit field again with his fellow foxes.

I wiped my eyes angrily. We weren't in the clear yet. "Danial, do you need blood?"

He lay still again in my arms, unresponsive. Elle began crying in the bedroom.

I lost it. Quickly opening Danial's mouth with one hand, I sliced open my wrist on his upper fangs, letting out a shriek at the pain. Then I pressed my wrist to his mouth. As he had that fateful night we'd first met, Danial's hand clamped onto my wrist like iron, as he sliced my wrist deeper with his fangs to get at more blood. I gritted my teeth, whimpering with the pain.

He fed only a short time and then held his mouth over the wound, healing it. After, Danial released my wrist and opened his eyes. His color was much better, and his eyes were alert.

"Where is Theo?" he said, tired but still strong.

"He didn't come back yet," I said, scared.

"He wasn't wounded as I was," Danial said, getting to his feet angrily. "He should have been back by now."

Elle cried loudly from the bedroom.

"Danial, what are we going to do?" I pleaded. "I need Elle's things. She needs food."

Danial opened his phone and called a number. "Harv, it's me, Danial. You're welcome. Remember you said if I ever needed a favor? I need one now." He gave Harv directions for getting to our plane and for bringing our stuff back to the hotel. Then Danial called room service and ordered me some food.

He went into the shower and reappeared four minutes later, dripping wet, just as someone knocked on the door. He grabbed a robe, put it around him, and answered it. I kept Elle quiet in the bedroom, watching through the door crack.

"Yes?"

It was the hotel manager. "I'm sorry, but you have to leave. You've already checked out and we need to rent the room."

"We originally booked the room for another two days," Danial retorted. "Business has determined we need to stay one more night."

"There is also the disturbance in the lobby last night—"

"We will pay for tonight and all of next week, if you allow us to stay until tonight," Danial said flatly. "Do you need my credit card again, or can you access my account without it?"

"No, sir," the manager said respectfully. "You've done business with us a long time. I know your bill will be paid. The food will be sent up immediately. Thank you." The door shut, and Danial locked it.

"I was so worried we'd have to leave," I said, coming out of the bedroom.

"He wanted more money is all," Danial muttered as he dried off his hair. "Come out, the food is here."

Danial opened the door and grabbed a wheeled tray, handing the waiters their tip without letting them inside. Elle bounded out, purring happily. I chewed up some of the hamburger and steak for her, and she wolfed it down. Together, we made short work of the food. After, she plopped down on my lap and fell asleep.

"I'm so scared," I whispered.

"We're going to be okay," Danial said, sitting down beside me. He slipped his arms around Elle and me. "Come." He picked us both up and carried us into his bedroom. After putting the gun within easy reach with the safety off, he pulled me into his arms, Elle resting between us.

"Try to sleep," he said gently. "I'll watch over you both."

I cried in his arms from tension, wondering where Theo was, why he wasn't back yet. After sleeping briefly, I was awakened by a loud banging on the door.

"Stay here," Danial whispered to me, then left with the gun.

A moment later, he was back. "It's okay, it's Harv," he said. "You can come out."

I got up, Elle in my arms. Harv was bringing in our luggage, with the help of two other men who tried not to stare at us. Elle's food and her crate—two huge holes in the side—and our bags were quickly piled on the floor. Except for the crate, nothing much was damaged or missing, at least at first glance

"Lass," Harv said in greeting. He was a big guy, somewhat like Danial, but with short gray hair, an Irish accent, and a cold glint in his blue eyes. He shook Danial's hand.

"Thank you," Danial said. "We're even."

"Hardly seems fair, Dan," Harv said.

I did a double take. Dan? I'd never heard anyone call Danial that, not ever.

"If possible, leave a few men outside the door today," Danial said. "Let them keep watch. We'll need an escort when we leave tonight to the airport, as many men as you can spare. Then, consider us square."

"Aye," said Harv. "I'll do that." He turned to me. "You've had a right hard time of it, lass. Go get yerself cleaned up and don't worry. Me and the boys'll watch yer back." He left with a grin, shutting the door quietly behind him.

Danial bolted it, then turned to me. "Sarelle, go shower. I'll watch Elle."

"I want to wait—"

"Go wash off the blood. When Theo comes back, I'll send him into you," Danial said, handing my bag to me and giving me a push.

I went into the bathroom, stripped off my clothes, and took a long, hot shower. I began crying part way through and didn't stop until almost the end. I was terrified Theo wasn't coming back. Danial had said he hadn't been injured and that he had been okay. Theo should have come back by now if he was going to.

I had a pounding headache from all the stress and the crying. I washed my face a few more times, took three aspirin, and put some lotion from my bag on my raw face. Then I put some antiseptic on my claw wounds from Elle and conditioned my hair, more to make myself feel normal than anything else. Needing additional comfort, I put on some sweat pants of Theo's and one of his sweatshirts. They smelled like him, the smell of open air and forest groves. Tears slid down my face thinking of him, and I wiped them away angrily.

I went back out to Danial. Elle was sleeping beside him. Her litter box was set up in the corner.

"Thanks," I said wearily.

"Come lay down," he said, beckoning. "Rest."

I went into his arms. The nearness of him comforted me, and I fell asleep.

* * * *

When I awoke, it was night again, and Theo had still not returned.

Danial was dressed and ready to leave. "I called Theo's cell hours ago, and I've kept trying every hour," he said. "It keeps going to voice mail. I've called the phone company, reported it missing, and they've triangulated it to an area about a hundred square foot, close to the Peterson building, where I went last night with Lander and Theo. I'm headed there now."

I grabbed him. "There's no way in hell I'm not going this time."

Danial gave me a gun. "Then come on."

I left Elle sleeping on Danial's bed, praying she'd be okay until I returned. We rode down with Harv and two more of his men. He left the initial two men he'd arrived with still guarding the hotel room door.

We finally made it to the area where the cell phone was located. I was surprised to see no police cars cruising the area, though one was parked in front, lights flashing but no siren.

I turned to Danial hopefully. "Could Theo have been arrested?"

"Unlikely. Theo trained for situations like this. He should not have been caught. If he had been, he or someone else would have called the hotel by now from the police station, asking for a lawyer or for a ride back to the hotel."

My shoulders slumped, my hope squashed.

"Go in from that side entrance," Danial said to Harv. "Sar and I'll wait at this end. Call if you find anything."

Harv and his men dropped us by the other end of the street, and we got out, walking slowly toward the building the signal was coming from. We walked inside, and I let my eyes adjust to the gloom. There was no sign of Theo or anyone. No blood on the tile, nothing. I turned to check the adjoining room, and Danial screamed.

I ran in his direction, my heart in my throat. Danial was on his knees, a sprawled body dressed in denim in front of him on the tile in a pool of blood. A cell phone lay broken near its outstretched hand.

"No! This can't be possible." Danial shouted. "No! Theo!"

I ran to his side and fell on my hands and knees. The body lay on its stomach, a ragged hole where the heart should have been. The head was missing.

I turned away, and everything I'd eaten came up. I fell onto my side, heaving. Danial was still keening.

I pulled him close, holding him tightly. "It's not him, Danial," I said, eerily calm. "It's not him."

Danial sobbed and squeezed me so hard something cracked in my back.

I didn't understand why he was so upset. That wasn't Theo. It couldn't be Theo. I loved Theo. We were going to get married. He had a daughter who

50

needed him, who he loved. This was his last job. He was not lying there on the ground, dead and headless.

"Get up," I said firmly. "We have to go. The police out front will make their way here. They had to have heard you screaming."

Danial drew a ragged breath. He called Harv, telling him to meet us at the back immediately. Then he got to his feet.

"Sar, you have to accept it," he said softly, helping me up. "It is Theo."

"No," I replied, looking him in the eye. "It's not."

We walked together back to the car. He helped me into the back seat and asked the men to take me back to the hotel. Driving away, I looked back to see him on his cell, watching me drive away as he talked, Harv standing near him.

Harv's men escorted me up to the room. I went inside to find Elle still asleep. I ordered room service and then fed Elle. After, I played with her, while I waited for Danial to return. Eventually, I slept, Elle at my side in Danial's bedroom. When I awoke, it was day again and Danial was back, his arms around me. I turned to him, putting my arms around him and went back to sleep.

When I awoke, Danial was gone. Elle was biting my fingers, telling me she was hungry. I again ordered room service, fed her, and cleaned her box. After, I quickly showered and then put on some jeans and a sweatshirt. A peek outside the door verified Harv's men were still in place.

Now that I was clean and full, worry again consumed me. Theo had been gone more than forty hours now.

Danial came in abruptly. "Are you packed? We have to leave within the hour."

"I'm not leaving until Theo comes back," I said defiantly.

Danial led me out of the bathroom and sat me down on the bed. "Sar, Theo is dead. You must accept it."

"No," I said calmly "That wasn't him, Danial."

"You saw the body—"

"It wasn't him," I said angrily. "Don't tell me it was, because it wasn't."

Danial looked at me seriously, took a deep breath, and then slapped me hard across the cheek. I fell back on the bed, my cheek stinging.

"I'm sorry to hurt you," he said seriously, "but you have to snap out of it."

"You bastard," I spat at him. "You wanted to get him out of the way. Maybe you were the one who shot him in the back. Don't think I can't see how you planned this out."

Danial glared at me, red tints in his eyes, his fury building. "Sar, he's dead. We need to go home. We won't be safe until we're back in my territory."

"No, he's not dead," I yelled.

Danial sneered, as he tossed something at me. "Catch."

Reflexively, I caught it. In my hands was a velvet box. Inside was a diamond ring, about a half carat. The diamond was set into the gold so it wouldn't catch on anything. Bought by a man who knew what it was like to need to work with your hands, who had wanted a ring for his wife-to-be that she could wear all the time and not have it catch on anything, no matter if she was cooking, handling steel, or chainsawing wood...

"It was in his pocket," Danial said. "I'm sorry."

I felt the world cave in as a scream from the depths of my soul tore out of me. Danial grabbed hold of me, as I hit at him and screamed louder. He held me as I kicked, flailed, and fought him.

"No, this can't happen. Not now. Not again."

Hearing myself utter that word, I remembered its other meaning, and realized I'd never hear it uttered to me in the same way ever again. Something broke completely inside of me.

"He said he was coming back. He promised he was coming back," I screeched.

Danial didn't speak, but his eyes were mirrors of my own, weeping tears.

I cried for a solid two hours, using up a whole box of tissues. Danial stayed with me, stroking my hair, holding me. Finally, I stopped, mostly because my eyes were too swollen to see.

"We have to leave now," Danial whispered gently. "As it is, I may need your help to avoid burning. We're just going to make it."

I didn't reply.

Danial picked me up, still sniffling, and carried me in his arms out of the hotel and down to the waiting limo. Elle was put sleeping into her crate by Harv, and his men drove us to our plane. I don't remember much about the flight, or the landing, or takeoff. Elle was scared, and I remember holding her. Perhaps I slept. We made it back to Danial's home just in time for him to take shelter from the sun.

Danial carried me inside, laying me on his bed. Cia was there hugging me, her face swollen with tears. She was pregnant now with her and Aran's first child, due in late December. She told me quietly they were hoping it would be born on the date they had been married one year earlier. I couldn't think about that or be happy for her. I didn't reply.

She cared for Elle that night. I lay on Danial's bed and cried myself to sleep, waking sporadically throughout the night. Every time I woke up, my first thought was confusion at not being home. Then I remembered the headless body in a pool of blood and it all would come rushing back. I'd be hit all over again with the pain, remembering Theo's blue eyes, his smile, his wiseass comments, and the way his body had felt with mine. The way it would never feel again. Danial did not enter or appear at all that night.

At eight the next morning, Cia knocked on the bedroom door. "Suri's at your house, taking care of your pets."

"Good," I said tiredly.

"Your boss is on the phone. He wants to know if you're coming in today."

It couldn't be Monday already? We'd come back a day early, and the weekend was still to come, right? Maybe I had lost some days?

"Tell him," I said, "the love of my life just died. I won't be in for a few weeks. It's okay if they replace me."

I stayed that way most of the week. I cried, resumed taking care of Elle and went about the chores of showering and eating like a zombie. Suri came in once and tried to talk to me about attending a funeral. I wouldn't look at her, wouldn't talk to her, and she finally left in a rage.

Danial reappeared on what I guessed was the following Monday night. "May I join you?" He spoke softly.

"It's your bedroom," I said, getting up. "I'm the one who should leave."

"Please stay," he said, enfolding me in his arms.

I stood there, tensely.

"Please tell me your words were from grief," he said, very upset. "I would never have hurt Theo. He was my best friend."

"I know that," I said, relaxing slightly. "I'm sorry I said what I did."

"I'm sorry I hit you," he whispered. "I was terrified it wouldn't be hard enough, yet scared more I'd hurt you."

"You didn't," I assured him. "I needed something to break me out of it. We'd probably be dead if we'd have stayed another night." I looked up at him. "Do you think it was Samuel?"

"No," Danial said reluctantly. "I wish it had been. There are laws I could reference to have him punished. No, Peterson somehow surprised Theo or someone else did."

"Do you think it was someone wanting his rank?"

Danial nodded. "Likely. Those who've had their ranking a short time are big targets. Some get their rank because of luck, as Theo did last Christmas."

I pushed past him. "I guess it doesn't matter."

Danial followed me. "Where are you going?"

I began to pack up mine and Elle's things. Most were still packed, so it didn't take long. "I'm going home."

"What? Are you crazy?" Danial said incredulously.

I walked out the two bags and loaded them in Theo's truck. "No."

Elle would have to ride with me in the cab. First, I'd have to find her. "Elle?" I called loudly. "Elle!"

"She's out walking with Cia," Danial said, grabbing hold of me, "but that doesn't matter, because I'm not letting you leave with her, not in your condition."

"I'm functioning," I said defensively. "I've spent enough time in your bed, Danial."

Danial let out a breath slowly. "Be reasonable, Sar. You need people around to help you take care of Elle. What are you going to do with her when you're at work, lock her in her crate?"

"I quit, Danial," I said heavily. "I'll be with her all the time."

Complete shock registered on his face. "Just like that?"

He and I had fought before because he wanted me to quit my job, and I'd refused. It had been so important to me then not to give it up. Now I couldn't think why.

"Yes."

"So you have no job, but you're leaving anyway?" he said, sarcastically.

"I have to go home. My pets are there, and it was Theo's home with me. I have to go and deal with it. I can't hide here with you, much as I'd like to." Danial opened his mouth to talk, but I talked over him. "I've been through grief before, this same kind of grief. I can get through it, but it's going to take time."

"Why not go," he said bitterly. "I wouldn't want you to be playacting here with me, wasting your time."

"I'm sorry I hurt you," I said sadly. "I shouldn't have gone out with you that night. It just made everything worse. I'm sorry I wore the dress."

"Don't be," Danial said, hugging me. "It was good to see you in it again, if only for a little while."

"Do something for me, please," I asked, opening my purse.

"Anything," he said tenderly.

"Test Theo's DNA against the body." I handed him some of Theo's hair I'd carried in my purse next to his picture.

"Sar—" he began.

"Do it, Danial," I said harshly. "Do you really believe Theo could get shot in the back so easily? I know you've waited to bury the body. You got it back here from Europe somehow. Test it."

"If Theo's alive, where is he? Why hasn't he contacted us?" Danial retorted.

"I don't know, but I do need to know for certain the body we saw was his." I swallowed hard. "I can't explain it, but I feel as though he's still living. Something inside me tells me he's alive, even if everything else points to him being dead."

He took the hair from me and nodded. "If it will help you come to terms, yes."

The front door opened. "Danial?" Cia called. "We're back."

I hugged him quickly, grabbed up Elle, and left for home. When we arrived, Suri came out to greet us. She hugged me, and that small act from her who'd always been so hard and strong made me cry again.

"Will you stay?"

"Of course," she said, nodding. "I heated up some soup. Come in and have some."

After a quiet meal, Suri went downstairs to sleep, and I began the process of introducing my pets to Elle. Elle liked the cats and dogs, but they didn't like her. They were wary of her, the way they had been at first with Theo. She kept trying to play with them but they just growled or hissed at her. She finally curled up in a ball in the corner of the room, looking forlorn. I felt so sad for her I let her sleep with me. After setting up her litter box in my room, I fed her. A short time later, I fell asleep holding her.

A week passed and then two. I finally told Suri it was okay if she left. I'd gotten Elle on a schedule now and was able to take care of her, my pets, and myself. Suri looked at me with worried eyes, but she left that night, telling me to call her if I was lonely. I wanted to tell her I was lonely, but the person I was lonely for was gone. I didn't want anyone else's company but his and Elle's.

Danial called later that night, excited. "Sar, you were right. The body wasn't Theo. He may be alive," he said hopefully.

"What can we do?" I said, the spark inside me rekindling.

"I am going back to Europe, Sar. If he is there, I'll find him."

"Danial, be careful please," I said, worried. "I don't want to lose you too."

There was silence. "You will never lose me, Sar," he said softly. I've got to run. I'm flying out tonight. Take care."

I hung up, musing. Someone had gone to a lot of trouble to make us think Theo was dead. Why? Who did it?

I immediately thought of Samuel. He had known there was something more between Theo and me than guardian and guardee. Would he have killed him?

Elle crawled up onto my lap. I petted her, and she purred, still a small rumbling sound more like a far-off blender than Theo's deeper and full-throated purring. I smiled, thinking how much I loved her and how much I loved her father. She was growing at a phenomenal rate and was now about fifty pounds. If she got much bigger, she wasn't going to fit in my lap. I was glad, too. The cats and dogs were starting to accept her.

With effort, I brought my thoughts back to Samuel. He was a man who cared deeply about the whole oath/choker tradition. He'd thought me to be cheating on Danial with Theo, which had to have pissed him off. Could he have tried to kill Theo or taken him to punish? He could have. He had the power and resources to do it. Enough men against Theo, and he'd have fallen. He wasn't invincible, just resilient. Yet Samuel should have been angry with me as well as

Theo. Instead, he'd been the picture of politeness. Further, what reason would Samuel have to interfere with a fellow Ruler's errant lover and her bodyguard? We weren't his subjects.

Aside from Samuel, who else might want Theo dead? Whoever was below him in ranking, the sixth through the tenth, which made five people total. They should be easy to discover because they would have to brag or at least admit to killing Theo to move up in ranking. I'd have to ask Danial where those bodyguards were ranked.

In addition to the six suspects I already had, there were probably a lot of people who had it in for Theo. Danial had many enemies now as Vampire Ruler of the U.S. Logic told me those would have killed Theo in an easier way and not tried this elaborate scheme.

That left me with the single most probable killer: Tawny's husband. He'd had reason to want Theo dead and could have easily tracked him and me when we'd brought Elle from the hospital. Still, it made more sense Tawny's husband would have wanted payback on Tawny…

I sat bolt upright. Had Tawny's death been accidental? From Terian, I knew there were potions that could be given to induce what looked like a heart attack.

I tried Terian, but got no answer. I left a message, telling him Theo was missing and asking him to call me as soon as he could. Then I called Danial and left a long message relating my suspicions about Tawny's husband.

The next day, I went in person to see my boss to explain what had happened and to ask him about coming back to work. He was apologetic, understanding the circumstances, but said things had needed to go on without me and my job had already been filled by another person. I asked my boss to call me if that didn't work out, and he said he would. His eyes said I'd let him down. There had been one too many times where he needed me and I hadn't been there.

Dejected, I drove home dry-eyed. I'd reached that familiar plateau where nothing hurt because everything felt as if it was happening to another person. My job was gone; so what? I'd have to find another one soon, but it could wait for a little while.

The month passed slowly. Danial called most every early morning from Europe before he slept to tell me how things were going. He'd spoken to Samuel, but Samuel had denied doing anything. He'd also spoken to someone involved with the ranking and been assured though Theo had been officially removed from the ranking, no one had come forward bragging about killing him. Those below Theo had moved up, but it was normal succession, as when a ranked person died from natural causes. He'd agreed with me with those two possibilities cleared, Tawny's husband was the prime suspect. Danial was working on tracking him down, but as Theo had been listed as Elle's father, he had no name to go on.

"The hospital had Tawny's address, but it's a dead end," Danial continued. "It was an apartment, in Tawny's maiden name. I'm not sure if her husband even knew of it." He sighed. "Someone cleaned out all of her belongings long before I got there. The landlord doesn't remember seeing anyone come get them. It's entirely possible he sold them for back rent."

"Didn't Theo have anything with her info on it? A phone number?"

"Her number wasn't in his cell phone, even though I had the memory chip accessed. He didn't have a phone outside of that. It doesn't matter anyway, as Tawny didn't have a regular phone in her apartment, only a cell phone, whose number has long since changed hands"

"What can you do?" I asked.

"I have one lead left: Tawny's landlord thinks she had a sister. However, he didn't know her name, or where she lived. He had only her maiden name to go on, the same as Tawny's." He sighed. "I have all of Europe to search."

"Danial, maybe you should turn this over to someone else there—"

"I will not," he replied, his tone like dark freezing water. "Theo would not give up looking for me, if I were the one missing."

My anger sparked hearing him suggest that had been what I'd meant. "I'm not advocating we give up," I yelled into the phone. "You can only work at night, and you've got no one watching your back."

"Suri, Ivan, and Demetri are here with me," Danial replied patiently. "They are doing most of the legwork during the day. Feel free to calm down anytime."

"I'm sorry," I said, relieved. "I didn't know."

"I know you're worried, but I have to do everything I can before I give up," Danial said bleakly. "I want badly for you to be right, for him to still be alive."

"I don't have words for telling you what it means to me that you're still there looking," I said softly.

"He was my best friend, Sar. I could do no less for him. Take care, until tomorrow."

I hung up with a sigh.

The phone rang immediately. It was Terian.

"Thanks for calling me back promptly," I said sarcastically. "I need to know something."

"I'll be by tomorrow," he said quickly. "I'm sorry I haven't called back until now. I just got your message today." He paused. "Have they found him?"

"No," I said heavily.

"They will," he said resolutely. "Get some sleep. Expect me about noon."

* * * *

Terian was there promptly at noon. He hugged me tightly, telling me again he was sorry. Then we sat on the deck and watched Elle play on the lawn with Ghost and Darkness.

"She's getting big," he said in admiration.

"Be careful, Terian," I cautioned. "She still likes to be picked up. She's about seventy five pounds now."

"I can probably still manage to lift her, Sar," Terian said with a laugh.

"I forget how strong you are," I said with a smile. He smiled back, his cherry wood eyes sparkling. "How is Sundown?"

"I'm thinking about proposing," he said hesitantly. "I'm not sure if I should. I'm immortal and she's not. What do you think?"

"Ask her, but first be honest about your immorality. If she says no, tell her you still want to be with her. Don't be afraid to tell her because of what Danial and I went through."

Terian gave me a considering glance and nodded thoughtfully. "Why did you ask me to come over?" he said, after a pause.

"I wanted to see you," I said, not wanting to admit I'd have settled for talking on the phone, and he had kind of invited himself over.

"That may be, but that familiar note means you need my help with something is in your voice. What is it?"

I relayed my suspicion to him about Tawny's heart attack. "Any ideas?"

He considered it. "I know of several things might have been used. How will this help you find Theo?"

I handed him my phone. "Call Danial and leave a message with the names of the potions that could have been used and the names of whomever you know in Europe who could have made them. Danial can track them down and see if they have any record of someone purchasing a potion in the four months leading up to Tawny's death. She wouldn't have been able to hide the pregnancy after the fourth month. She hadn't told her husband, but he might have suspected the child wasn't his."

"The potion would have only been good for a few days after creation," Terian said quickly. "He would have had to buy it and give it to her in the span of seventy-two hours."

"Please call Danial and tell him that." I dialed the phone and handed it to him.

He took it and shortly began talking quickly, dictating a list to one of Danial's foxes.

When he finished I took the phone back. "Stay for dinner? I've made lasagna."

"Of course," he said, grinning. "I was hoping you'd ask."

After we'd finished the meal, he headed out, saying he had a lot to do on the way home. "Most of all, I have to come up with a way to tell Sun I'm part demon."

"If she loves you, she'll accept it," I told him. "I accepted Theo being werecougar."

"Sar, I'm so sorry about Theo," he said softly, hugging me good-bye.

"So am I," I said to him sadly. "Good luck."

* * * *

Danial called back later to thank me for the information, and he would get started on it right away. I wanted to ask him if he had appointed someone else to run his business since he'd been gone so long from his territory. Part of me worried irrationally Devlin might have been left as makeshift regent, ludicrous as it was. More likely, Danial's life had been put on hold the way mine had been.

Another week passed. With me not working, I was able to get a lot of work done in preparation for winter. The garden Theo and I had planted last spring had taken a turn for the worse while we'd been gone, but with Elle's help, we got it under control. She was also able to help me cut wood, by rolling pieces with her paws and moving logs over, so I could cut them through. Despite her youth, the intelligence in her eyes revealed she was more than animal. My only concern was how limited her cougar form made communication between us. She still had not changed form yet to human once.

I called Cia the next day, explained my concern and asked her for advice. She told me to bring Elle to see her that night.

We drove over to Danial's home after dinner. Seeing the house again, I was struck by the feeling if I could only go inside, Theo would be there waiting for me. He had just been away on a long assignment. He would be so happy to see us; he would relish seeing how Elle had grown and there was so much he could teach her...

Tears slide down my cheeks and I wiped them away angrily, driving past the house on to the fox communal compound.

Cia was overjoyed to see us and gave us both a big hug. She took us to her room, and then Janice came in dressed in a robe.

"I can't change, Sar, because of the baby," Cia said apologetically, "but Janice will."

Janice disrobed and gradually changed into her fox form. She did it deliberately slowly, as Elle watched her with wide eyes. She wasn't scared as I expected her to be. Janice barked once, and Elle came over and sniffed her. They ran around a little, and then Janice changed back to human. Again, she did it slowly, deliberately. Elle watched, but she seemed not to know what to do.

Cia shrugged her shoulders. "She just must not be ready," she said, as

Janice got back into her robe.

"How long did it take you to learn to change?" I asked. Cia was the only werefox I knew for sure that had been born were.

"I changed when I was five or six, I think. It's hard to remember."

I leaned over and whispered to her "Cia, if she takes that long, her vocal cords may not develop correctly. I'm worried—"

"Sar, if you rush her, she might be hurt then, too," she replied. "So what if it takes her a little longer to speak?"

"You think I shouldn't worry?"

"Do you see how big she is?" Cia said meaningfully.

"What are you saying, Cia?"

"I'm saying Elle might only be a few months old, but she's maturing at the rate of a cougar, not a child."

Realization swept in, and I felt shock. Why hadn't I noticed? "You mean—?"

"Yes. Elle might change and be five years old already," Cia continued.

My eyes closed, as I fought to control myself.

"Relax, Sar, you are doing the best you can," Cia said, trying to comfort me.

I remembered Theo saying those same words to me and began to cry. Cia held me to her, not speaking, her thoughts likely the same as mine.

Even if we eventually did find Theo, even if he somehow found his way back to me, he'd never get this time with his daughter back. I worried she was already forgetting him.

* * * *

October came and once again, I found myself scurrying to be ready for winter. The garden had done well, and I busied myself putting up vegetables Theo and I had planted, the same ones he'd never seen grow into fruition.

I also decided it was time to face facts. I had to find work soon.

My SUV had died a month ago. I had been saving up to buy a new car since the spring, but I had needed that money in the last months to pay my bills. It was now early September and winter would be here soon. I had Theo's truck, which was almost new, but my other savings were also nearly gone. With careful scrimping, I had enough money left to see Elle and me through this winter. Then I was going to have to get another job, and this one would have to be a full time one.

I had debated trying to use some of Theo's money. He'd had a bank account somewhere, but I'd found no paperwork on it in his belongings. Aside from his clothes, guns, and woodcarving equipment, there was not as much as a photograph. I could've asked Danial to access it, sure, but that made me feel like I was giving up on Theo, declaring he was dead. I wasn't ready to do that,

60

not while I still had money of my own. There was also the worry I wouldn't be able to get Theo's money, anyway because he and I hadn't married. There was no death certificate for him, and his daughter was for all legal purposes a cougar. Elle's paperwork from Europe didn't include so much as a social security number.

I had a lot to worry about, especially when I considered my responsibilities to Elle. Yet I tried not to think about them, pinning my hopes on Danial. He would find Theo and everything would be all right. I also devoted myself to spending time with Elle to teach her human words for the world around her even if I couldn't teach her to speak. She had grown fast in the last month and was almost one hundred pounds now, all of it muscle. I was beginning to worry about leaving her alone with the cats, but she'd given no sign she thought of them as anything other than her family. In the way she watched me, she understood my words to her and knew to nod or shake her head if I asked her a question or to indicate she wanted something with her paw and a look. She'd been housebroken for some time now, but she still had not changed form yet.

Danial called late in the last week of October. "I found Tawny's sister. She gave me the name of Tawny's husband, but said she had no idea where he was. She hadn't seen him for months."

"Does she know about Elle?' I said hesitantly.

Tawny's sister was blood relation to Elle. I wasn't. I was afraid of losing her.

"Sar, Tawny's sister didn't even know about Theo," Danial said with a sort of disgust. "I didn't mention Elle. She's staying with you, no matter what."

"Thank you," I said gratefully.

"I do have real news. She showed me a picture of Tawny's husband," Danial said oddly.

"What is it?" I asked intently.

"This man, Tawny's husband, was named Will. In build and size, Will was a dead ringer for Theo."

"So the body we found was—"

"Will, yes. That was why the head had been taken. We'd have known it wasn't Theo at once." He paused. "I always wondered how Peterson knew of our true natures. It's not something Theo or I advertised. Will was the one who betrayed us, Sar. He told Peterson what we were, and that's why they asked us to be there that particular week."

"He found out about Tawny and Theo?"

"He may not have known Theo by sight, but he knew who Tawny had been stepping out with those nights she wasn't home. He had to have known for some time, he arranged for this setup months ago—"

"So who killed him and planted Theo's stuff on him?" I interrupted.

"Sar, if I knew that, I'd be able to tell you what happened," Danial said in exasperation.

"I'm sorry, Danial, please go on," I said, chastened.

"My guess is Will knew Theo would be coming for revenge when we got away at the airstrip. He went to Peterson and got one of the prototype guns. He waited until we'd finished with Peterson and were leaving. Then he confronted Theo, and Theo shot him."

"Theo would never have shot him in the back," I said, horrified.

"Yes, he would have. Theo was practical, Sar. He would not have wanted to look over his shoulder for the next fifty years or put you and Elle in any danger. We went there that night to ensure we'd all be left alone. That means you kill everyone, not just the ones who shoot at you."

"I understand that," I said softly. "It's just repugnant to me."

"You'd be a little less ethical if you'd been hunted yourself," Danial said darkly. "I hope you never are, but this is the real world." He paused.

"It means someone else was there waiting for Theo that night. They captured him somehow after he shot Will. They took the ring from him, his phone, and wallet and planted them on Will's body. Then they kept him. Whoever it was either has him or has killed him."

"For what purpose?" I asked. "Wouldn't they have gained more by asking for a ransom from you?"

"I don't know the purpose," Danial said. "Ransom would have been the most lucrative, yes, but they didn't want me to know he was alive, so that's out. It makes no sense at all. I keep wishing Theo were here to help me. I counted on his planning skills so many times, on his ideas and conclusions." His voice broke a little at the end.

Tears slid down my face. I'd counted on Theo. too. He'd always had a plan, or some logical place to start one. He'd helped me prepare for anything and everything I'd ever had to face, except losing him.

I wiped at my eyes. "Could it have been Peterson? You said he wanted to test the guns he was making."

"He's officially out of the weapons business," Danial said darkly. "His team who designed his guns are dead. I personally destroyed his plans, all of them, including infecting his company computer with a malicious virus that wiped everything in the database."

"He could start again—"

"He's a drained husk," Danial said, sneering. "He won't be starting anything ever again."

"Oh," I said softly, chilled.

"You should know something else, Sar," Danial added. "Will did kill Tawny. I spoke to the druggist who made him the potion. He said Will had told him it was for an old dog he had that was failing, to ensure a quick death."

Horrible as that was, I didn't care at all about Tawny. "What will you do now?" I said. "There seem to be no leads left to follow."

"I'm coming home, Sar," Danial said, thick with emotion. "I've done everything I can here. Samuel's promised to notify me, if any news of a werecougar reaches him."

"Come and see us when you are rested," I said sadly. "I've missed you."

"I miss you too, Sar. I'll be there next week to see you and Elle."

I hung up, feeling terrible. My hopes had been dashed by Danial's failure. Worse, I couldn't even mourn Theo, when everything pointed to him being alive somewhere, captive.

I sat before the fire with Elle, resisting the urge for a glass of wine. I had to be strong for her; I couldn't be drunk or even tipsy.

"Danial's coming to see you next week," I said to Elle softly.

She looked at me curiously.

"You met him when you were first born," I said. "You might not remember him by sight, but you'll remember his scent."

Elle nodded, then bared her fangs in a grin.

"Time for bed," I said. "Do you need to go out?"

Elle shook her head.

"Go into bed then," I said. "I'll be in after getting the dogs settled."

Elle nodded and trotted off to the bedroom.

I watched her go, letting worry creep back into my face. In this last week, our finances had gone from bad to worse. I'd forgotten we owed the workmen for the updated plumbing, the new roof, and the kitchen remodeling they'd done a few months ago. Theo had been going to settle up with the contractors when we'd returned from Europe. I'd left it to him to handle and hadn't given it another thought. They'd finally come calling, irate, one after the other. I'd paid everyone off, but it had taken the rest of my savings. I needed money for next month's bills, especially for Elle's food. She had graduated from a steak a day to a roast and a chicken two times a day. Suri had taught her to catch mice in her time with us, but that was more a learned skill than a way to keep Elle fed. When he came, I needed to ask Danial about the money of Theo's. Hopefully, there would be enough to last the winter. Well behaved as she was, I didn't want to leave Elle alone for hours until she was older.

* * * *

Finally, it was Halloween.

I had made Elle a little costume, a cape and a tiara. She liked it, preening as she looked at her reflection in the mirror. I laughed and took her picture with my camera as she posed.

Later on, I made some popcorn and tossed pieces to Elle as she lay beside me. We were watching a bad Sci-Fi movie about a town that got flooded, and its residents were evil monsters. It was bad, but in a comforting way. I'd had a scary enough life lately. I didn't want to watch anything that was going to make me truly afraid.

There was a knock at the door. I got up to answer it and found Danial standing there. He looked the same, still beautiful, with just a trace of arrogance.

I smiled at him. "Come in."

He did, handing me his coat. "I didn't call, but I figured you'd be home."

Elle had followed me to the door along with the dogs. The dogs welcomed him, tails wagging, but Elle hung back, her eye watchful.

Danial kneeled down. "Hi, Elle. Do you remember me?"

She slowly inched forward, stretched out her head, her eyes wary, and sniffed him. Then she bounded to him, almost knocking him over in her urge to rub against him, purring loudly. He hugged her close and looked up at me, tears in his eyes.

I wiped at my filling eyes. "Come into the living room."

Danial picked Elle up, all hundred plus pounds of her and followed me into the living room. "Are you watching another of those awful movies?" he said with a smile, setting her down.

"Want to kill a few more brain cells with me?" I offered.

"Sure." He smiled and sat down. Elle quickly sprawled on his lap, taking up most of the couch, so I squeezed into the small section on the other side of him.

The movie was awful, but we had a good time laughing about it. When it was over, I told Elle it was time for bed, to go into the bedroom.

She shook her head, then pointedly looked at the woodstove.

That meant she wanted to spend tonight out here in the woodstove room instead of with me. More and more, she was distancing herself from me at night. I didn't know if it was because she liked the heat or because she was getting too old to sleep with me.

"Okay," I said, "but you have to go to sleep. No sneaking out and watching TV."

She nodded and then curled up. I fed the fire one last time, then turned to Danial, standing by the door.

"I should go," Danial said reluctantly. "It's late."

I stopped him, my hand on his arm. "Please, stay with me a little while."

"Sar—" he began warily.

"Please, Danial. I have to talk to you. Come with me." I held out my hand.

He sighed and took my hand. I led him below to the bedroom that had been his not long ago. Danial sat on the edge of the bed with me.

"She understands us," I said quietly. "I didn't want to talk in front of her."

"What is it, Sar?" he said tiredly.

"You remember the Hallows party a year ago?"

"Of course," Danial said with longing. "I remember being so nervous, worried you wouldn't show. I remember how you looked in the dress, dancing with me." He paused. "Why do you bring it up?"

"Because you must be going to have another one soon, unless you're skipping this year."

"Yes, in late November," Danial said edgily. "I closed the business while looking for Theo and am going to reopen it next year. I need the last months of this year to finish up loose ends of old business." He sighed. "I also need to hire someone to replace Theo, if such a thing can be done."

"I want to be there, Danial," I said. "If you would permit me to come."

"I had hoped you would," Danial said, kissing me gently on the forehead. "I wanted to invite you, but wasn't sure you'd want to—"

"I know you will invite Samuel," I said forcefully. "I want to question him about Theo—"

His eyes tinted red immediately. "Sar, that is not what I had in mind. I have already talked to him. He said he did nothing."

"I don't believe him, Danial. You weren't there when he and Theo had words."

"That doesn't matter," he retorted. "He is a Ruler. You cannot question him as if he were a mere human."

"I certainly can—"

"Sar, I forbid it," Danial said arrogantly, grabbing hold of me, "and that's the end of it."

"Who are you to forbid me anything?" I said furiously.

"I'm a man who loves you," he said furiously and kissed me hard, pulling the length of his body against mine as we fell backwards onto the bed.

I struggled, but he kissed me more thoroughly, his lips and body cool against mine. I shuddered in his arms, the feeling of being held and desired making me weak with relief and happiness.

Danial moved, rolling me from my side unto my back, his kisses intensifying. He shifted suddenly, pressing down with his hips. I felt his erection pressing firmly to my belly and shuddered, My mouth opened to let out a gasp. He saw the opportunity and took it, sliding his tongue into my mouth to taste me. I trembled and then kissed him back for all I was worth.

Danial broke the kiss, his black eyes staring at me beneath him as he pulled off his shirt. I arched my back, pulling my sweater off over my head. All I'd needed to do was kiss him. I wanted him so badly I could taste it.

He pulled off my jeans and underwear with one quick tug. I unbuttoned his pants, but he pushed me back and pulled down his jeans, yanking them off in a swift jerk. I unhooked my bra, tossed it aside, and then he was on me, thrusting into me with a loud eager cry before covering my mouth with his own. Then he drew back to watch me under him, my body moving with his as I groaned with pleasure.

I couldn't get enough of him. I clutched him close, my mouth devouring his, my eager cries of pleasure sounding with each thrust of his body into mine.

He broke the kiss and pushed up with his forearms, his fangs bared. I reached up with one hand to clasp the back of his neck loosely, then looked into his eyes and nodded once. I threw my head back, baring my neck for him, and he struck fast, sinking his fangs into the unmarked side. I cried out in pain, and he shuddered, beginning to make the soft cries of pleasure I loved to hear as his movements intensified. Hearing him, feeling him jerking within me, pushed me over the edge.

"Danial! Oh, Danial! Danial!" I came screaming his name.

Danial climaxed, his wordless shout matching mine in volume. He squeezed me tightly, his body giving a few last jerks. When our breathing quieted, he spoke. "You have never said my name before, Sar," he said tenderly.

"That is only one of my regrets," I said gently, kissing him. "There is a lot I'm sorry for with you, Danial."

He looked at me in surprise, blinking.

"I'm sorry," I said quickly. "What I'm trying to say is I should not have left you like I did. I should have stayed with you to work it out. It wasn't your fault, what happened to me or to our baby. You did the best you could, Danial. I'm sorry."

He hugged me. "No, I didn't, Sar. I should never have pushed you, should never have made so many demands. I wanted you like I hadn't wanted anything in so long. All I thought about was having you with me, making you mine. When you said you needed more time, I wasn't willing it give it to you. I never thought much about the life you had until you met me. I thought too much about what I wanted and what I thought was best for you." He paused. "I should never have bedded Angelica. I did it out of jealousy, out of loneliness, because I knew how you felt about her, and I knew it would hurt you."

He was right about all of it, but I had something to apologize for, too. "I never should have slept with Theo, either, Danial, not the way I did." I let out a long breath. "I should have waited to talk to you, to give you the ring face to face. I owed you that at least. I should have called you on your cell the night I saw Angelica and asked you, if only to hear it from you, if what she said was true. I was hurt, and all I wanted was to get away." I looked into Danial's eyes. "Did Theo tell you what happened to us, what really happened?"

"Yes," he admitted. "One night in June, I finally asked him to his face how he could have done to me what he had done. He told me everything." Danial paused. "It matters to me that you stopped him that night on New Year's Eve. Even though you were half in love with him, you still stopped him, because you had given your word to me." He kissed me then and sighed contentedly. I settled into his arms.

"Sar, what did you want to talk about?" he said finally. "Or was that an excuse to get me down here?" He hugged me closer. "Not that I mind at all, if it was."

I did not want to talk about money now, not like this, but I thought of Elle upstairs and knew I had to. "Danial, you know I quit my job." I began, hoping he would help me by guessing what I had to say.

He hugged me, but didn't say anything.

Well, there was no subtle way to say this. I might as well be blunt. "I need access to Theo's money, for Elle and me. I've gone through my savings, and I don't want to leave her—"

Danial moved back abruptly, pushing me on my back. "You mean all this time you've been subsisting on your own money?" he said furiously. "Why didn't you tell me?"

"Yes, I—"

"Why didn't you say something, Sarelle? I thought you were thinner than I remembered you being."

My eyes were filling. "Danial—"

"What do you think the money was for? It was for you and Elle, if something happened to him. He put it in both your names."

"He never told me how to access it," I sobbed, tears leaking out of my eyes. "Maybe he planned to, after we got married, but he never got the chance—"

Danial shushed me, stroking my hair. "Sar, I'm sorry, please don't cry. I'm sorry. I can get you access tomorrow. There's enough there you don't have to worry for a while."

"I knew...I'd have to ask...if we decided he wasn't coming back," I heaved the words out, then took a deep breath. "I didn't want to face he wasn't coming back, but I have to now because he would have come back if he could have. So he has to be dead, Danial. He has to be dead."

"I know," Danial said softly. "I did everything I could to find him, to find out what happened to him. But the trail ended with Will. There are no leads left to follow."

"You did your best," I said, running my fingers through his hair.

He sighed. "I did, because every night since he was taken I have blamed myself for my jealousy. You spoke the truth that I wished somehow he was out of the way so I could be with you." He laughed wretchedly. "I've gone through most of Europe trying to alleviate that guilt."

I hugged him and didn't speak.

"It hurts me to know you would never be here like this with me if he was alive," Danial continued. "It still hurts that you picked him over me. That you decided to die being loyal to him rather than oath to me when I tried to save you from Devlin."

I went still, anger filling me. Either he was making a point or he wanted to start a fight. I was betting on the former, seeing as we'd just made love.

"Can you forgive me for what happened that night?" he whispered. "Can we start again, you and I?"

"I forgave you," I said softly, my anger lessening. "You tried everything to stop Devlin, but he was too powerful for you to fight. There wasn't anything more you could've done."

Danial took my hand. "You know I love you, Sar. You know I want you with me. Will you come and be with me now? Let me help take care of Elle and you?"

"Do you really want to try again, after all that's happened?" I studied his face. "I'm no closer to handling your immortality than I was six months ago."

"You need me like you didn't before," Danial answered. "Being a parent alone is not the same as being on your own. I was a father once, a good one. Elle doesn't just need food and shelter, she needs love and guidance."

"Yes," I said softly. "I want to try again, but I'm afraid how this will affect her if it doesn't work out between us."

"It will work out," Danial said firmly. "I'm not asking you to oath to me, or to give me any promise. I'm asking you to let me help you raise Theo's child, to come and live with me until she's grown." He kissed me gently. "If you want to, view it as duty. I feel responsible for her. You do not have to share my bed."

"Like I'm going to live with you and be able to resist," I said with a chuckle.

"You said it, not I," Danial said huskily. "Though of course, I'd welcome your affections."

"What if Theo somehow returns?" I asked. "Could you let me go, if he did?"

"You would still want to leave?" Danial said unbelievingly.

"Depends on his reasons for not coming back," I replied. "I can't say, not for sure."

"Do you expect me to be that cold?" Danial said, closing his eyes and grimacing as if in pain. "To say such things to me as if I had no heart?"

"I don't mean to hurt you," I said apologetically. "I meant to be honest." I reached out to him and touched his face. "I can't truly let him go, not knowing what happened, if he's dead or not. Do you understand?"

Danial sighed. "I understand you want him, not me."

"Don't give me that," I said angrily. "Do you understand I'm upset? My life fell apart. This is the second time I've lost a loved one in two years." I moved to get up. "This is probably the wrong time for another try, Danial. It's not going to work."

Danial moved fast, gathering me in his arms. "Don't say that. I'm sorry I got angry, but it's hard to have just made love with you and listen to you talk as if I don't matter to you at all."

"You do matter," I said softly into his neck. "I'm just a wreck. Why would you even want me like this?"

Danial hugged me. "When I saw the ring he was planning to give you, I knew any chance I'd had with you was over." He kissed me. "I'll take whatever you can give me, Sar, for as long as you'll give me. Please let me help you. If you don't want me, that's fine. Do it for Elle."

"I'll come," I said softly, "but not just for Elle. I'll come because I want to be with you."

"Say that again," Danial said huskily.

Hearing that word, I felt as if I'd been kicked in the gut. I began sobbing uncontrollably.

Danial immediately panicked. "Sar, what's wrong? What did I say? Sar?"

The urge to throw up rose within me, and I quickly clambered out of bed.

Danial grabbed hold of me, pulling me back. "Sar, say something? What is it?"

I forced myself to breathe deeply. "I'm okay," I said finally. "I'm sorry. It's because it's the first time I've been intimate since…um, again, it's something he used to say every time…" I trailed off.

"I will never say that word, not to you like this. I promise," Danial assured me.

"I feel like I'm falling apart," I said tearfully. "Like everything's wrong, and I'm so scared it won't ever be right again."

"It will be, in time," Danial said. "You're still grieving. Lean on me. I'm here for you. I'll not let you down."

"Please love me, please," I whispered to him, kissing his neck. "Hold me."

"I have never stopped loving you, Sarelle, and I never will," Danial said compellingly. He pushed me back gently, spreading my thighs and sliding into me in one quick motion. I began kissing him urgently, moving with him.

The cellar door opened and something tumbled down the stairs. Danial rolled off me immediately, so his body was in front of mine.

From the foot of the stairs came the sudden cry of a little girl.

Chapter Four

I jumped out of bed, grabbed up Danial's shirt and put it on. He slipped into his jeans and followed me to the foot of the steps, where I reached down, gathering a sobbing Elle into my arms.

She was in human form, somewhere between four and five. Her hair was long and blond, like mine. She was naked, and her arm looked broken, hanging at an odd angle. She was crying loudly.

"Shh," I said.

"Give her to me," Danial said as he came up behind me.

I handed her to him. He took her in on the bed and laid her down.

"Hold still," he told her. "This will hurt, but it will help."

Elle stopped crying long enough to nod, her eyes shut tight. With a swift jerk, he set her arm. She screamed. We both comforted her as best we could while she healed. When the bruises faded, Elle opened her eyes and looked at us.

I gasped. She had Theo's eyes, the medium gray blue of a cloudy overcast day.

"Mommy?" she said, her voice raspy and uneven.

Hearing that one word, I suddenly knew who I was more than I ever had before in my life. I gathered her into my arms and held her, tears coursing down my face. "Yes."

Danial picked us both up and laid us in bed, cradling me against him with Elle in the middle. I couldn't stop staring at her. I'd wanted to see her for so long as a human. Now that she was, I didn't know what to say first.

Danial, gentleman that he was, took up my slack. "Do you know who I am?".

"Danial," she said, making it sound like Danielle.

"Danial," he corrected.

"Danial," she said again, saying the correct 'Dan-yal' pronunciation.

"Good." He smiled at her. "Do you know who that is?" he said, pointing to me.

"Sarelle. Mommy. Mother," Elle said slowly, trying hard to get the right emphasis on the words.

"Do you remember how to change back?" I said to her, my eyes searching her face.

"No," she said, tears filling her eyes.

I hugged her again. "Shh. It's okay, Elle. I just wanted to know what happened."

"I heard you crying. I heard Danial, um, upset. I needed to get to you, to help you. I needed to open the door."

For never speaking before, she was doing a fantastic job of it. I'd been talking to her for months, trying to expose her to as many words as I could, so when she finally did change to her human form, she would know as much as possible. I was glad of it now.

"I couldn't um, grip the door. I reached for it and my paw became like yours," she said finally. "I remembered what you did and turned it and pulled, but when I started forward, my legs wouldn't work right and I fell."

Elle had never walked on two legs before. I looked at Danial. He had eyes only for her.

"You were very brave," I said. She hugged me again.

"I need to go outside," she said to me suddenly, a look of panic on her face.

I gathered her up quickly and raced for the stairs. Danial followed, mystified.

We got to the bathroom in time. I showed Elle what to do, and she did it. Then I showed her how to work the sink, and she washed her hands. She was still naked, so I got her a sweatshirt of mine to wear and a pair of leggings. They were too big, but it was the best I could do.

I sat her on the closed toilet seat and helped her dress. Then I helped her to the couch.

After sitting her down near Danial, I went to put on some clothes myself. I brought back Danial's shirt to him, and he put it on. We spent the rest of the night teaching Elle to walk.

She didn't know how to change back, and I didn't know how to help her do it. So we had to make sure she could get around on her own. I was worried she'd fall down the stairs, or something worse. Initially, I put Ghost on one side of her and Darkness on the other. Then I called them, and they steadied her as she walked, holding onto them. It worked for a few steps at least, but she kept losing her balance and falling. Then Danial and I tried. We each took one of her hands and helped her walk alongside us. Soon, she was able to walk, just holding lightly to our hands. She beamed a huge smile at us, and I had to blink back tears yet again.

Faint daylight was showing through the windows. I took care of the cats and dogs while Danial took her below with him. While my pets were eating, I checked the Weather Channel, becoming depressed to know they were forecasting snow for the coming weekend.

Snow plowing season was here. In addition to dismay, I was excited. Elle had never seen snow before. I couldn't wait to see her face when she saw it for the first time.

I let the dogs outside, and they did their business. That was what Elle had meant by saying she had to go outside. She'd gotten too big for her litter box, and I'd trained her to go outside like the dogs did. I'd felt bad, but the other weres did that in animal form. There had been no way for her to use a toilet in cougar form.

When the pets were settled, I went back downstairs to Danial and Elle. Danial held his finger to his lips as I entered. Elle was asleep, nestled in the crook of his arm, her head on his chest. Her eyes were closed, her hair fanned across his arm that held her.

I crawled next to Danial's other side, and he put his other arm around me, pulling me close to him. He kissed me softly, and we all settled down to sleep.

We slept until dusk, when Danial's cool lips woke me in a gentle kiss. "Wake up, Sar."

I opened my eyes to find him grinning at me. He had smiled before, but never with this much happiness.

Elle was awake and jumping a little on the bed. "Mom, can we get up now?" she yelled.

"Yes," I winced. "Not so loud so soon." At least she'd slept as long as she had.

Danial offered me his hand and helped me up. I gave a big yawn and covered my mouth. Elle gave one, too, imitating me. She covered her mouth, too. I grabbed her and tickled her, and she shrieked. Danial laughed then, and I'd never heard him laugh like that, so light, so happy. I turned to behold him grinning ear to ear.

"Come," he said. "You and your mother should eat."

We each took her hand and went upstairs. "What would you like?" I said to her.

"Chicken," she said, licking her lips.

"Try some eggs and bacon instead," I offered. "Then you can have chicken. Okay?"

"Okay," she said dubiously, "but you only gave them to me as a treat, um, before."

"We're celebrating," I said. "Give me a few moments."

Danial played with her while I got breakfast ready. I sat her at the table when it was time, and she wolfed down her eggs and bacon, after Danial helped her to use her fork.

"Some more?" she said, looking at me hopefully.

I made her some more, eating some myself as I cooked. When she'd had another two platefuls, she finally said she was full. I put the dishes in the dishwasher and told Elle we needed to think about showering.

"I don't want to get wet," Elle said, crinkling up her nose.

"You don't want to smell bad, do you?" Danial said.

"No," she said slowly, looking at him.

"When you look like this, Elle, you need to bathe," Danial said patiently

"Okay," Elle said reluctantly, drawing it out.

I put her in the guest shower with me and showed her how to wash her hair, how to rinse off, and how to use the soap. I'd never had cause to give her a bath before this. She watched me comb out my long hair, and I handed her the brush when I was done, so she could do the same to her hair.

"Your body looks different from mine," she said haltingly.

I thought desperately I needed a break about now. I had no idea how to answer her. "I'm older than you, Elle," I said finally. "When you get older, your body will look like mine."

"Will I have—?"

I cut her off. "Yes, exactly like mine, but that's not for a long while. I have to tell you something else too, Elle, and I want you to understand I'm not upset or angry with you. You need to understand it is not okay to talk about things like this with anyone except me and Danial."

She looked sad, and I kicked myself. "Elle, I want you to ask me any questions you have. I'll do my best to answer them as will Danial. I just want you to feel comfortable around other people. If there are other people around, whisper in my ear what you are thinking of saying before you say it, and I'll let you know if it's okay to say." God, I hoped I was handling this the right way. What if I were traumatizing her?

"Okay, Sarelle," she said, looking up at me.

I thought about telling her to call me Mom, but decided not to.

"Was I called Elle, um, by you?" she said haltingly. I realized then she knew words she'd heard around her often, but only the ones I'd taught her. I was glad again I'd talked to her so much in the last few months. I helped her out of the shower and handed her a towel. I helped her dry off, and she hugged me.

"Was I called Elle by you?" she said again.

I wrapped a towel around my head and another around hers and led her into the bedroom. Danial, going by me into the shower, kissed me. Hoping there was enough hot water left for him, I sat Elle down on the bed beside me.

"Your father, Theo, called you Elle. He named you Elle, which means he called you that first, and said to everyone they should call you that. Do you understand?" I said gently.

"Did he call me that because of you?" she said then.

"Yes," I answered, remembering and trying not to be sad.

"Mommy, why are you always sad thinking about him?" she said, hugging me.

"I loved him very much, Elle," I said, choked up. "I miss him."

"You often told me he loved me," she said in a small voice. "Where is he?"

"We aren't sure, but we think he died," I said, holding her close. "Right after you were born, he disappeared. Danial has just returned from searching for him, having given up."

She looked up into my eyes with Theo's eyes. "Why did he die?"

"Sometimes it happens," I said quickly, thinking of Tawny's tangled web of lies.

"Are you going to die? Is Danial?" she said, panicked.

"Elle, I am not going to die for a long time. Danial is not going to die, um, for a long time either." This was not the time to talk about vampires. There would be enough time for that later.

"Am I going to die?" she was still panicked.

"Elle, remember downstairs? How you fell?"

"Yes," she said, considering.

"Remember your arm, how it felt?"

"It hurt a lot," she said loudly.

"Remember how Danial straightened it, and it felt better?"

"Yes." She was thinking hard now. "He fixed it."

"You are a werecougar, like your father was," I said. "Like him, you can heal almost any wound. It is hard to hurt you, unless you get hurt here." I pointed to her heart.

"Is that where Theo got hurt?" she replied.

She was quick. "We think so," I said slowly. "Come and get dressed."

I put her in one of my short sweaters and a short skirt. They were huge on her, but it would do until I got her some clothes. I put on a sweater and some jeans and conditioned my hair. Elle wanted some, when she saw me doing it, so I gave her some.

I looked in the mirror then, really looked, as I hadn't since those days in the hotel in Orleans. I was thinner, as Danial had observed. Not supermodel thin, but there was thinness about me that had not been there before from lost muscle and fat. That wasn't due to lack of food, as he'd implied, but lack of my old routines; I was no longer lifting steel routinely or practicing with a gun once a week. I vowed to start working out and to teach Elle to shoot in the near future.

In addition, my hair hadn't been highlighted in months and had grown out, my roots dark around my face. I would need to fix that as well. Strangely, my face itself looked the same, not etched with all the sadness of the past few months. My green eyes stared resolutely back at me, undefeated.

Danial yelled in alarm from the other room. Turning around, Elle had vanished. I ran into the guest bathroom to see him wrapping a towel around himself. He was as close to total embarrassment as I'd ever seen him.

Elle was looking at him hard. "He looks different than you and me, Mommy."

"Because he's a man, a male," I said, trying to stifle my laughter. "You and I are females, girls, women."

Elle opened her mouth again, and I held a finger to her lips. "What did I say?" I said gently, and she immediately hushed.

Danial had regained some of his composure in the meantime. He kneeled so he could look into Elle's eyes. "You need to knock if you go into a bathroom and someone is in there," he said gently. "You need to ask if you can come in and only enter if they say it is okay. Okay?"

"Okay," she said. "I'm sorry."

Danial hugged her. "It's okay." He kissed her forehead, "We need to get you some clothes that fit you." He looked at me. "Let's meet at the truck in five minutes?"

I nodded, and he went back in the bathroom.

"Where are we going?" Elle said, her eyes sparkling. "For a ride?"

"We need to get you some clothes, Elle, and some shoes."

"Toy for me?" she said, excitedly.

I cringed a little at the choice of words I'd taught her, but I'd thought of her as both daughter and animal. I kicked myself. I should be ecstatic she was able to speak as well as she did. Sure, some of her inflections and vowels were coming out wrong, but it would get better with practice. What was important was that I could understand her enough to know what she was trying to communicate to me. It was amazing she could remember so much from her other form. It made sense. She didn't change once a day or once a week. Her cougar form had been her form her whole life until now. Her memory would be normal memory, like I remembered yesterday and the day before.

"Mom?" Elle was still looking at me expectantly. "Toy?"

"Maybe we will get a toy for you," I said, smiling at her. "If you are a good girl."

She beamed up at me. Again I saw Theo in her so strongly I felt I'd been kicked in the chest. "I will be good," she said seriously.

Danial came out, the picture of composure. "We've got to hurry; they'll be closing the stores soon."

He scooped up Elle, who shrieked in joy, and carried her out to his waiting SUV. I locked the front door and followed them.

Danial drove us to the closest mall and hurriedly carried a shoeless Elle into the store. We went to the shoe department first. The saleswoman hurried right over, eyeing Elle's outfit.

"Can I help you?"

"My daughter stepped in dog poop, and we had to toss out her shoes and socks," I replied. "We need to buy more."

"We can't let her try on shoes without her wearing socks."

"Then bring us socks, and we'll purchase them first," Danial said pointedly. "Now."

Danial bought Elle ten pairs of shoes and socks. She wore the sneakers she liked best, and the rest he arranged to have shipped to my house. Then we quickly looked at clothes, and he bought her ten outfits, mostly jeans and sweaters, plus underwear and a winter jacket. Again, he had everything shipped to my house except what Elle wore. She picked out the colors herself, favoring blue and green as her father had.

After leaving the store, we stopped at the food court for a late lunch. Danial, of course, did not order any food. I waited for Elle to ask about that, but she didn't.

Even at ten p.m., many people were out and about. As we ate, it became apparent some were staring at us.

"Why are they watching us, Mom?" Elle said, eating her second hamburger.

I looked to Danial, not sure of what to say. The three of us together were eye-catching, to say nothing of the scar on my neck that no matter what I covered it with would never look like anything other than a bite mark.

"They are watching us because we are beautiful, Elle," he said, looking at her lovingly. "People like to look at beautiful things."

"I am beautiful?" Elle said. "Like this?"

"You are the most beautiful, next to your mom," he said with emotion, gazing at her. Then he met my eyes, inclining his head slightly. "I need to excuse myself for a bit."

He was likely starving. He would have to leave the mall and the video surveillance to do what he needed to do.

"Elle, come with me," I said, holding out my hand. "We're going to look at toys. Grab our plates and we'll toss them out."

"What about Danial?" Elle said immediately, looking from him to me.

"He will catch up to us," I said, taking her hand. "He has to go eat."

'Why didn't he eat with us?" she said, as I dumped the trash in the nearby bin.

"He needs other special food," I said, "but he'll find us, in an hour or so."

She came with me, but watched Danial walk away from us with a little fear in her eyes.

* * * *

Danial caught up to us an hour later in the toy store. Elle had been worried about him and ran to him as soon as she saw him.

He hugged her. "I told you I'd be back soon."

Elle's eyes widened as she drew back from him. "You smell of—"

"Elle, what did I say?" I said sharply.

She came close and whispered. "He smells of blood, fresh blood." She was scared, but the smell of blood had excited her, too, being part cougar.

Sigh, *oy vey*, and every other expression of angst. Time to explain vampires. "You know how we need food to live?"

"Yes," she said.

"Danial needs it to live," I said. "He can't eat food like you and me."

"Will he take, um, mine?" she said hesitantly.

"No," I said, kissing her, "but he will take mine from time to time. You don't have to worry, it's okay."

She looked dubious.

"I give it to him willingly. He enjoys taking it from me," I said. "Understand?"

"I guess," she said. "Does it hurt you?"

"Not the way he does it," I said, giving Danial eyes over Elle's head. "Now which toy do you want?"

Danial interceded. "She means which ones, Elle. Let's get a cart." He then proceeded to buy Elle at least twenty new toys. She kept her favorite—a stuffed cougar—with her, and he sent the rest to my house.

"You're going to spoil her," I said to him in a half-serious tone as we walked outside.

"Good," he said, putting his arm around me. "I tried to spoil you, but you wouldn't let me."

"Maybe I will this time," I said quietly, leaning into him.

He looked over at me, considering, but didn't say anything. The drive home was also quiet; Elle's throat was sore from talking so much, and Danial and I were relieved to have a few moments with no questions. All too soon, we arrived home.

Danial walked us to the door. "I have to go, Sar, but I'll come back in a few days if that's okay."

"What about, um, what we talked about?" I said pointedly. I wanted to know if he had meant what he had said to me last night, but felt uncomfortable asking him to take care of Elle and me, especially in front of her.

He opened his wallet and handed me a card. It was a black MasterCard with my name and his on it and the emblem of his company, with "Solutions, Inc." written across the side. "I got these last year. We never used them, but they're still good. Use it for whatever you need. There is no limit."

"Danial, thank you, but I didn't mean that," I said, flushing.

"I meant everything I said downstairs," Danial said, taking me in his arms. "Give me two weeks to build onto my home. Elle needs a room of her own, furniture, and a tutor."

"Do me a favor," I said, "buy a new bed."

Danial looked pained, but nodded. I kissed him to soften my words, and he pulled me close, his tongue slipping inside my mouth quickly. I broke the kiss and gave him a look of chastisement.

"I'll be back in a few days." He grinned at me widely. "Maybe sooner."

I was struck again by how happy he was as he swung Elle up into his arms to hug her good-bye. A few seconds later, he drove off.

We went indoors, where I started a fire to warm us. As I did, I showed Elle the procedures. Danial was right; now she was in human form, there was a lot she needed to learn.

After taking care of my pets, Elle and I got ready for bed. We'd forgotten to get any pajamas for her, so I gave her one of my T-shirts, and put on a nightgown myself. I put her in my bed because I didn't think she should be alone in the cellar. It seemed wrong to have her curl up with the dogs in human form. She was asleep when her head hit the pillow. I fell asleep beside her soon after.

I awoke the next morning to her already wide-awake and bouncing, talking loudly about breakfast. I gave her tired eyes, but got up. She took a shower by herself, likely mostly for Danial. Halfway through, she got soap in her eyes and began screaming. Rushing in, I helped her rinse it out. As she dressed, I started a fire and saw to the pets.

"Mom, I'm hungry."

I rubbed my eyes, already exhausted and wished Danial was here. "That's next."

"Mom, are you going to shower?"

"No," I replied. "I'll wait. Let's eat. We have a lot of work to do today."

An hour later, she and I brought over more wood. For being as small and young as she was, she was quite strong. We got two loads of wood and stacked them in the basement. Then she helped me bring more wood upstairs.

She was ravenous by lunch, eating an entire small chicken I had roasted, while I had a sandwich. After lunch, she took a nap. I slept too, as I was exhausted myself. Elle was back up at three p.m., when her clothes and toys were delivered. She spent the rest of the afternoon playing as I napped on the couch, after finding room for her clothes in my closet.

Danial called that night to say the construction had started. "How much space should I add?"

"Why not two rooms, one for Elle and one for pet stuff? You don't have an attic and your cellar is full. We'll need storage space and living space, as well as litter box space, reluctant as I am to mention that."

"I'll make sure there is enough room for everything," he answered, pleased. "And everyone."

Sudden worry about how happy he was acting made me distance myself. "Your purchases arrived. Elle's been having a great time."

"Good. I look forward to seeing you both tomorrow night. I've checked into hiring a tutor for Elle. I should have news tomorrow."

"Isn't it a little early for that?" I said, leery. "She's only a few months old."

"She needs schooling, Sar, especially at the rate she's growing."

"I agree about her being tutored instead of in public school. She might change in front of someone, but isn't she too young?"

"No. This tutor comes recommended by a were-family I know. There won't be problems. He will live here on my property and stay in the fox compound."

"Okay, then. Come by when you want to tomorrow. We'll be here."

"I will," he said happily "take care, both of you."

I sat down Elle after dinner and told her we would be moving soon. "We are going to live with Danial. I know it's not home—"

"Good," she said, smiling hugely. "I like him."

Well, that had been easy. "You'll have your own room, a place for your clothes and your toys and books. There will also be a person coming most days to teach you things, like I just taught you about starting the fire yesterday. There is a lot for you to learn about the world."

"So long as Danial is there," she said flatly.

"Yes," I said with relief. "He will be."

Later, as she slept beside me, worry again ate at me. Was I doing the right thing, running to Danial? Sure, it made a bad situation easy, but was it the best thing for Elle?

I told myself it was, then rolled over, and went to sleep.

* * * *

79

The next day, I gritted my teeth and took Elle to see my parents. I'd kept her existence hidden from them, not wanting them to meet her until she was in human form. Now that she was, it was time for the insurmountable task of breaking the news I both had Theo's daughter and she and I were going to move in with Danial.

The first part was easy: my mother loved Elle at first sight. When they went for a walk, I broke the news to my stepfather.

"I'm moving in with Danial, Stepfather Dear. Elle needs a father figure in her life."

"This is more than Elle, it's because you've given up on Theo," Chris said.

"I guess I have," I said sadly. "Danial chased down every lead It's been four months now. I can't pretend anymore that he's going to walk through my door if I just keep waiting."

"It also means you and Danial are involved again. He cheated on you before. Can you trust him?"

"Yes," I said slowly. "We are being honest with each other like we should have been a year ago. What happened last time was my fault, too."

"Honestly, I think you shouldn't do it, Sarelle," Chris replied. "Your mother and I are always here for you. Call us if you need us." He hugged me. "Can I take Elle fishing?" he said, hopeful. "Theo and I only went that one time."

I laughed. "Of course, if she wants to go."

"You're sure this is best for Elle?"

"Elle needs a man in her life, and Danial wants to be that man. You should see the way he is with her—"

"What?" my mother screeched. "Don't tell me you are back with Danial. Are you insane?"

"Mom, I love him—"

"You loved Theo, too. Danial didn't just cheat on you Sar, he hit you once, remember? This is a mistake and you know it."

"It's not a mistake," I said angrily. "It's what's best for Elle."

"You are disgracing Theo's memory," she said nastily. "Danial is scum, and he'll never be good enough for you. Do you really need a man that badly in your bed?

Elle was in the next room and, with her extraordinary hearing abilities, she was hearing all of this. "Mom, I'm doing this with your support or without it!"

"It's without then," she said, glaring at me.

"We'll be leaving," I said frostily.

"Please don't say bad things about Danial, Grandma."

My mother and I turned. Elle stood there behind her, tears in her eyes. I scooped her up in my arms and we left.

She was silent all the way home. When we got home, I sat her down on the couch.

"I'm sorry you heard all those things your grandma said, Elle."

"Were they true?" she said softly.

I took a deep breath and let it out. "Do you know what 'cheat' means?"

"Yes. You sang a song to me often about that. Did you smash up Danial's truck like in the song?"

I stifled my amusement. "No, I didn't. Do you understand what 'jealousy' is?"

"It's what the woman who sings the song feels. She wants what she thinks is hers and is mad someone else has it."

God, she was so smart. I sighed and stroked her hair. "Danial was jealous. He cheated because of it. After, he regretted cheating. Do you understand 'regret'?"

"He was sorry?" she offered.

"More than that, he wished he could go back and choose not to do what he did."

"Why was he jealous?" She gave me a hard stare.

I was just as pinned by her gaze as I had been by Theo's. "Because I'd fallen in love with your father." That was a lie. It had been Terian who'd made Danial jealous, but I didn't want her to think there was anything between Terian and me because there hadn't been, not like that.

"I think he was right to be jealous," Elle said angrily.

"Danial was wrong to do what he did." I put my head in my hands and sighed. "I was wrong for what I did. We were both to blame."

"Did he hit you?" she said softly. "Hurt you?"

"Yes," I said agitatedly, remembering.

"What happened then?' She looked, afraid.

"Your father and Danial fought. Your father won, and he and I left."

"Theo beat up Danial?" She was incredulous.

I only had the one picture of Theo, the one in my wallet. I took it out, and showed it to her as I had so many times when she was a cougar. "Your father was strong and fast."

She hugged me hard, tears on her face. "If he was so strong and fast, how could he have been killed?"

"The truth is we don't know," I said, hugging her back. "He went out to protect you and me, and he didn't come back. He loved us. He would have come back if he could have."

"So he might be alive?" she said, both hopeful and worried.

"Sweetheart, if he could have, he would have come back," I said, taking a deep breath. "He must be dead." I looked at her and kissed her forehead.

"Remember he loved you, Elle. There was nothing he wouldn't have done for you."

* * * *

After Elle was in bed, I made a call to Terian's cell, breaking the news of Danial to him. I hadn't seen him much in the last few months, but we'd talked on the phone. I wanted to tell him I was moving and give him Danial's number.

His reaction was as expected. "Sar, are you insane?" he yelled at me. "You are going back to that vampire after all Theo and I did to help you get free of him?"

"I didn't expect you to approve, but I still love him. Besides, this is best for Elle."

"Is it really?" he said sarcastically. "You'll be wearing a collar before you know it."

"I already am," I said flatly, "but that was my choice. You don't have to worry."

I'd put it back on the night Danial had told me construction had started. It had gone on easily, and the familiarity of it soothed me, just as if Danial's arms had been around me.

Terian swore. "I'm already worried you're his slave."

"I can take it off at will," I retorted. "Stop having hysterics."

"Are you going to give him your oath?" Terian said in a strangled voice.

"No. Danial wants me to live with him until Elle is grown. There aren't any promises between us."

"He's agreeing to that only because he believes Theo to be dead. You've got to know that."

"Part of me still hopes Theo is alive, but he would never have stayed away so long, Terian. He would have left a trail of bodies to get back to us."

"I believe that, too," Terian said heavily.

"How is Sundown?" I said after a while.

"We broke up yesterday." Terian began sobbing.

"I'm sorry," I said sadly. "Do you want to talk about it?"

"Sar, it was terrible. I asked her to marry me, and she looked at me like I was crazy. She said there was no way she'd be my wife. She said she could feel the evil inside me. She left and doesn't return my calls."

Bitch. Self-righteous, bloodless, heartless bitch. "Then she didn't deserve to be with you. You're a good person, not evil."

"I'm tired of being alone. Some of what I said just now is jealousy, that you always seem to have someone, and I don't—"

I had a thought of pure genius suddenly. "Terian, come and work for Danial. He needs someone to replace Theo, someone to watch out for us. He said he was going to look into—"

"Sar, I don't know much about weapons—"

"You know sorcery, enough to protect us, and you aren't a novice with guns or knives. I remember you fighting Danial more than a year ago."

"Danial might be my ally now, but he was jealous of you and me before. Is he going to want me around you that much?"

I knew when he said that, he was interested in the job. "Go with me tomorrow night, and we'll ask him. It can't hurt."

* * * *

The next night, I drove Terian to see Danial. Elle came as well.

"I should have driven," he grumbled ten minutes into the journey.

I ignored him and kept driving the speed limit. I'd called Danial before we showed up and explained why I was coming to see him. He'd been dubious, but had agreed to see Terian.

When we arrived, Cia came to take Elle to the werefox compound. Terian, Danial, and I went into Danial's great room and sat down, Terian and Danial faced each other, and I was off to the side. I couldn't help remembering the last time we'd been here and everything that had happened. Maybe they were thinking about that, too.

"So, Terian, you want the job?" Danial said, looking at Terian over steepled fingers.

"Tell me what it entails," Terian said seriously.

"Protecting Sar, myself, and Elle at all costs, whatever it takes." Danial replied.

By the way he said it, he meant more than killing attackers; he meant 'sacrificing your own life for one of ours if you have to.' Terian was immortal, though. Even a blast at close range with a gun equipped to kill weres and vampires hadn't killed him. I'd missed his heart, true, but not by much. Danial's words likely didn't give him the same chill they gave me.

"I can do that," he said, holding Danial's gaze.

"You would need to study tactics and do some weapons training," Danial continued. "You would be second in command under me, not just for my business, but in terms of my family and home. You would assume control of the werefoxes and run the guard detail. You would need to travel with me on business, depending on the level of danger."

"Danial, I don't have a lot of experience—" Terian began.

"Neither did Theo, when I met him," Danial said, interrupting. "He studied and learned a lot on his own. Some was trial and error. He wanted to do this so he did it. Do you?"

Terian was silent for a few minutes. Danial watched him, a calculating look on his face.

Finally, Terian broke the silence. "I can do all that." He met Danial's eyes with his red ones. "I will not kill for you, Danial, not for profit and not for justice. Self-defense is one thing, but murder is another. I know what Theo was, and I am not going to be an executioner."

Danial's smile didn't reach his eyes. "Theo said much the same thing to me when I offered him the job more than fifteen years ago, Terian. I'll say to you now what I said to him then. The line blurs if you do this sort of thing enough."

Terian gave him a look of distaste.

"So you don't want the job?" Danial said.

"I'll take it," Terian said coldly. "On one condition."

"What is that?" Danial said, equally cold.

"Sar told me you aren't pushing an oath on her this time. If that changes or she ever wants to leave, I expect you to honor your word. You aren't going to keep her with you against her will, not with me around. Is that understood?"

Danial's face softened, as he looked at Terian with respect and a little admiration. "I would expect nothing less from you, Terian," Danial said. He held out his hand, and they shook on it. "I would expect nothing less."

"What is the salary?"

Danial named an astronomical salary. "That figure okay?"

Terian flashed a smile. "More than sufficient. Does that include room and board?"

"Room and sustenance goes with the job. Tell Suri your food preferences, and she'll take care of it. Do you need any extra room besides a place to sleep?"

"I'd like a lab set up, to stay current with my alchemy and sorcery."

"I have a room that can be converted. I'll have the workmen do that as soon as they finish our new addition." Danial handed him a stack of books. "Here is some beginning reading on military strategy and a few thinner books on weapons, primarily handguns, but also some assault rifles, and other weaponry. Can you start in two weeks?"

"That will be fine. I need time to do the prep work and to get my stuff moved here."

Relieved, I watched them shake hands.

* * * *

I drove Terian back to my house after collecting Elle, thinking about the exchange. I hadn't thought about Terian's living arrangements. He'd be living on Danial's property. The more I thought about it, the better I decided it was.

"You're quiet," Terian said, glancing over at me. "We're almost to your place and you haven't said a word."

"Just relieved. I'll feel safer, knowing you're going to be around," I said, giving Terian a smile.

He gave me one back. "I appreciate Danial's offer. I won't be alone anymore; I'll be with all of you. Thanks for setting this up."

I parked, and we both got out, Elle bounding out after me.

I turned to Terian. "Thanks for agreeing," I called. "Have a good trip home."

He waved, then started down the driveway in his truck.

After he left, Elle and I got ready for bed. Resolving to get her some nightclothes as soon as possible, I quickly called Danial and thanked him again for offering Terian the job.

"It is I who should be thanking you," he said warmly. "Terian is an excellent choice. He has more than enough power and intelligence for the job." His voice dropped an octave. "More importantly, I trust him completely. I know he will protect you and Elle, having seen first-hand what he did defending you the last time you were threatened."

Uneasy, I changed the subject. "How is the construction?"

"Slow," Danial said grumpily, "but I'm bringing in more help tomorrow. It will be done in another two weeks, come hell or high water. Pack whatever you are bringing a few days before. I'll have Suri and Ivan come for you, Elle, and your pets."

"Will you be coming before then to visit? Elle was upset she couldn't see you tonight."

"Tell her I missed her too," he said lovingly. "Regrettably, no. I'm doing all I can to handle the addition and get business caught up. Put her on, I'd like to talk to her, just to say goodnight."

I called to Elle in the bedroom, my heart comforted that I was making the right decision.

* * * *

The day before we were set to leave, I packed up with Elle's help. It was hard to know what to bring, but I brought everything I thought I'd need for the winter, deciding to leave the summer stuff here until I saw how much storage space Danial had.

Next, I packed the food, all of it except the meat. Suri and Demetri, who had something going now, were coming to stay at my home this winter. They would look after my house. If we came back to stay sometimes in the spring, the house would be ready to be lived in.

Lastly, I picked up the cougar from the mantle; the one Theo had carved for me. I handed it to Elle, and she took extra care packing it away in wrapping paper.

"That's everything," I said. "Did you leave out clothes for the morning and pajamas?"

"No pajamas," Elle said, making a face.

"I'll grab something from my dresser," I said. "Come, let's go to bed.

Tomorrow is going to be a busy day for both of us."

I opened the drawer to grab her a T-shirt and, instead, opened one of Theo's drawers. Hands shaking, I picked up one of his shirts and smelled it. The scent of wide blue skies, forest, and prairie grass brought tears to my eyes.

"Mom, are you okay?" Elle said worriedly. She ran to me and hugged me.

"I'm okay, Elle." I sat down on the bed and handed her the shirt I was holding. "Sniff."

She brought it to her nose and inhaled deeply, as she had seen me do. "What is it?" she said. "It smells good."

"That is what your father smelled like," I said softly.

"Mom, did you love him like you love Danial?"

"More," I said softly. "I loved him more."

"Can I keep this?" she said.

"Yes," I said. "Pack it in one of your boxes."

She carried it out of the room, still sniffing it. I pushed aside my robe and the box with the engagement ring Theo had gotten me and got another shirt from the drawer. I held it to my face, remembering him.

Would I be over Theo before I reached the limit of clothes stored here that still held his smell? It seemed important somehow to preserve his scent, so I could return, pull out one of his shirts out, and remember him. Time invariably would make the scent of him fade. I took one last long breath, trying to commit the scent to memory. Then, I put the shirt back and closed the drawer.

* * * *

The next day, Elle and I moved in with Danial.

There was plenty of room now. Off the great room, next to his bedroom, was a small closet, and on the other side was Elle's room. Facing it was a room for pet stuff and another room at the end of the short hallway for storage.

"I've never heard of getting an addition up and finished in such a short time. This is perfect, Danial."

"Ruling has its perks," Danial said arrogantly. He took my hand. "Come see what else I did for you."

He led me into his bedroom. He had added on a small living space with a woodstove for us off his bedroom. In his bathroom, there was now a Jacuzzi tub for two like the one at my house. The wardrobe I'd used was again in his room, along with a small dresser.

"This is wonderful," I said appreciatively. "Thanks for the dresser. I forgot to mention it."

"You brought more clothes this time," he said meaningfully, "and it matched the new bed. Hopefully you brought your paint clothes, unless you want everything to remain white." He gave me a teasing smile. "That is, if you'd like the job."

86

"We can get started on that tomorrow," I said enthusiastically. "You know I like to paint."

"I do," he said, hugging me. "Make yourself at home and alter what you like. If you need me, I'll be in my study working."

The next day, Elle and I bought paint. The next week was spent painting the new rooms starting with hers, which we painted blue. I added clouds on the ceiling and helped her to put some grass on the bottom of the wall as a finishing touch. As soon as it was dry, Danial arranged delivery of a canopy bed, a vanity, her own TV, and a slew of videos.

To balance Danial's largesse, I made sure Elle had chores, such as vacuuming, doing dishes, and dusting, in addition to helping me paint the other rooms. Danial was set on spoiling her. That was okay, so long as she appreciated what she got. Mary was still working for Danial, but she was fast near retiring age and glad to give up some of her responsibilities to Elle.

The pets, on the whole, adjusted well. Ghost and Darkness were ecstatic to be back at Danial's house. Both dogs dove back into their old schedule of running with Ivan or Aran in the mornings and sleeping away the nights. Every day there was also a walk with me, short or far, as well. I'd ignored them last time and paid the price, both in them ceasing to see me as their pack leader and in losing their affection and trust.

The cats took a little more time to get used to Danial's home. Asher scratched a hole in the arm of the couch, upsetting me more than Danial. To make up for that, I sewed up slipcovers on the sewing machine I'd brought.

Elle's tutor showed up the second day, introducing himself as Bill. He began with an hour at a time, as she was uneasy being away from me at first. She adjusted quickly, and he took her for greater periods each day, a relief to me. Even though I loved her, spending all day with her every day wore me out. Also, I was needed elsewhere.

I discovered that a week after we'd moved in, the first night Elle slept in her own room. I waited for Danial for an hour before coming upstairs to see what was keeping him.

It was hard to see Theo's desk, even with it cleared off in preparation for Terian's arrival tomorrow. I averted my eyes to Danial, hunched in his chair.

"Are you coming to bed?" I spoke gently.

"I can't, I've got too much to do," he said wearily.

I moved behind him and began massaging his shoulders. He groaned. I worked his muscles until his knotted shoulders had relaxed.

"Thanks," he said.

"How can I help?" I said.

"I'd love if you filed a few of those finished cases," he said hesitantly, indicating an overflowing box and the nearby filing cabinet.

I was tired to begin with, but managed to get all his filing done and up to date within a few hours. Danial remained in front of the computer, typing and clicking rapidly.

"It's almost two," I said flatly. "Come to bed. I'll help you more in the morning."

"You go on," he said. "I'll make a list for you and be right down. I'm beat."

Danial joined me sometime before dawn, not waking me. In the morning, he was sleeping soundly, dead to the world. After Elle went to her lessons, I took the list he'd left me and got to work.

Over the next week, together with Terian, we started to make headway. At night, Danial did the correspondence, programming, and conference calls only he could do. During the days, I updated the office billing and various secretarial tasks that had lapsed. After a few days, the work was caught up enough so Terian and Danial began work on the new, more pressing cases.

A few days before Danial's party, Solutions, Inc. work was current enough I convinced Danial to take a night off.

"Terian's in his lab," I said temptingly, "and Elle's in bed. Want to join me in the tub?"

"No," Danial said seductively. "Put one of your silk shifts on for me, the red one."

I looked at him in surprise. "I didn't know you still had them."

"They were yours," Danial replied easily. "Of course I kept them."

"I thought you gave them away," I said delicately.

"Come here," he said, chastising me. He took my hand and drew me near. "The truth is Angelica saw your robe on the back of my door and asked to wear it. In a fit of anger, I told her she could have it. I was disgusted she was so petty as to want it."

How petty had he thought me when I'd shown up and demanded it back? I flushed red.

"I want you to forget what happened before and here I am dredging it all up," he grumbled. "I shouldn't have—"

I put my finger to his lips. "If you'd like me to wear it and you have it, I'd be glad to. Tell me where they are, and I'll get them."

"On the back of our bathroom door," he said hesitantly. "In the large garment bag."

I went down and unzipped the bag, lifting out the clothes he'd bought me almost a year ago now. Some jeans, a few sweaters, and the two silk shifts, along with a bunch of sexy underwear, most of which I'd worn once, if at all. I put everything away in the wardrobe and dresser, laid the red shift on the bed, and then went to fold away the garment bag. Something was in the bottom, weighing down one side.

I opened the bag to find a familiar red velvet box. Inside was the ring Danial had given me when I'd gone with him to Switzerland. He hadn't given it to Angelica as he'd said cruelly to me once. He'd kept it all along.

I blinked back tears. I'd made Danial out to be a villain in the saga of Theo and me. It had been easier to consider him that way; to not care I was hurting him, to forget I loved him.

I took out the ring and put it on.

Chapter Five

I undressed and slipped on the red silk shift. Then I quickly fluffed my hair and got in bed, striking a seductive pose. Danial came in a few moments later, pausing in the doorway to look at me.

He moved fast, shedding his clothes and climbing into bed, his kisses eager and excited. I kissed him back hungrily, rubbing my body against his. Danial let out a groan, then rolled me on top of him. Holding me by my hips, he moved into position and thrust into me. I let out a loud cry, throwing back my head as I moved on him with abandon. He let out another groan, this one almost pained. I looked down at him, his eyes black with lust, his lips parted, fangs bared slightly. I kissed him, and he opened his mouth wide on mine, his tongue teasing my lips. I let out a moan and slid my tongue into his mouth in response. His hands tightened on my hips as he thrust faster.

I came quickly, screaming his name. Before I'd finished, he rolled me over on my stomach and covered my body with his. Grabbing both my hands in his, Danial held me to the mattress as he pounded himself into me, his movements rapidly quickening. Abruptly, he stopped.

I turned slightly, looking up as him. "What is it?"

He raised my hand, the diamond sparkling on my finger. "Why are you wearing this?"

"I'm sorry," I said softly. "I found it in the bag."

He withdrew, moving his body so he was lying beside me and didn't speak.

I sat up and moved to take off the ring, but Danial stopped me. "You don't have to take it off, Sar. I just was taken aback to see it on your finger."

I sighed and took it off anyway, placing it on the nightstand. "I'm sorry. I don't know why I did." I paused. "That's a lie. I did it because I wanted to give you me, the way I was when we were first together and we were happy. Before

90

everything happened."

"I don't want you as you were," Danial said gently, hugging me. "I want you as you are, right now, and how you'll be tomorrow, and the day after, and next year, and the time that comes after. We can be happy now, Sar, if you'll let me make you happy." He took the ring and gently placed it again on my finger. "Please wear it always, even if it's not on your ring finger."

He went to kiss me, but I stopped him. "Wait."

Danial looked at me, the old wariness back in his eyes. "What?"

"Am I right in thinking your annual party is this weekend?"

"Yes, on Saturday night. You and Elle should sleep all day and night before it to make sure you are able to make it through."

"You want Elle to attend?" I said surprised.

"Do you think we can stop her?" he said, rolling his eyes.

"No," I replied. "She can be persistent, and I don't see any harm in it."

"Why do you ask about this now?" he said carefully.

"I still intend to ask Samuel a few questions," I said just as carefully. "Discreetly, I promise. He will expect you have marked me, as you told him you were going to. I think you should."

"I can," Danial replied, "but it will hurt. I'm going to have to be very careful with you now we're together again. My blood is a lot more powerful than it was. Though I can still drink from you, I'm not going to be able to heal you like I used to. My taking your blood will have to be shallow cuts, and the mark will have to be shallow as well—"

"I want you to make it as deep as Devlin made his," I said firmly.

His eyes widened. "You'd never be able to remove it," he whispered. "Never."

"I'd carry it the rest of my life," I said, holding his gaze.

"It will hurt a good deal," Danial said cautiously. "I've never bitten you that deep, Sar. No amount of sex will dull that kind of pain."

"I know," I said, letting out a breath. "Will you do it?"

"Only if it's what you want," he said carefully.

"It's what I want, and it's safest for us all."

"You're safe enough without being marked," Danial said seriously. "I am Lord here, and you wear the choker."

Watching him, it was apparent he was balking. What I didn't comprehend was why. "I understand it will hurt. I'm still asking you to do it."

"Not because you want to be mine," Danial said softly. "I never wanted the farce I had to play out under Devlin and now Samuel, Sar. I don't want you to pretend with me, now that I have a choice."

"I'm not pretending," I said angrily. "I'm here in your bed because I want to be here. I'm asking you to give me a mark I'll never be able to remove because I want that from you. I'm going to carry a mark made from hate for the rest of my life. I want one from love!"

"Do you love me?" he said stridently.

"I never stopped," I said, swallowing my guilt over Theo. "You keep telling me you want to make me happy. Don't you understand I want to make you happy, too?"

"You don't have to do this to make me happy," Danial said, embracing me.

"It's because you tell me I don't have to that I want to." I kissed him gently.

"You're sure?" Danial said urgently. His eyes sought mine, his breath coming fast.

I nodded. "Do it," I said softly.

"I'm sorry in advance for the pain," he whispered. He turned me over onto my stomach and began again, his thrusts measured. Yet this time, Danial was so excited he was shaking, kissing and nuzzling me. In a few minutes, he shuddered, screaming my name. His excitement stoked me, and I climaxed again, arching my back with a sharp cry.

Danial struck, biting me so deep his top and bottom fangs were completely buried. I let out a scream of pain, but he covered my mouth, silencing it. My climax ebbed in seconds, the nerve endings in my neck radiating damage. I panted hard, trying to hold still, every fiber of my body wanting to fight him. Danial shuddered with wave after wave of pleasure, his body moving involuntarily on mine. As he did he sliced deeper with one of his fangs, causing me to jerk in his arms. I pushed back from him, suddenly afraid.

Danial crushed me to him and pulled my top half upright as he continued to feed, still shuddering. I let out whimpers, tried to pull away, and then gave a cry as I cut myself again on his fangs. Danial let out a muffled groan of sheer joy, and his mouth clamped down tighter, still swallowing.

The pain dulled, my fear deadening with my senses. A few seconds later, I went limp in his arms, nearly unconscious. Danial abruptly withdrew, laying me back gently, then went for the bathroom. In a grey haze, I watched as he tended to my bites with gauze and gentle kisses. As the fog in my mind cleared, the pain returned, throbbing.

Danial handed me some aspirin and water. "These are prescription strength for me. Please take them and tell me when they wear off."

I swallowed the pills and water and lay back gently. "Thanks. You were right about the pain. Does it look okay?"

"Yes," he said quietly, his tone odd. "It looks fine."

I looked over at him. He looked back worriedly.

"What's wrong? Did you take too much?" I said, searching his eyes.

"I wanted to take it all," he admitted, drawing back from me. "That's never happened to me before. I could feel you fighting me, and it didn't matter."

"You're scaring me," I said softly. "Do you still want to?"

"No," he answered. "As soon as you went limp, the feeling passed." He gave me an agonized look. "I wanted to give you my blood, enough so you'd waken." He wiped at his eyes. "I'd have turned you."

I was silent, watching him, my chest heaving in fear.

"Ever since draining Devlin, I've had this desire before to share blood with other donors, when I took a lot of their blood," Danial continued. "Dr. Camlyn said it was a normal desire to procreate for those vampires with the power to turn others. He said the urge would abate in time. I thought it had."

"Why didn't you warn me?" I whispered.

"I wanted to mark you badly as you asked," Danial said, moving still further back. "I've never bitten anyone that deep I wasn't trying to kill." He paused. "I've never lost control like this with anyone. I'd not have risked doing this tonight if I'd had."

"You stopped in time," I said slowly. "You didn't give me any of your blood, right?"

"No," Danial assured me. "My saliva still heals you to a lesser extent It just doesn't take away your pain. I used the minimum, to be safe. You'll be fine."

"Then why are you on the far edge of the bed?"

"I could smell your fear, taste it in your blood. I don't just feel awful for the terror I caused you, I feel terribly guilty I enjoyed myself so much at your expense." He let out a breath. "I've never enjoyed inflicting pain. I'm worried Devlin's blood has somehow corrupted me."

"If it had, you wouldn't be thinking recriminating thoughts now," I assured him. "His blood has changed you, made you more powerful. It makes sense that power comes with a price."

"I'm sorry," he said haltingly. "I wanted you to feel safe in my arms, not afraid. I didn't want you to be scared of me, after what happened before—"

I reached out and brought his hand to my cheek, covering it with my hand. "I asked you to mark me. Nothing that happened here tonight changes what I feel for you."

"Even telling you all I did?" he replied, surprised.

"I asked you to tell me everything, to keep no secrets," I answered. "I trust you more, knowing you told me the truth, as hard as it was."

"We don't have to share blood again," Danial said quickly, moving closer.

"We can, though it won't be so much," I said, managing a smile. "Probably not soon, either or I'll have to take some of those awful blood replenishing packets."

"Do you forgive me hurting you?" he said, serious.

"I forgive you. Let it go," I said gently and kissed him. He cradled me to him, and we slept.

* * * *

The bite opened in the night, but Danial stopped the bleeding with pressure. In the morning, it was scabbed over. Examining it, the wound was deep, as deep as Devlin's had been, the four punctures a purplish red on a background of blue purple, from bruising beneath the skin. There was some pain, but with the aspirin, it was manageable.

"It will scar," Danial said from behind me.

"I've always wondered why, when you bite, you don't bite with all your teeth?" I said hesitantly. "It feels like your incisors are all the way in, but they must not be."

"I'm not biting to eat flesh, like a mouthful of chicken," Danial said, cracking a smile. "I'm biting to open a vessel to drink from."

"Then why the four marks, instead of just two?"

"It's theorized the lower fangs are for opposing the uppers used to pierce a vein, to provide a counterpoint to the pressure."

"To hold a person still, so they can't dislodge you, no matter how hard they struggle."

"Yes," Danial said with a sigh, "but that's false. You remember when I bit you a year ago, when I was dying? The wounds were ragged because you were struggling and I couldn't hang on. My best guess is evolution: four fangs instead of two increased the accessible amount of blood from a single bite."

"Was biting easy to learn?" I blushed. "What I mean, is it must be easy to sever or slash instead of pierce. It must have taken, um, practice to do what you did last night."

Danial nodded. "Yes. Willing donors hold still, so they usually only have two or four shallow cuts." He cleared his throat. "The idea of the mark originated from the Oath; equal restraint. No human could withstand a bite so deep once, much less twice, if he or she didn't do it from love. No vampire could bite that deep and not kill, unless it was out of love."

"In that way we are oathed, then," I said quietly. "Both of those things were true last night."

"We're in love again," Danial amended quickly. "Come, Elle will be looking for us."

* * * *

Terian gave me a narrow eyed look when he showed up for work, but didn't say anything. Irritated, I pulled him aside. "I didn't give Danial an oath, so stop glaring."

Relief passed across his face. "It's not my business," he then said loftily, moving away.

Time kept passing and I found my new routines both enjoyable and reassuring. Elle was happy, and so was I. I hadn't expected to enjoy the busy work I did for Danial, but I found satisfaction in helping him with his e-mail, phone calls, and filing. There was always a lot to organize and collate, so when Danial awoke for the night, he could get right to work instead of spending half the evening chasing down a client who had left a message during the day or finding the right phone number to call back someone. In turn, it gave him more time to spend with Elle and me.

I still took time for myself. Sometimes I baked or read, but not to the extent I had before when living with Danial. I wanted this to work, which meant I needed to keep myself busy. Between Danial's business, Elle, the pets, my target practice, and my hobbies, it was easily accomplished.

My only sadness was my mother had not called me in all this time, a first for her. I finally broke down and called my stepfather. I told him everything was fine, we were all settled, and we'd like to come for Christmas, if it was okay. My mother called back later to say Elle and I could come, but she didn't want Danial to darken her doorstep.

With heavy heart, I told him the news that night. Oddly, he wasn't upset like I was.

"They remember what happened," he said sadly. "I don't blame them for not liking me. I know how much they liked Theo."

"I don't feel right about them excluding you."

"Go. Elle needs to see her grandparents. Besides," he said, pulling me to sit on his lap "this way we don't have to worry about my not-eating being a problem."

Elle was less cooperative. "I'm not going. I don't like Grandma. She's mean."

"You are going," I said sternly. "We're going to pick you out a dress tomorrow."

"I'm not."

I let it go, with Christmas still a month away. There was time for her to come around.

Later that night, I mused over the real trouble. Elle loved Danial the way he loved her; completely and utterly. She did not want to hear a word against him. He was her hero, her father in all ways but the biological one. When she had a nightmare, it was him she cried for to soothe her. When she learned something new, she always made sure he was there to hear it. When I put her to bed, she wouldn't fall asleep until he came in and kissed her goodnight.

Danial was the same; Elle was first in his world. No matter how full his schedule was, he made time to read her a story, brush her hair, or spend time talking to her about what she had done that day. He was never too busy for her, or cut her short in favor of more pressing matters.

Some of this was hard to watch. I was now a third wheel to their twosome. I handled it as gracefully as I could, devoting extra time to the dogs and cats or spending time with Cia. As much as I felt excluded, I also relished they had bonded so quickly. Seeing them together, I knew I'd been right to come live with Danial. However, their relationship also raised an important question. If Theo returned now, how would Elle take it? In her eyes, she already had a father she loved. She was not the cub she once was huddled in Theo's arms.

* * * *

The night of the party came. At Danial's request, I wore my red dress with the fox head choker and earrings. Danial had bought Elle a red dress with a sweetheart neckline and matching red shoes. She was twirling around in the great room, watching the skirt flare out to settle around her legs as we waited for Danial.

Danial came out from his bedroom at last, buckling a sword and belt onto his waist. He was dressed in his red swordsman's shirt, black jeans, and those thigh high leather boots I loved.

"I thought this wasn't a costume party this time?" I said, eyeing the sword.

"I needed it the last party, Sar," Danial said grimly. "I would prefer to have it and not need it, then need it and not have it."

"Point taken," I said, grimacing in return.

"Danial, are we ready to go?" Elle said excitedly.

"Almost," he said, going to one knee before her. "I have something for you." He handed her a blood red velvet box.

She opened it and let out a shriek. "I love it." She tossed the box aside and held up a tiny gold fox head on a short wide gold chain. The pendant was identical to the one at my throat, down to its ruby eyes.

She tried to put it on immediately and couldn't. "Why won't the clasp work?" she said in frustration.

"I must fasten it," Danial said lovingly. "Hold still." He slipped it over her head and fastened the miniature choker in place.

Elle ran to the mirror in the entryway to admire herself. "Wow."

"I thought I'd better," Danial whispered to me. "Some vampires like children's blood."

"It was good of you to think of it," I replied, grimacing again. "Let's go."

Terian drove us to the party, not speaking. I wondered if he was nervous. This would be his first real job as head of security for Danial.

The drive brought back thoughts of Theo. Again, I was sad, missing him and then pushed away the thoughts.

We arrived in good time. As we were early, almost no one was here yet.

The band was just setting up as we walked in to the convention center. The tables were spread with food while waiters and bartenders stood ready.

"Everything looks great," Danial called to an approaching figure.

It was Tatiana, again in silver, her hair in ringlets. "Thanks, Danial." She embraced me. "I'm glad to see you," she said formally. "This is a welcome surprise." By the way she said it, she knew all about Theo and what had happened between Danial and I.

"It's good to see you," I said stiffly.

"Who are you?" Elle said, her eyes wide.

"I'm Tatiana, a friend of Danial's and your mom's."

"Are you a witch?" Elle asked bluntly. "Do you do bad magic?"

Tatiana looked at her in shock, her mouth open.

"Elle, what did I say?" I said sharply.

"I'm sorry," Elle said quickly to her.

"It's okay, Sar. Yes, Elle, I'm a witch," Tatiana said with a smile. "A good one."

"You're more than your average witch," Terian said with an appreciative smile.

"Wouldn't you like to know." She winked at Terian. He winked back at her and smiled.

Danial, meanwhile, had walked over to the band and asked them to test their instruments. I smiled as the first strains of "Lady in Red" sounded.

He picked up Elle. "Care to dance, my Lady?"

"Yes," Elle shrieked.

Danial held her in his arms, and moved to the music with her. She swayed in his arms as Terian and I watched.

"Sar, you were right to do what you did," Terian said emotionally. "He loves her like his own child."

I nodded, watching them sway to the music, pushing away a slight feeling of jealousy. When the song ended, Danial brought Elle back to us, and she and I quickly got something to eat.

The guests began to arrive. Terian took up a position somewhere out of the way, Aran and Demetri with him. Several other foxes stood near the doors. Before long, we were surrounded by people, all of them vying for Danial's attention.

I'd been nervous attending this party last year. Yet this year I felt comfortably in the background, content to look after Elle and not try to be especially witty or smart. Elle was very well behaved, responding politely to questions as she held my hand or Danial's.

The night wore on, and my face began to tire from constantly smiling. To give us a break, I danced with Elle a few times, and then we returned to the tables for more food. By the time we'd finished, most of the human guests had left. Around us were only our guards and a few scattered vampires, but more were coming in.

Elle sniffed, then pressed herself to my side. "I smell blood, Sar. Fresh blood," she said quietly.

"They are like Danial, most of them," I said softly. "Some might be weres, but don't believe any are good like he is, Elle."

"Danial warned me not to," she said, scared.

"Don't worry," I reassured her. "We're going to stay over here and watch. There is just some ritual usually, and it doesn't last very long."

Danial came over to us. "Are you ready, Sar?"

"Yes," I replied. "Is there anyone Elle and I should be careful of?"

"Devlin wasn't invited," he replied, waving to a man who'd just entered. "There are a few who have come from outside the US to be here tonight, like Samuel, but they aren't going to be trouble. You will notice more have come, close to a few hundred."

"You once told me there were about five hundred vampires in the United States. Did most not get invited?"

"Some I don't trust at all or want around Elle and you. They were not invited."

"Won't ignoring them aggravate them?"

"It is my choice who to invite. If I summon them here, as I did for a couple, they have to come or face death as penalty."

Most of the guests had gathered around Danial by this time. On some unspoken cue, they bowed to him as one. He inclined his head slightly in response and then beckoned to me.

Danial kissed my neck, and then reopened the partly healed wound on my neck, drinking only a little before kissing it enough to stop the bleeding. "The customs have been honored," he said commandingly. "Please enjoy yourselves. If I asked you to see me, please do so immediately."

Everyone bowed again, and then they broke up, some going to dance and others feeding either on collared humans they'd brought or some humans Danial had provided for the party. A few vampires reluctantly went towards Danial now in the center of the room.

I'd missed this last year when I was in the bathroom with Tatiana. Elle pressed herself to my skirt, watching with wide eyes. "Is that what Danial does to you?" she whispered.

I glanced around. Everyone was conducting himself or herself appropriately. No one was screaming in pain or half-unclothed, and there was little blood.

"Yes," I said. "Don't be afraid. No one's going to do anything to you or me."

"Good Evening, Sarelle," a voice said from behind me. I turned to find Samuel standing there. "You look lovely, my dear," he said warmly. "I must compliment Danial on his handiwork."

Here was the moment I'd waited for all night.

I smiled at him, extending my hand. "Elle, this is Samuel, Vampire Ruler of Europe. Samuel, this is my daughter, Elle."

Samuel looked down at Elle. He looked up at me, anger in his eyes. "So I was right. Your oath was a lie," he said coldly, his blue eyes chill.

I didn't reply. I gazed back at him, thinking his eyes were cold, that they had never been kind eyes at all. I'd just seen what I wanted to that night he'd saved me.

"Your guard was your lover," he continued. "Why does Danial permit you to keep her?"

"He loves her as a daughter," I said quietly, hugging Elle.

"Then I'm glad her real father is dead," he said cruelly.

I stepped into him suddenly and shoved hard. While he was far stronger than me, he wasn't expecting that. He fell backward to land on the floor on his rear.

"Tell me what you did to Theo," I shouted furiously.

All conversation stopped in the convention center as all eyes focused on us.

"I did nothing," he said coolly, his eyes tinged red. "I don't answer to you, whore."

Danial's voice sounded behind me, cold as a winter wind. "How is it you know for certain he is dead?"

"No were survives his head removed for long."

"Why did you not tell me that when I asked of Theo?" Danial said, coming to my side.

"You already knew it," Samuel said casually.

"Tell us what you know," I shouted.

"I'll tell you nothing. You two make a mockery of our traditions." Samuel rose to his feet.

Terian was behind him suddenly. There was a loud click as he disengaged the safety. Samuel froze.

"Tell them what you know."

"I will not." Samuel glared at Danial with red eyes. "You are dead the next time you come to Europe," he snarled. "You dare threaten me, a fellow Ruler?"

There was a low growl. I looked down. Elle's eyes had changed to golden yellow, and her teeth were bared to reveal cougar fangs.

Samuel looked down at her and recoiled. "A werecat!" he said in disgust.

"How dare you say that?" Danial roared. "Theo was my best friend for more than a decade. How dare you insult his child and my lover, to say nothing of insulting me. I am Master here. It is my territory. You seem to forget tradition easily enough when it suits you."

Samuel met Danial's eyes, and slowly the red faded. Dawning realization Elle was Theo's, but was not my biological daughter followed. "I apologize, Racklan."

Danial's eyes were still red. "Tell us everything you know."

"I thought your Sar and Theo were lovers. I was angry, especially knowing you two were oathed and how much you cared for her. So I decided to remove Theo from the equation. I sent a man to kill him, and he came back to report Theo was already dead. He had seen a headless corpse with a fatal chest wound from one of the new guns." He paused. "I did not know he was your friend. I am glad I was not the one who ended his life."

My big plan had flopped. Samuel didn't have the answers I wanted. He just knew what we already had. My shoulders slumped.

"That was not his body," Danial said. "It was another werelion's body, a man by the name of Will. He had his own reasons for wanting Theo dead. We assume Theo shot him, but aren't sure."

"I'll check this," Samuel said. "There are persons in Europe who would pay to have a pet werelion."

I gripped Danial's hand hard, dizzy with the implications.

"I'd appreciate that," Danial said coldly.

"I insulted you and your lover at your own party. It is the least I could do to make amends," Samuel said, lowering his eyes. "Vampire law demands it. Adieu." He turned and made his way to the exit with a few men and two vampires taking up flanking positions behind him.

I looked around, suddenly noticing the silence. All the guests were looking elsewhere as if nothing had happened. It made sense they wouldn't have wanted to get involved in a fight between the two most powerful vampires in the room.

"Sar," Elle said in a garbled voice.

I looked down. She was still half changed to cougar, her fangs protruding.

"Danial, we'll be right back. Come." I led Elle to the bathroom.

"Sar, what do I do?" she wailed, her words still garbled. "I can't talk."

"Shh, I'm right here. No one is going to hurt Danial," I said calmly. "Breathe and think about how much fun you had tonight dancing with Danial." I held her, murmuring words of encouragement, and slowly she changed back, her eyes darkening to blue, her teeth receding.

I had her look in the mirror to see she was back to normal. "See? All set."

She smiled at me, relieved. "I'm sorry."

I hugged her. "You're okay, Elle. Your dad changed like that, too, when he was really angry."

"Really?" she said, looking relieved.

"Really," I said, giving her a smile.

"Touching," a cold voice said. I looked up in fear to see Devlin standing in the doorway. He was just as gorgeous as ever, but diminished, no longer the picture of power and arrogance. Yet he was still strong enough to break my bones with one blow. A river of fear like ice water went down my back.

"Are you lost? Get out of the women's room." I shouted at him.

His golden eyes narrowed. "I was looking for you, Sar. You are the hostess, right? I just wanted to give you a little kiss, to thank you for all you've done for me."

"Get out of here," I said loudly, glad I sounded brave.

"No," he said, pushing me hard. My back hit the wall, and Elle let out a scream. Devlin turned, reaching for her, and I pushed him, putting him off balance. He staggered, but caught himself, then grabbed my wrists, slamming me up against the wall. I pushed against him, but his strength kept me pinned like a captive butterfly.

"Let me go," I said, hatefully. "Don't you dare touch me."

"I'm doing you a favor, Sar. I'm here to give you information," Devlin said scathingly. "Don't you want to listen?"

"Stop it, please!" Elle cried out, tears in her eyes.

"Run, Elle," I said urgently. "Go get Terian or Danial."

"You move, Girl, and you'll come back to a broken mother," Devlin threatened, turning to Elle. Elle stayed where she was.

"What is it then?" I spat at him. "Tell me and get out."

He pressed his body to mine. "Aren't you going to tell me you missed me first?"

I recoiled, turning my head so I wouldn't have to look at him. He leaned in closer, his breath soft on my neck.

"Theo's alive," Devlin whispered in my ear. "He's being held in Europe, which is why he never came back to you. He's being used by a breeder of fighting dogs for practice. He's torn up almost on a daily basis, but he regenerates. He's alive, Sar. At least, for now."

I fought not to cry, not to believe him. Yet hope rose within me at once. "You're lying. You hate me and you hate Theo. All you sow is evil. You are just saying this to hurt me."

"It's not a lie," Devlin said, his golden eyes staring into mine. "Theo isn't invulnerable. He can't sustain too much more damage without dying. It's a matter of days, Sar."

My heart was beating out of my chest. I had to save him. I had to find him.

Devlin let out a shriek of pain. His grip on me abruptly loosed, as his body jerked, then fell away from mine. Terian stood there, his prototype gun smoking. Devlin was on his knees, glaring up at Terian, a huge hole in his chest to the left of his heart. As we watched, the wound filled in.

Devlin regained his feet. "Demon," he hissed, baring his fangs. "I owe you from before—"

"Where is Theo?" Terian said calmly, his gun steady on Devlin.

Devlin glared at him and didn't reply.

"I will shoot you as many times as it takes for you to tell me," Terian continued, his eyes cold. "Until you die or I have to leave you here in pieces to get more ammo."

"Somewhere in Germany," Devlin spat out, his golden eyes filled with hate.

"Sar, go get Danial," Terian said. "Quick."

I left, giving Devlin a wide berth and grabbing Elle's hand to pull her with me. We raced back out to the convention room. Craning my neck, I located Danial. He was with two vampires, the ones I'd met last year: Van and Erik. Dark haired and eyed, both of them looked somber in matching forest green shirts and black pants. I hurried toward them, pulling Elle with me.

"Van, Erik, you remember Sar?" Danial said pleasantly.

They both took my hand one after the other, and kissed it.

"Good to see you," I said politely. "If you'll excuse us?"

I pulled Danial to the edge of the room. We weren't remotely out of hearing, but I didn't care. There was nowhere we could go inside the building where someone wouldn't hear us.

"Devlin accosted Elle and me in the bathroom. He said Theo is being held in Germany by a person who breeds fighting dogs. They are using him for practice. He only has a few days before he won't be able to regenerate anymore." The last sentences came out as a sob.

Danial held me to his chest, trying to calm me. "Breathe, Sar."

"We will help," Erik said suddenly from behind us, glancing at Van. "For a price."

"Find him, dead or alive if at all possible," Danial said over my head to them, "and you can name your price."

"I owe you for Erik," Van said in an emotionally charged voice. "You helped negotiate his release those many years ago. It will be the usual price between allies."

"Go tonight," Danial replied urgently.

They nodded to him and left immediately.

"Can you trust them?" I was finally regaining my composure.

"They are two of the best trackers I know. If he's there, they will find him," he said convincingly, as he led me to the bathroom. "Now let's find out what else Dev knows."

Terian and Devlin were just as I'd left them. The latter didn't have any new holes in him, just the one round patch near his heart. He looked sly and full of himself standing there, even though Terian still had the gun trained on him. Hate still smoldered in his golden eyes.

"I shouldn't be shot for crashing a party I ought to have been invited to," Devlin stated. "Your whole staff is infected with bad manners, Danial."

"Dev, how is it you know this information?" Danial demanded.

"You think I ruled for centuries and didn't make acquaintances?" Devlin said sarcastically. "I know who deals in live black market goods in Europe, goods like captured wereanimals and collared female vampires, names all your investigating couldn't acquire. I know a few months ago someone sold a werelion to a dog fighter in Brussels."

I staggered. Danial held me up, supporting me against him.

"You will give me the names of every buyer and seller of wereanimals you know," Danial said with authority. "Now."

"Of course I will, for a price," Devlin said with a smile.

"What do you want?" Danial replied.

"I want you to share some of your power with me, Danial. I have no standing now, none. I want you to give me standing. I want respect again. I have too many enemies to appear weak."

Danial looked at Terian and then back to Devlin. "I can't give you some of my power. I can't trust you around anything I care for. However, I'll give you some of my business. I often get contracts for jobs I no longer do, like guarding the rich, seeking private justice for the wronged, and putting fear into those who prefer to cause it in others. I'll pass them onto you, if you give me your assurance you'll do the jobs and not fuck up or hurt anyone more than necessary to do the job."

"That won't give me power," Devlin said angrily.

"It will give you both respect and fear, which carries limited power," Danial said forcefully. "It also will give you a solid tie to my business, which commands a very healthy respect since last August."

Devlin looked inward, considering, as we waited.

"It's a deal," he said, reaching out a hand to Danial.

Danial shook it. "The names."

Devlin reached into his shirt pocket and handed Danial a computer generated list. A glimpse revealed names, addresses, and what they'd bought or sold in the last year.

"Take Elle to the car, Sar," Danial said, his eyes still on Devlin. "Terian, go with her. I have some unfinished business here."

I gathered up Elle and took her to the car, glad the party was done. Terian drove us home, not speaking.

Later, after I'd put Elle to bed and showered, I lay in our bed thinking. What if Devlin had lied? What if Theo wasn't in Germany? Danial said Van and Erik would search all of Europe, but how long would it take?

Danial came in, his hair still wet from the shower.

I sat up, relieved. "I'm glad you're okay. I was worried leaving you there with Devlin."

"The other guards were there," Danial said reassuringly. "Despite my ominous tone, most of what we spoke of was just catching up. We haven't spoken since I returned from Europe."

"I know he's your brother, but I don't want him to come here," I said softly.

"It's because I want to keep you separate that I stayed there to talk," he answered. Lying beside me, he opened his arms. "Come, please."

I went into them gratefully. "I'm scared Erik and Van won't be in time."

"Don't be afraid," he said. "They'll find him if he's there. They are already in route."

I broke down crying. "What if he's dead? What if he's dead because we took too long to find him?"

"Theo is strong," Danial said calmly, squeezing me. "No one who'd pay the high price a werelion would cost on the black market would weaken him to the point he couldn't regenerate. You've seen the foxes. Even with serious injuries, they are fine with food and a little rest."

Darkly, I thought to myself there were rich idiot men who'd buy an animal for the sheer pleasure of shooting it and mounting the head. Dogfighters were somewhere below them.

"Relax," Danial said tenderly. "We are doing all we can."

"Hold me for a while, please?" I said.

"Gladly," he murmured.

* * * *

The next day, Dr. Camlyn visited us. Danial was taking no chances after what had happened last year with me being cursed. Elle and I underwent an elaborate exam to make sure no one had tried to curse either of us. Elle was reluctant to participate, but once I told her what had happened last year, she was eager to go along with the exam.

Stephen found nothing on either of us. I was very relieved, to put it mildly. "Thanks."

"I'm glad no one had tried to hurt either of you. You both appear healthy. Still, as your doctor, I recommend you come in right after the new year to get your blood tested and a physical. It's been close to a year. Elle can wait for her checkup until mid-summer."

"I'll call for an appointment. Thanks again for coming."

After he left, I sought out Terian. He was in his lab, concocting some potion.

When I'd heard him request a sorcery lab a month before, I'd envisioned feathers, claws, skulls, and black drapes. However, his lab was well-lit and airy, with dried powders and plants labeled and stacked neatly on shelves.

"Hey, Terian," I said, entering.

He looked up and smiled. "Hi, Sar." He carefully measuring out some of a clear liquid. I waited until he was done and then came closer.

"Thank you for saving us last night."

"It's my job," he said with pride.

In the weeks he'd been here with us, Terian had been a lot happier. It was not being alone and maybe also because he knew we truly needed him. Danial may have been the hub, the center of Solutions, Inc., but Terian was now the frame that held everything around Danial together.

"What do you want, Sar?" Terian said finally. "You didn't come here to chat."

He knew me too well. "I want a potion that will let me dream of Theo like I did before so I'll know if he's alive."

"I don't know of one," Terian replied. "Not one you can take by yourself to share his dreams without any physical contact with him."

"Is there anything magical that will let us know?" I persisted.

"Sar, most of the ones that deal in dreams can mess you up big time if you have a nightmare instead of a good dream—"

"Terian, it's been months now. I can't live like this any longer. I decide he's gone and then something comes along. I'm so hopeful I can't eat or sleep. I can't live like this any longer without knowing."

"Well, you're going to have to," Terian said seriously. "I can't tell you if Theo is alive. Sorcery is imperfect." He touched my hand with his. "I can't tell you the future, Sar. If I could, I'd try to foresee mine."

"Is there anything you could think of that would help me accept that?"

Terian paused and regarded me for a moment. "I can make you forget him."

I visibly recoiled from his words. "No."

"You want peace. The only way you'll get it is by forgetting how much you still love him. You're obsessing over him, instead of focusing on the life you have now."

Terian was right, but I wasn't ready to let go. "No, Terian," I said softly. "As much as I hurt now, I can't do that." Some tears fell from my eyes, and I wiped them away. "I don't want to forget him. I'm fighting not to..." I began crying.

Terian came and put his arms around me. "Shh," he said, hugging me. "I won't make you forget if you don't want to."

I dried my tears and quickly stepped away from him. "Thank you for listening. I'd better go."

"Anytime," he said, going back to his work.

* * * *

In the first weeks of December, I started teaching Elle to shoot. We began with my revolver and shortly worked up to the explosive bullet gun. She was strong enough to handle the recoil from the first, but her aim was off. I practiced with her every day for an hour until she could hit what she aimed at from twenty feet away. After that, we settled for weekly practice. Terian joined us most times, his proficiency also increasing as the days passed.

A kind of peace descended slowly. The life I had was a good one. Elle was a wonderful daughter. My dogs were happy and the cats were behaving, scratching only their cardboard scratch pads and not Danial's furniture. Danial was all any woman could have wanted in a lover and partner. We worked well together, he loved Elle and his desires and wants were enough like mine we were both happy living together. He made time for us the way he hadn't before, and I tried to give more of myself to him. I hadn't realized I had held so much back, but it became apparent quickly.

A year before, I'd put up the tree with the werefoxes by day. This year, I, Elle and Danial put it up at night. As we three decorated the tree, I told Elle and Danial the story behind each ornament. The one I'd made in first grade from some poster paint and sparkles for my mother. The glass birds with hair for tails my mother had ordered for me when I'd been small. The ceramic ones I'd painted through the years—unicorns, birds, dragons, Pegasus, and cats. As was my tradition, we made Christmas spiders.

They both thought I'd gone crazy when I'd brought out glue, pompoms, pipe cleaners and sparkly string.

"Spiders, Mom?" Elle said skeptically. The look in Danial's eyes mirrored hers.

"There's a story behind it," I said, pulling Elle into my lap as Danial sat down beside me. "A long time ago, in a little village, there was a poor family who couldn't afford to celebrate Christmas. They cut down a tree from the forest, but they had no money for presents and certainly no money for decorations. They brought home the tree and put it in their home, but it made them sad because the branches were bare. They went to bed that night sad."

"Spiders in the house heard and felt sorry for the people in whose home they lived. So, they decided to do what they could to help." I had Elle's attention now and Danial's. "The spiders crept to the tree when the family was asleep and spun webs over it. They sparkled as only spider silk can sparkle. It was all the spiders had to give."

"Then God looked down and saw what the spiders had attempted and he was moved such small creatures had spent the whole night working to ease the sadness of one poor family. God turned the spider webs to gold.

"In the morning, the family came down to see the most beautiful tree anyone had ever seen before."

I had been working with my hands as I talked and had fashioned a black spider from pipe cleaners and a black pompom and a golden spider web from gold pipe cleaners and golden wire. Bending the spider's legs to attach him to the web, I handed him to Elle. She took it, enthralled.

I wiped away a tear with the back of my hand discreetly. I was a sucker for happy endings.

Danial hugged me. "I enjoyed that," he said, clearly moved. "Show us how you made it."

Together, we each made a spider and hung it on the tree.

Later that night, as we lay in bed, Danial said softly "Thank you for including me in setting up the tree. I loved your story of the spiders. It made me remember the night I saw you save one."

In that moment, I realized my thoughtlessness. Why was it always so hard for me to remember he had feelings just like mine? I'd set the tree up at night and not day because Elle had asked me to. It hadn't occurred to me that Danial would have been looking forward to helping or that he'd have been hurt to wake and find it already up. Yet it had occurred to her.

"You're upset," he said, moving closer. "What's wrong?"

"That was the night you asked for my oath," I said without thinking.

"Yes, it was," Danial said, drawing back a little. "I set a record for my pushiness."

"You were very romantic and not pushy at all," I said. "I'm glad you were there today with us."

"What would you like for Christmas?" he said, changing the subject. "I want to get you something special."

"No presents, please," I said chidingly. "You give me too much already."

"There must be something you want?" he said persistently.

"No." The one thing I lacked now was not in his power to give me.

* * * *

Christmas Eve came. I drove a sullen Elle to my parent's home. As soon as we went inside, I left Elle with my stepfather and took my mother aside.

"Listen," I said. "In private, you can say anything you want about Danial to me. It's your home, but don't say anything in front of Elle, please."

My mother glared at me. "Sarelle—" she began.

"Mom, do you want her to hate you?" I said bluntly.

My mother stopped, aghast.

"She loves Danial like a father, and she remembers all the things you said last time we were here. She didn't want to come, Mom. Nothing I said could persuade her. It was Danial who told her she had to come, Danial who said he'd be disappointed in her if she didn't."

"Sar, men don't change who they are," my mother said sadly.

"Men act according to how they are treated. So do women," I countered. "Please, for me, for Elle?"

She sighed, and we hugged one another. "Okay."

Christmas dinner went well. Elle was polite, if a little detached.

Opening the gifts afterwards was fun. My parents had gotten me some bath stuff and some slippers. For Elle, they'd gotten a small flat screen TV. She'd been wanting one for her room. I'd had to stop Danial from buying it for her so there had been something she wanted she didn't already have.

For me, my mother had made me a scrapbook of my baby pictures, and I'd made her a quilt of patchwork velvet. Elle had helped to piece it together, and Danial and Terian had even helped cutting out the squares. My mom was touched when I told her how we'd all worked together to make it for her. She ran her fingers over the velvet and finally smiled at me. As for my stepfather, Chris, Elle promised to go fishing with my stepfather, which pleased him more than the bottle of ten-year Lagavulin I'd gotten for him.

Driving home, Elle was silent. I didn't push her, deciding she would talk when she was ready. She had hugged my parents goodbye, though she was clearly ill at ease hugging my mother. It was a good beginning.

Danial was downstairs feeding when I got back. Elle went to her room to put away her presents. I got a glass of wine and sat down with Cavity in my lap.

"You've gained weight at Danial's," I scolded. "You're cutting off my circulation. No more treats."

Terian came in and sat down across from me. "How did it go Sar?" he said apprehensively.

"Really good, actually," I said. "We made peace, if not amends."

"I'm glad," he said, touching my hand with his. "I know you were worried."

"I have something for you," I said, moving Cavity off my lap and rising. I handed him a package from under the tree.

"I have something for you, too," he said sincerely.

"You first," I said, grinning at him. "Open it."

Terian opened the package to reveal a cape with a sparkly brass colored pattern of moons and stars on a dark brown background, lined in brown satin.

"Try it on."

As I'd hoped, it fit him perfectly, falling to just above his boots. The brass color brought out the cherry wood color of his eyes. He quickly went to look in the hall mirror with me following.

"This looks great." He put up the hood. "It fits perfectly."

That was a relief. There had been no way to get his measurements without giving it away so I had to guess. Lucky for me, he was not much different from Danial in build and height.

"Sar, I love it," he said joyfully. "Thank you." He hugged me and then looked again in the mirror.

"Every sorcerer should have a cape," I said knowingly.

"And every wish in your heart should be granted." He took my hand and placed a vial from his pocket into it.

I remembered the last time I'd drunk from a vial like this. I held it as if it contained a deadly plague. "What's in there?"

"You said you didn't want to forget," Terian said. "I can't bring Theo back to you, Sar, but I can help you remember him."

I eased myself down onto the stone bench, before I fell down. "What are you saying, Terian. What will this do to me?"

"You'll relive the dream Theo and you shared. It won't be any different, just a replay of what you dreamed last time. However, it will be as real as it was last time you dreamed it."

To feel Theo again with me, loving me...I closed my eyes. If Terian had not been with me, I'd have downed it immediately. As it was, my hand brought it involuntarily to my lips.

Terian saw the look on my face and grabbed my hand. "No, not tonight. Save this until you can't remember the dream clearly anymore, until your memories of Theo are almost gone. I can't do this for you again, not ever. This will use up the last of the bond between you and Theo, and he's not here to renew it with you."

"What are you saying?"

"When the dream is done a second time, it will start to fade immediately like a normal dream does. You may even wake up without remembering," he finished sadly. "I'm sorry."

"Don't be," I said finally, wiping away tears. "Thank you, Terian." I hugged him.

He moved back. "Have a good night. Thanks again for my cape. It should be a big hit."

"Where are you off to?".

"The werefoxes are throwing a party," he said. "See you tomorrow."

I bid him farewell with a smile, happy he wasn't alone and he had friends expecting him tonight.

There was a noise from downstairs. I went to the window. Ivan was leading an unsteady brunette out the back door to a waiting car. Jealous, I wondered if Danial had given her a bonus for coming on Christmas Eve. I pushed away the unkind thought, telling myself sternly she deserved something extra for coming out here in the cold tonight of all nights.

I finished my wine quickly, got another glass of wine, and went into our bedroom. I didn't want Danial to see Terian's present. I'd have to explain what it was, and he didn't need his feelings hurt again. I took the glass vial, wrapped it up, and put it in my sock drawer, cushioned safely. Then I took off my clothes, slipping into my robe. Terian was right; this night was for living, not remembering the dead.

Chapter Six

Danial came up the cellar steps a few moments later, the luster on his skin shining.

I gave him an appreciative smile. "You look very good."

"Where is Elle?" he said, tilting his head, his eyes darkening with desire.

"In her room," I said, patting the couch beside me. "Come sit."

He came over and sat next to me, slipping his arm around me. I leaned into him. Together, we watched the tree twinkling, the lights blinking on and off. We were both remembering a year ago, when he and I had oathed to one another beside the tree, but we didn't speak of it.

"How did it go with your parents?" he said tentatively.

"It went well," I said, "considering my mom was herself."

"Do you think she'll ever like me?" he said, hopeful. "It was nice having family to visit the Christmas we went there together."

"Give her time," I assured him. "She'll come around sooner or later."

He held me and stroked my hair. "I hope it's sooner than the next decade—"

A sharp knock sounded and we stared at each other. We weren't expecting anyone. Hope rose in my heart as the same hope leapt into his face. We rushed to the door. Danial threw it open quickly. Erik and Van stood there, supporting a man in their arms.

It wasn't Theo. My heart sank, my hopes dashed.

"Come in," Danial said, ushering them inside. I shut it behind them and took their hats and coats, wondering why they needed them, as cold didn't bother vampires very much.

"It's beginning to sleet," Erik said grumpily.

"Which I why we dressed up," Van finished. "We'll have a hell of a time getting home."

"You may stay in my guesthouse if you wish," Danial offered. "Now please tell us who this is."

"His name is Nineva," Erik answered. "He is the werelion held by the dog fighter for practice."

I studied the battered African American man before me. He sat on the stone bench, clearly hurting. In spite of the sliced up face and many scars from old wounds, he looked to be only twenty-five or so. The wounds would have had to be very bad for them to have scarred and not immediately healed. Yet Nineva's brown eyes were clear, as he gazed at me with something close to recognition.

"You must be the one called Sar?" he said. "May I have some water?"

A tremor went through me. No one outside of my friends and family knew I liked to be called that,. Well, Devlin too, who was neither. "How do you know that?"

"He has a story to tell you," Van said. "Let's all sit."

They went into the great room and sat down. I brought Nineva a glass of water, and he drank it all. Then I sat beside Danial as Nineva began his tale.

"I was vacationing in Europe with a friend, a woman called Fay. We had been childhood friends, and we'd always wanted to see Paris. After we'd saved up the money, we finally booked a trip. On the second night of our stay, while we were out at a club, we were taken."

"Taken by whom?" Danial asked.

"We didn't know, at first," Nineva said. "The last thing I remember about the night was drinking and dancing. I guess someone slipped something in our drinks. We woke up in chains, in separate but adjoining cages."

Danial's arm tightened around me, pulling me closer to him. I took a deep breath as Nineva continued. "A man came. He was not were or vampire, but he had an aura of power around him, at least one I felt. He said his name was Gene. He asked us what animals we were. When we refused to answer him, he shocked us until we changed form."

I felt my stomach heave and closed my eyes. Danial was still as death next to me.

"Once he knew what we were—lion and hyena—he arranged to sell us to the highest bidder. Unluckily for Fay, we were both purchased by the dog fighter. Fay didn't last long. She was never very strong anyway, having had polio when she was young. They tore her to pieces."

Nineva wept briefly, the tears sliding down his face. I got up and handed him a box of tissues, saying a silent prayer Elle stayed in her room for a while.

"I was always strong though," he continued. "I fought well, and so I was valued and kept alive. After each fight, I was given a period of time, a few days usually, to regenerate, but I wasn't given near enough meat for my body to fully heal. If your emissaries hadn't rescued me, I'd have died in a few more weeks."

I wanted to scream at him "What about Theo?" but remained silent.

Erik and Van looked at each other and rose. "We will leave now," Van said, "We have already stayed too long. The night is waning."

It had nothing to do with the storm. They were leaving because they knew Theo had died. My heart sank lower, if that was possible.

"Thank you," I whispered.

"I know the man he speaks of, Gene, and the dog fighter have been dealt with," Erik added. "This sort of trafficking is abhorrent."

"You'll be paid in the usual fashion," Danial said, rising to see them out. "I thank you again."

They inclined their heads to him, nodded to me, and then left. Danial shut the door, took my hand, and led me back to Nineva. He was looking at the tree, a slight wavering smile on his face.

"I lost track of time," he said, his voice cracking. "I didn't know it was close to Christmas already."

Danial sat down and pulled me down on his lap, holding me to him tightly. "Please, tell us what you were brought here to tell us. The entire thing, no matter what reaction we have."

Nineva began speaking. "I had been there only a few hours when another man was brought in. He was dark blond, handsome, about twenty-five or so, dressed in denim. He had a partially healed gunshot wound to his arm, but was otherwise unharmed. His eyes were blue."

Tears were already sliding down my face.

"He refused to change as we did, and he was also shocked until he changed. He was a lion, but not African, like me. He was a North American lion, a cougar. Next to Fay and me, his form was a rare one. Gene was delighted. He'd been told to expect another African Lion, not a cougar. He sold him within a day. After they led him out in chains, I never saw him again."

I was sobbing into Danial's chest. "He's dead. He's dead, Danial."

"You spoke to Theo," Danial said through gritted teeth. "You knew of Sar."

"Yes, we spoke," Nineva said. "He said his name was Theopolis. He'd been taken during a fight. They'd mistaken him for the African lion, and shot the man by mistake. Gene had been promised a were, so his men took Theo, knowing he was some type of were by the fast healing gunshot wound on his arm."

"Who was to blame?" Danial rasped out. "Who was behind this?"

"Theo said Peterson had set it up. The African Lion, a man named Will, told Peterson what you were for a small fee. Peterson then set up a meeting, planning in reality to test their weapons on you. Will never suspected Peterson had double-crossed him and was going to sell him off to Gene as soon as you had all been killed."

"I saw how close the two men looked," Danial said. "In the dark, it would be easy for Gene to mistake Theo for Will. When he saw them confronting one another, Gene acted to protect his investment, shooting Will instead of Theo. What else did Theo say?"

"He said he had to get free. He had a daughter, newly born to care for and a beautiful fiancée he loved. He'd sworn to come back to you, and he would do it or die trying. He said Sar was the most beautiful, funny, and loving woman he'd ever met. He told me how she'd saved his daughter, shielding her with her own body. He told me of you, Danial, that you were the most loyal and trustworthy man he'd ever met, despite you being vampire."

I couldn't take anymore. My heart was breaking all over again. "Please stop."

"Go on," Danial said with authority.

"There is nothing more," Nineva said sadly.

"Finish it," Danial growled. "Now, Nineva."

"Before we left, Fay and I overheard Theo had been sold to a sadist, one who had a predilection for weres. According to Gene, Theo attacked the sadist the first time he tried anything. He was beaten within an inch of his life for it and then allowed to heal slightly. That would repeat itself until he finally died, Gene said. Then he was to be stuffed and mounted."

"Do you have his name?" Danial hissed in a voice from the bowels of hell.

"Erik and Van found him, after torturing and killing Gene," Nineva said. "He's dead. They beat him to death with his own whip."

"That gives Sar and I some comfort, to know justice has been done," Danial said. "Did they find Theo's body?"

"Although they searched the house and grounds, Van and Erik found no trace of Theo. The man had many were trophies, heads, skins, etc., even stuffed weres in their animal forms. There were no cougar trophies of any kind."

A small part of me still had hope Theo was alive. The rest of me was weary, tired, and emotionally drained. At that moment, I gave up my last bit of hope and closed the love I felt for Theo away in a corner of my heart.

"That's all," Nineva said. "Now I've told you my tale, what do you intend to do with me, Lord?"

"You are a guest, not a prisoner. You may leave or stay here as you like," Danial said after a moment. "You said you were a good fighter. I can always use help."

"I will stay long enough to recover, but then I wish to return to Africa," Nineva replied. "I am in your debt forever, Lord. Ask of me whatever you will, and I'll do it gladly."

Danial nodded, already on the phone to Terian. "Come and show Nineva to a spare room in the compound." He hung up his cell. "Feel free to call your relatives tonight," Danial said, putting his hand on Nineva's shoulder. "Talk as long as you want to. We owe you for this information. Now we have another piece of the puzzle."

Nineva nodded. "Thank you, Lord."

Terian arrived in a few minutes, with Aran in tow. "Easy does it," Terian said, helping Nineva to his feet. "Lean on us. We'll transport you by car to your room."

Danial shut the door after them, then came and picked me up in his arms. Instead of bringing me to bed, he placed me in front of the woodstove and started a fire.

"Stay here. I'm going to put Elle to bed. I'll be right back."

I nodded. There was no way I could open presents anytime soon. That would have to wait until tomorrow.

Danial strode away. I curled up in front of the fire. With so much going through my mind I cried a little, thinking about someone hurting Theo, my Theo, who'd been so funny, lovable, and brave. The minutes passed. Lulled by the fire's warmth, I fell asleep.

I woke up to find Danial curled next to me, his arms around me. It took me a few seconds to wonder where I was, why my body was so still. Then all Nineva had said came rushing back.

"Danial?" I said in a tiny voice.

"Yes, Sar?"

"Tell me what happened that night."

"It wasn't pretty. I'll tell you if you wish, but I want to forewarn you."

"Tell me."

"Theo, Lander, and I went to Peterson's building to erase their computer files and demolish the building, planning on finding some of the attackers lying in wait. We weren't disappointed. They were armed with their prototype guns. Lander was killed right off.

"Theo and I separated; I took the front way, and he the back. I got shot a few times, but drank from the men I killed and began healing at once. My body can heal bad wounds fast if I drink deeply." He paused. "Yet there is only so much damage I can heal in a short time because in that time I can only drink and process a certain amount of blood. When I got shot again in the chest a few moments later, it slowed me down enough that I got shot twice more in succession. Luckily, Theo and I had gotten them all or so we thought. I loaded up the virus, launched it, and then got shot again in the chest. Theo killed the man who'd shot me and then helped me get to the street just as their servers were blown to pieces."

115

"At the street, Theo told me to go. He said I was too wounded to help him anymore. He was worried we'd left you alone with no food or no guards. He said he would walk back because it wasn't far or get a cab. He knew there was one more person at least in the back of the building. He said he couldn't rest easy knowing they might try to hurt us again. Then he was gone. I made it back to you unseen by luck with the last of my strength." He paused. "The rest you know."

"Thank you for telling me," I said.

"What Nineva described happened in the space of a few weeks at most," Danial said, resigned. "Theo either escaped or was killed back in early August. He would have contacted us by now if he escaped."

"I know. Please let's not talk anymore tonight."

Danial held me, and we sat watching the fire for some time in silence.

* * * *

The next day, I went through the motions of taking care of Elle and myself. She knew something was wrong, of course, but didn't ask me straight out. I couldn't bring myself to tell her about her father. I was too busy working on getting from one moment to the next. Fortunately, Elle wanted to see Cia, who had delivered her baby boy, Aran Jr., a few days early. I let her go with little persuasion.

That evening when she returned with Terian, Elle opened her presents from Danial, Terian, and me. Danial and I had gotten her some books and toys, which she was excited about, but the best present was Terian's. He had made her a potion for wings like the one he'd given me almost a year ago. Elle shrieked with joy, running around the great room, her huge butterfly wings knocking lamps and pictures over as I ran after her, trying to keep the chaos to a minimal level. It was her favorite gift. Her joy in her first Christmas cheered me even if the slight taint of sadness remained.

As Elle readied for bed, I pulled Danial aside. "I've got to talk to you. Elle went to see the baby earlier."

"Good. Have you seen Aran Jr. yet?" Danial asked.

"Not yet," I replied. "How is Cia doing? Aran's got to be happy."

"To my relief, the delivery was smooth, no problems. Aran is proud and seems to be inches taller now from gathering compliments from everyone on his son."

"Elle wanted to see him badly. I think she's lonely. I feel bad there isn't anyone here for her to play with." I turned to Danial. "Why haven't there been any children before Aran, Jr.?"

"The werefoxes are all young, and I don't encourage breeding without responsibility," he answered. "Not that any of the current foxes are loose so to speak. I certainly don't expect them to be celibate, but they live here for one reason; to watch my back. If they want to have families, they don't enter this line of work, as a rule."

He had a grim undertone. I changed the subject. "She said she had questions to ask you tonight. I thought you should know so we can discuss what to say and what not to say."

Danial didn't hesitate. "Sar, I think we have to think of Elle being about four to five years old. She clearly matured at the rate of a cougar and now is maturing much slower at the rate of a normal human child. She's very smart, so she can handle the basic concept that Aran and Cia were in love, and Aran helped to make the baby in Cia."

"I agree. I just don't want to give her too much information and scare her."

"Things were different growing up on a farm. Animals were around and it was easy to see nature and not have to talk a lot about it. My talk from my father involved having me watch him breed his favorite stallion and mare. When it was over, he asked me if I had any questions."

"What did you say?" I said, curious.

"I told him I didn't think I could stand up for long in that position, without falling over," Danial said, laughing. "Come on, let's go tuck her in."

Right as we walked into her room, Elle asked the question I'd been dreading: "Mom, Danial, how did the baby get inside Cia in the first place?"

Danial glanced at me, then said, "Aran helped to make the baby in Cia, because he loved her."

Elle switched her attention to me. "Mom, can you have another baby, if you wanted one?" Elle didn't know I wasn't her biological mother. I'd seen no reason to tell her until she asked. Now was the time.

"Elle, I have something to tell you," I said, sitting down beside her. "I didn't have you the way Cia had Aran Jr. You are Theo's child, but you didn't come from my body. You are the daughter of Tawny, a woman Theo knew in Europe."

Elle was floored, but she did her best to hold it together. "Where is Tawny, Sar?"

"She's dead, Elle. She died giving birth to you," I said, squeezing her hand. "I'm sorry."

"But you are my mom?" she said.

"I'll always be your mom," I said, kissing her on the forehead. "It doesn't matter that you didn't come from my body. I love you, Elle."

"Why?" she said, puzzled. "I'm not your child, Sar."

Because you are Theo's child and I loved him more than my life. Because I promised him I'd keep you safe. Because I see so much of him in you sometimes it hurts to look at you.

Danial nudged me gently.

"Because I love you," I said. "You know Danial is not your real father, Elle, but he loves you just as much as Theo did. You are mine in all the ways that matter."

"Can I still call you Mom?"

"Only if you want to," I said, hugging her.

"I want to," she said, hugging me back. Then she paused. "Can I call Danial 'Dad' then?"

Her hesitant question hit Danial with the weight of a train going full speed. He leaned heavily back against the wall, his eyes guarded, waiting for my answer.

Part of me desperately wanted her to call Danial "Dad" because it would make him so happy. Part of me rebelled against it, reserving that privilege for Theo alone. However, it wasn't my call to make really; it was hers.

"If you want to," I replied, trying to sound calm.

"I want to," she said, turning to look at Danial. "Goodnight, Dad," she said softly.

"Goodnight, my daughter," he said emotionally. "Sleep well." I moved to turn off the light.

"Could you have a baby, Sar, if you wanted one?"

"Yes," I said, before thinking why she was asking.

"Could Danial help you make one?" Elle asked hopefully. "I'd like someone to play with."

"Sar can have a baby easily, Elle, because she's human," Danial answered quickly, "but I am not. I can't help to make a child inside her."

"Why not?"

This was getting better and better. I sighed softly.

"Because I'm vampire," Danial answered sadly. "Go to sleep, Daughter. Save your other questions for tomorrow." He shut off the light and led me back to our bedroom.

"I'm sorry, Sar," Danial said, stirring up the hot coals. "Sit down. I'll put on some more logs."

"I'm sorry, too," I said, coming to hug him. "Thanks, I'm not ready to sleep yet."

We sat before the fire, basking in its warmth as the logs caught. Suddenly, Danial brought out a box from behind his back and gave it to me. "Merry Christmas," he said, grinning.

I opened the box to find some Godiva chocolate. "You have captured my heart, Danial," I said, immediately seeped in chocolate lust. Tearing off the wrapping, I surveyed the contents, took out a piece, and ate it with relish. "How did you know I liked these?" I said, pleased.

"I asked Cia," he said sheepishly. "She told me you liked them."

I ate another piece and then put them aside before I exceeded my saturated fat RDA for the day. "Thank you. I have something for you, too," I said, turning to him with finality.

"What is it?" Danial said anxiously.

I took his hand and looked into his dark eyes. "Danial, if you want to try again, I'll try with you to have your child."

He froze, staring at me. "Sar, please, don't say it unless you mean it."

"I mean it, Danial," I said, kissing his hand. "This isn't because of Elle's talk tonight. I've been thinking about this for the last month."

"What if we find Theo?" he said.

"We aren't going to find him," I said hopelessly. "It's been almost six months."

"Why do you want to now?" Danial said. "You didn't want to before."

"You didn't give me a choice before," I said carefully, trying not to fight with him. "I am getting older. You were right, there isn't much time, especially if it takes a few years. Theo is dead, and he's not coming back to me. I decided I want a child, if you'll try with me to have one. I'm scared to, yes, but after how I feel about Elle, I want to try, before it's too late and the chance to have one of my own, one of our own, is gone."

"You know what this means to me, that you are offering to do this?" Danial said unevenly.

"I know," I replied. "I want to do this for both of us. I see the way you are with Elle. You are a good father, Danial."

"And you have made a good mother," Danial said tenderly.

"I wonder sometimes," I said sadly. "I think I could do better."

"That is the sign you're getting it right," Danial said, hugging me close.

"Maybe."

We fell silent for a few moments.

"I'm prepared to try," Danial whispered gently, "but I have a condition. Actually, two."

"What conditions?" I said uneasily, worried he was going to demand we Oath again.

"If you get pregnant, I expect you to do exactly what I say, no matter how strange or unnecessary you think it is at the time, until our child is born."

"That's fair," I said slowly. "I admit, I'm afraid. I've never been pregnant before, and I'll need your help."

"Which I'll gladly give," he assured me. "It means that if we find Theo somehow, or he comes back during that time, I will not let you see him, not until you've had our child. Not for any reason."

"That's fair too," I sighed. "What's the second condition?"

"If we should ever part, the child stays with me." He paused. "I know in

119

these modern times women are usually favored to retain custody. Understand, please, I say this because we are not oathed, and—"

"And I've left before," I finished coolly. "I get it."

"Do you?" Danial said bitterly. "I lost many loved ones over the years. Many of them met tragic ends. Some still haunt me hundreds of years later, but I'd not survive losing a child again." He looked away. "I wouldn't want to."

"We already lost a child," I said quietly.

"There is a difference between losing a child you've never spoken to or held and one you have," he replied emotionally. "I hope you never have to experience that difference firsthand."

"Are you worried I couldn't handle it?" I said angrily. "You're acting as though a woman raising a child alone increases its chance of dying. For God's sake, you just told me I was a good mother."

"You are," he said soothingly. "I'm telling you, albeit rather badly, I couldn't go through with this, have it work, and then have you decide one day you want to leave and take our baby with you. It would destroy me, Sar."

"I promise you, right here and now, I will not do that," I said resolutely.

"Then I will go to Terian tomorrow," Danial said happily. "Come, we need to get some sleep. It will be dawn soon."

* * * *

First thing the next morning, Danial summoned Terian to request the potion. Terian came straight from there to find me. We met a few hundred yards inside Danial's woods on one of the many deer paths.

"Hi, Terian. I decided to take a walk with Ghost and Darkness first thing, before it snows again—"

"He wants me to make another fertility potion for him," Terian interrupted. "He said you agreed. Did you?"

"Yes," I said, nodding. "I want to try."

"Have you given up?" Terian said, his eyes searching mine.

I relayed the story Nineva had told us last night. As I told of Nineva's and Theo's torture blackness seeped out of Terian to fill the room. I shivered in its embrace and quickly finished the narrative.

"So he is dead then," Terian said with a note of finality.

"He has to be," I said, mirroring his sadness. "I don't have any reason to hope otherwise."

Terian hugged me. "I'm sorry, Sar. I'd hoped for a better ending for you and him than this one."

"So did I," I said sadly, as we released each other. "I'm hoping for a new beginning with Danial."

"I'll get started right away."

"Is there anything I should be aware of, outside of normal pregnancy stuff,

I mean?"

"Not that I know of," Terian replied. "It should be a normal delivery, like Cia's was."

"Were you there in case something went wrong?"

"No, I wasn't there, and I wouldn't have been much help if I had been. I don't really have any healing powers. My power is more suited to destruction and illusion, sad as that makes me. Most of my creations are temporary, like the wings I made for you and Elle." He shrugged.

"Then who was on hand?" I asked worriedly. "Dr. Camlyn might not be able to make it here in time if I went into labor early—"

"Sar, wait until you get pregnant to worry," Terian reassured me. "It will take a while to make Danial fertile—" He stopped abruptly, coloring.

I looked away from him so as not to make him more embarrassed. "You're right. I'm just worried."

His reminder also gave me something else to consider. This time we had to be sure Danial was completely ready before trying. I'd concluded a possible reason for my past miscarriage was because   Danial had been between stages; fertile enough to get me pregnant, but not changed enough his semen was capable of helping create a healthy fetus. Even if that wasn't the reason, I was not taking any chances that it might have been.

* * * *

Two weeks later, far before dawn, Danial came early to bed. "Terian gave me my first dose earlier tonight." He paused. "I've not told Elle. She'd expect you to produce a sibling in a few months' time."

That was true, but he was really worried I might be unable to get pregnant again. "I won't mention it to her, either."

Danial began unbuttoning his shirt. "I hope you're not too tired. I came down early in hopes of celebrating."

Time to bring up protection. "I'd like to use condoms until Stephen pronounces you fertile," I said quickly.

Danial gaped at me. "Sar, I don't want to use anything with you. I don't see the point."

I looked at him silently. What words wouldn't hurt, wouldn't make him feel I blamed him for what had happened last time?

Danial resumed unbuttoning his shirt. "This is just your nerves talking, sweetheart. There's no danger from us being intimate."

"Last time, Stephen said you shouldn't have been able to get me pregnant," I persisted, "but you did. I think maybe there was a problem, because you had just started taking the potion and the change wasn't complete—"

"Are you saying what happened last time was my fault?" he said, offended and hurt. His eyes were red tinged, his mouth a grim line.

Sigh. "No, it was not your fault. I went to a doctor back in January to get checked out myself. After he pronounced me fine, I told him what happened and asked for his opinion on why I'd miscarried. He said there had to have been something wrong with the baby."

"Something must have been and it had nothing to do with me."

"Danial, I don't want to argue with you. This is how I feel—"

"Fine, Sar. We just won't have sex again until we know for sure I'm ready to get you with child." He stood there watching me, obviously waiting for me to back down.

Ouch. I stood by my guns. "I respect that if you feel that way," I said softly.

He turned from me and slammed out of the room, the door hitting the frame so hard it bounced back open. Very faintly, I heard the sound of an engine started on one of the SUVs followed by the sound of tires spinning and catching in the driveway.

Disheartened, I decided to go and see if Elle was still awake. I found her in her room, looking through her baby book.

"You were so small." I sat down next to her, peering at the pages of pictures as she slowly flipped them. There she was, the first day we'd come home to my house. A picture of her trying to make friends with Ghost and Darkness, and them avoiding her. A picture of her asleep, her paws outstretched lying on my bed. Pictures of her in her Halloween costume I'd made her, then her first picture in human form, of us painting her room, paint everywhere, even in our hair. Pictures of her shooting and posing next to the time she'd put the whole clip of bullets inside the target. Lastly, a picture of the three of us, Danial, me, and Elle sitting next to the tree the night we'd put it up. Cia had snapped it for us.

"Mom, how old am I?" Elle asked.

"It's hard to say," I said vaguely. "You matured as a cougar your first few months. Now that you are human, you are aging a lot slower. You should be about five or six, at least that's what we think."

"When was I born? How many years ago?"

Damn you, Danial, for leaving and not being here to help me answer this. "Seven months. You were born in August. You are a Leo, like me."

"I'm not even a year old?" she said in shock.

"Elle, you are just as you are supposed to be—"

"There's something wrong with me," she cried, throwing the book hard against the wall.

I grabbed her, holding her still. "There is nothing wrong with you," I said to her calmly, a good deal more calmly than I was feeling. "You are just the way you are supposed to be."

"I can't remember how to change. How I did it. I was a cougar for so many months, and now I can't be one, no matter how hard I try." She began sobbing, and I let her, telling her that it was okay, that she was okay.

Suddenly, I had an idea. "Elle, there is a man staying with us who is also a lion."

"Like me?" she said quickly.

"No, but close. He's an African Lion, not a cougar. He'll have a mane and a tufted tail, like the pictures you've seen in books. His name is Nineva."

"Can I see him?" she said.

"Tomorrow, I'll take you to him," I assented. "I'll bet he can give you some pointers about changing."

She hugged me so tightly I gasped. "Mom, I would love that. After breakfast?"

"I'll have to ask him and see. You have to realize Nineva was hurt badly. He may need some time to heal before he's able to teach you anything."

"But I can see him tomorrow?"

"Yes, tomorrow," I said, relieved.

"Mom, I love you," she said, releasing me to look up into my face.

"I love you, too, Elle," I said, kissing her forehead. "Now let's get you tucked in."

"Danial has to come in and kiss me goodnight."

"He's out, but I'll remind him, as soon as he returns."

She snuggled in to go to sleep. "Goodnight, Mom."

Emotionally exhausted, I decided to go and sit in the Jacuzzi for a while. I turned on the water, checked on the pets one last time, and returned to a brimming tub. The hot water felt wonderful as I slipped in. I turned on the jets, letting the water pound away at my aching muscles as I thought about Elle.

It was true something was unusual in terms of her development, even taking into account being werecougar. Theo had said she should have been born human. Whatever was unusual about her had accelerated her growth, not just in her body, but also in her mind. It didn't affect how I felt about her. I just thought of her as gifted.

My thoughts brought back other memories of her, like the first time she had seen snow. She'd tried to eat it and then spit it out when it didn't taste like ice cream. For some reason, she had expected it to.

Elle's eating habits were like mine now, though occasionally she ate raw meat. I encouraged that, remembering how it had always helped Theo to stay healthy. That and Chinese food. I smiled, thinking of him wolfing down quarts at a time…

The bedroom door opened and closed.

Quickly, I climbed out and dried off. I put on my pajamas I'd left warming in front of the woodstove and went into bed. Danial was already there, his back to me. I knew he wasn't sleeping, but I said nothing, just lay down beside him and went to sleep.

The next morning, Elle and I went to see Nineva at the fox compound. He was reclining on the couch, watching some TV, his expression intent.

"You look better already," I said looking him over.

"I ate a side of raw beef last night," he replied. "It speeded the healing process. Now who might this be?"

I brought Elle over closer. She looked at him shyly. "This is Theo's daughter, Elle."

"I see the resemblance," he said, touching her face. Elle shifted her feet nervously, but she let him touch her.

"Elle, this is Nineva."

"Pleased to meet you," she said politely, giving him a tentative smile. He smiled back at her.

"Nineva, you said if there was anything we needed from you, you'd be glad to help," I said boldly. "Elle could use some pointers on how to change form, when you're well enough."

Nineva didn't look shocked or apprehensive. He didn't ask how old she was or anything else I'd expected. Instead, he just took her hand and drew her close to him.

"Reach inside yourself," he said to her softly. "Can you feel something inside you, something that wants to come out?"

"No," she said worriedly.

"Concentrate, Elle. Close your eyes. Breathe in and out, slowly and deeply. Look inside."

Her eyes closed, and so did his. He kept holding on to her, her hand in his. "Can you feel it?" he said, after long minutes had passed.

"No," she said, with tears in her eyes.

"Shush," he said gently. "Don't worry. There is a way to bring the change that never fails between great cats. I'll change form myself and bring you with me."

"Should I leave?" I said tentatively to Nineva.

"Don't leave, Mom," Elle said nervously.

"I'm not embarrassed if you aren't," he replied.

I was embarrassed, but Elle had asked me to stay. "I'm okay."

Nineva slowly got up and with difficulty lay down on the floor on his side. He had Elle lay down also, so she was facing him.

"Hold on to me and close your eyes," he said. "I can help you; I'm male to your female."

Though the sexist remark annoyed me, I kept my mouth shut. This mattered too much.

Nineva began to move, his body twitching. His back arched, and his fangs began to lengthen. Elle's mouth was open as well, her fangs were growing. Clothing ripped, as shoulders and legs were suddenly too wide for the fabric. Fur sprouted, noses flattened, fingers shortened into paws, and tails grew. A few moments later, there were two lions lying on the floor.

Nineva raised his head, his huge eyes golden in his regal face. He shook his mane and rose slowly to his feet. He was absolutely beautiful, down to his tufted tail. Elle raised her face and looked at me with yellow gold eyes. She still looked for the most part like the cub she had been, but she was much larger now, easily three feet long. Her spots were lighter, but she didn't yet have the white patches on her face that Theo had.

She rolled to her feet and rubbed against Nineva, purring. Her purr had deepened a bit, but it was still high pitched compared to Theo's. Nineva purred, the sound a deep base, almost echoing in its loudness. He licked her head, and she closed her eyes, enjoying it.

I watched, enraptured, as Nineva began playing with Elle. He was still recovering, but he was able to hold her down with his paws while she growled at him and tried to bite him. He couldn't chase her, but he did roll her over a few times when she crawled over him. After only a few moments, he lay down with her and fell asleep, her small body curled next to his big one.

I watched them curled together; thinking about Theo, about what he had missed. If he'd been here, he would have been the one to teach her how to change. He would be sleeping with her now…

I woke up to Elle shaking me, holding a blanket around herself. Nineva was gone.

"Mom, I can do it!" She hugged me fiercely.

"I knew you could," I said, hugging her back.

"Nineva said I should come back every day until he leaves," she said happily.

"Good," I said, smiling. "Now come on, let's go find you some clothes."

* * * *

The problem with Danial was not solved so easily. What had begun as a simple misunderstanding easily stretched into weeks and then a month. He talked to me, but no longer touched me at all. When I tried to touch him, he held me at arm's length gently. Terian noticed, but he didn't say anything.

Elle noticed too and bluntly asked what I had done. It irritated me that she immediately took his side.

"I didn't do anything, Elle," I said, trying to be calm.

"You must have done something," she persisted. "Danial still hugs me."

"Elle, this is private between Danial and me. Go to sleep and please don't ask about this again." I kissed her quickly and then left.

I was reading in bed a little later when Danial stalked in.

"I'll thank you to not be telling Elle lies about me, Sar."

My eyes narrowed. "Danial, I said nothing—"

"She wanted to know if I had hit you again, Sar. She asked me."

Great. We were going to fight. "Stop saying my name as if it's a curse word."

"She said 'again', Sar," Danial said, deliberately ignoring me. "How does she know of this? What did you tell her?"

I put down my book and faced him. Despite him being an ass, he had a right to know what had happened.

"She overheard my mother a while back, yelling at me for going back to you after what had happened. She asked me later what was true and what wasn't. I told her you had hit me and now regretted it. I told her I'd also done things I shouldn't have, that the situation was of our making, not yours alone."

Danial sat on the bed, studying me. "I believe you," he said softly.

"Good for you," I said and picked up my book.

"Sar—"

"Don't 'Sar' me, Danial. You come in here and accuse me of badmouthing you to our daughter, when all I did was defend you. You were wrong to hit me, no matter what I had done."

I glared at him pointedly, then shook my head and looked away. This was pointless, bringing this all up again.

"What did you tell her, exactly?"

"I know how you feel about her. I didn't tell her all the sordid details." I put the book down, turned over, and lay there fuming with my back to him, too mad to read.

"You are right," he said softly. "It was right to tell her the truth and not to hide what had happened. I was wrong to hit you. I'm sorry, Sar, for what happened then and tonight."

"So am I, Danial," I said, my back still to him.

Danial took off his clothes and got under the covers with me. "Are you ever going to forgive me?"

His supplicant tone placated me slightly. "I already forgave you, like I've told you many times now. Please don't speak of it anymore."

"As you wish."

I felt his hands on me, pulling me backward carefully into his embrace. It had been weeks since he'd held me, and his body felt amazing fitting against mine. I sighed in pleasure. Abruptly, it came to me he was warm.

"You're warm."

"It's working."

"Are you, um—?"

"No, not yet. I am being tested daily now by Dr. Camlyn. He said it should be within the week."

To have him so close and know it was still a week until I could have him…I groaned. Danial shifted against me. With a jolt, I felt his hardness against my bottom, pressing through the thin cloth of my pajamas.

"Darling," he said to me softly, kissing my neck, brushing me with his fangs. I groaned again and reached back to run my hands through his hair. He pulled me against him tightly, flexing, making me painfully aware of how ready he was for me. I lay there aching for him as he moved against me.

His breaths came faster as he grew more and more excited. He turned my head and kissed me, his hands reaching around under my pajama top to caress my breast. His hips still moved urgently against me.

"Stop, please," I gasped.

He slid his tongue into my mouth, tasting me, filling me. I moaned, and he turned me over toward him and rolled his body on top of mine. He kissed me deeply, putting his hands under my buttocks to lift me and slid off my pajama bottoms. Before I knew it, they were off, and he began to slide inside me.

"No, wait—" I said fearfully, looking up at him, my eyes wild with wanting him and sudden panic.

"Sarelle, look at me."

"I am looking at you," I said, swallowing hard.

"Look down at me," he said, his voice husky with need.

I looked down and saw the condom encasing him. My eyes darted up, and I opened my mouth to speak. Danial drove himself into me in that moment, and my words became a cry of passion. He clasped me to him, moving as fast and as hard as he could. Then he was yelling out my name, jerking inside me as he climaxed.

He pulled out of me and stripped off the condom. "I was not going to last, Sar. All those nights of sleeping next to you, wanting you."

Danial kissed me eagerly, his fangs pressing gently. He moved lower and took one of my breasts in his mouth. He suckled me, and I arched my back, writhing. He broke away to put on another condom and then he was inside me again, stroking me, sliding over that particular spot I liked. I hissed, and he bit me gently, his tongue running over my skin. I rolled him over then, riding him. He thrust up into me repeatedly, holding my hips against him.

"Come for me, Sar," he said, his voice thick with love and lust. "I want to hear you."

I was close, so close I could taste it. Then he drove into me fast, holding my body tightly, and it was enough to send me over. I cried out wordlessly, screaming, my head thrown back, my eyes shut as the orgasm washed over me. He sank his fangs into me as I came, opening me, shuddering as he came again. He held onto me as his orgasm ebbed, drinking, making those pleasure sounds I loved to hear. I clasped him to me, trying not to move despite the sting, his muscles contracting under my fingers as he swallowed. The pain slowly lessened as he healed me.

Danial pulled out of me, cleaned himself off, and threw away the condom. Soon, he was holding me again. "I love you," he said softly.

"I love you, too, Danial," I said, kissing him.

There was a knock at the door then. "What is it?" Danial said.

"Phone call," Terian said, his voice sleepy but clear.

"Tell whomever it is I'll call them back," Danial said with annoyance.

"It's not for you Danial, it's for Sar."

Danial and I looked at each other quizzically. "Who is it?" I asked.

"She said her name was Kat," Terian said.

Chapter Seven

I got up immediately. Kat wouldn't be calling me here at this time of night unless it was an emergency. "Tell her to hold on."

I put on a robe and went to the door, opening it to take the proffered phone from Terian's hand.

"Kat?" I said.

"It's me, Sar," she said.

"What's wrong?" I asked. "You sound awful."

"Brett and I, we had a fight. He told me to get out. He said it was over between us." She sobbed, the connection becoming staticy.

"Kat, I'm sure he didn't mean it," I soothed her. "He loves you. You're his wife. Everyone argues."

"He was so angry though. Can I sack out on your couch?" she said quickly. "Just for the night?"

I covered the receiver with my hand. "She needs a place to stay for the night," I said to Danial, unsure of his answer. "Do you mind if she uses the guest room?"

"It would be simpler if she stayed in a nearby hotel," Danial said after a moment. "I don't want her to know my address. You may trust her, but I don't know her. I'd be glad to arrange a room. Terian can pick her up. Where is she?"

"I'm going to need to go, too," I said reluctantly. "She's really upset. She probably needs someone to talk to more than a warm bed."

"Then I'll be here waiting for you when you get back," he said, kissing me. "Be careful."

"Where are you?" I said into the receiver.

"A place called the Whitfield Hotel."

"That's just south of here," Danial said. "It will take about two hours to get her and bring her back to the local hotel in Alan's Creek. Take the Expedition with the GPS." He turned to me. "I believe there's a lounge inside the hotel. Tell her to wait there, if it's open."

"Kat, wait for me in the lounge. I'll be there soon."

"Okay. Thanks, Sar."

I hung up. "She sounds so odd. She must have been crying a lot. We need to leave now."

"I'll wait for you in the SUV," Terian said with a nod.

"Okay." I threw on some clothes, kissed Danial, and then went out to the SUV, where Terian waited.

As soon as I'd put on my seat belt, he stepped on the gas, sliding slightly on the icy drive before the tires caught. The truck lurched ahead.

"Always have to be a showoff." I grinned back at him.

He grinned back and then turned back to the dark drive ahead. Soon, we were on the main road. I settled back in the seat and looked out into the sporadically lit blackness. We would need to take some back roads until we got to the highway. The Whitfield Hotel should be easy enough to find. Terian was silent as the miles passed, the GPS assuring us at intervals we were headed in the right direction.

"Terian, are you awake enough to do this?"

"I'll be fine," Terian said, giving me a reassuring look. "I didn't know you had a friend, outside of your family and the people who live with Danial," he added, gently curious.

"Kat and I haven't spent a lot of time together lately," I said guiltily.

First, it had been because I'd been grieving Theo, then because of raising Elle, and then moving in with Danial. I hadn't talked to Kat in months, but it was her fault as well as mine. She obviously knew my number.

"So you're not close anymore?"

"That doesn't matter," I added. "She needs me and she's my friend."

"In case you're wondering," Terian said suddenly. "Asher's doing fine."

"Good," I said in relief. "I hoped she'd be happier with you. Elle's too much for her. Ash spends most of her time in the basement, afraid to come out from beneath the bed. She may not have had a great life at my old house, but she deserves to feel calm and secure."

"She's great. She sleeps with me, curled under my chin most nights."

I was instantly jealous; Ash had never done that with me, ever. "Good. Thank you again for letting her stay with you."

He was quiet for a while, then he spoke again on a completely different subject. "Sarelle, did you and Danial make up?"

"You know we did. You heard it all."

Terian flushed. "I didn't hear anything, but yes, I know you're being intimate again. I didn't mean to pry."

"It's okay. You can't help if your hearing is extraordinary."

"What did you fight about?"

Despite it being none of his business, I was too tired to care. "He wanted to have sex before we knew for sure the potion's made him fertile. I insisted on protection. He finally agreed tonight."

"Sar, you were most likely right in, um...sticking to your guns."

"You think the cause last time—"

"It's logical, yes, though there's nothing in any book to prove you right, but both times now I've made the potion exactly as it's described. There's no variation on the potion. It's always the same, no matter the source. An unwritten waiting period is the only variable I can think of."

"Where is the potion from?"

"It's listed in various spell books," Terian said vaguely. "Always the same."

Something was off here. I turned to him, searching his face. "If it's the same, he must have paid you a fortune again for it."

"He asked me to make it, and I said I would."

"That tells me nothing, Terian."

"Sar, this is between me and Danial—"

"And me, Terian. The baby will be growing in my body. Tell me whatever you're hiding."

Terian sighed. "Remember when I told you the potion used supernatural blood? That it was the most expensive ingredient?"

"Yes."

"That's the crux of it, the transforming agent, if you will; what makes it work. The rest is just details." He paused. "The potion is made from my blood."

"Your blood?" I said, trying not to grimace. "Demon blood?"

"Yes. Last time I made this, I thought he wanted it just to have sex with you, like some kind of supernatural Viagra. Because of my anger at him, I charged him what I wanted. I knew he'd have no choice but to pay it. Those alchemists couldn't make it for him. He needed me to do it. There was no one other than me willing to part with so much supernatural demon blood for any price."

"How much does it call for?" I asked uneasily.

"Enough to make me weak," he said meaningfully. "Enough to put me close to death, though not to kill me."

"I'm sorry," I said quietly. "I didn't know."

"How could you?" he said in a tired voice. "I didn't want to tell you. I thought it might put you off trying."

"Why?" I demanded. "Danial drinks blood. If you give him your blood willingly, why should it matter to me? It's like my blood I give him."

"No, Sar," Terian said, serious. "It's not." His eyes bored into mine. "It is my blood that is changing him, quickening his body, and making him able to get you with child." He paused. "There will be something of demon in the child, I think, something of me."

I went still hearing that. "Does Danial know this?" I said.

"He didn't last time, because I didn't tell him. This time he does," Terian said softly.

"Why didn't he tell me?" I demanded. "Why didn't you?"

"I asked him not to. I thought you might change your mind, if you knew. I want this child as much as Danial does. I'll never have a child of my own. This is as close as it will come for me."

I wasn't sure whether to feel: angry because I'd not known the whole ramifications of the potion or dumb, because I should have guessed most of them for myself without anyone having to tell me. We made the rest of the trip in silence.

Despite some highway construction, the sites were still empty at this time of morning, and we slipped though without delays. We got to the Whitfield Hotel about three a.m. Terian and I got out, and I went to the office to find Kat. I didn't see her car in the parking lot. The lounge off the office was closed, its innards dark and still.

Terian followed me to the front desk. I rang the bell.

A man appeared. He smiled at me and then looked behind me to Terian, who was glowering at him. "Room for two?" he said with innuendo.

"No, thanks," I said cheerfully. "A friend called me from here. Her name is Katrina. Can you see if she's registered?"

"Hold on a minute, I'll check," he said. He looked through the list of names. It seemed to take forever. I resisted the urge to tap my foot.

"I don't see her here," he said finally, looking back at me.

"Do you remember a blond woman, about my age?" I said. "She has eyes like mine, though she looks more, um…like a supermodel than I do."

He gave me a blank look.

I sighed. "Is there anywhere nearby where she might be? A bar nearby that stays open later than normal? I thought she'd wait in the lounge here, but it's closed."

"No," he said with a shrug. "I'm sorry."

I turned to go, and then blackness seeped into me, curling around my body.

"You're lying," Terian said softly.

The man suddenly smiled at him, then quickly brought up a pistol and fired. Terian pushed me down, and the bullet meant for me hit him instead. He staggered, but didn't stop. He fired, shooting the man in the neck. Blood sprayed like rain, leaving a red spatter across Terian's shirt, droplets scattering over my face.

Terian dropped beside me, then went motionless, listening.

"What do we do?" I whispered.

"There are at least four more of them. I hear three heartbeats outside, moving close to us. The other one is further away, somewhere in back of the guy I shot."

"Could that be Kat?"

Terian didn't reply.

Shit. This was no friend-in-need scenario. This was an ambush. They'd kidnapped my friend to get us here, whoever they were. I hoped Terian had memorized those books of Danial's. We were going to need expertise to make it out of here.

"Tell me what to do."

"Get behind the counter and grab the guy's gun. Stay here until I come for you."

His voice rang with authority the way Theo's had. I hurried behind the counter as he went outside through the office door. I gathered up the gun, crouching as I studied it. The gun was a semiautomatic, but not a familiar one. I didn't see a red dot, but logic said the safety had to be off. It was also still loaded with at least one bullet because the slide wasn't back.

Shots rang out, at least three. Then one, then another three. I stayed where I was, waiting and thinking. What if Terian had been shot? What would I do? I thought about looking over the counter, but knew I'd give myself away. I was supposed to be hiding.

I looked at the dead man beside me. Who was he? Who did he work for? He'd been aiming at me. I was the target here. Why? I expected attempts on Danial's life and attempts on my life when I was with him, but who knew of Kat? I hadn't called her in a long time, not since I was with Theo. I thought back, trying to remember the last time I'd seen her.

Theo, Brett, Kat, and I had gone out to dinner. We'd had a good time, though they were curious about Theo, and he didn't know how to answer their questions. They had wanted to know what he did and who he worked for like my parents had. That had been easy. Then Brett had asked him jokingly if he'd ever killed anyone.

Theo's eyes had gone cold then. "Why would you want to know something like that?"

Brett had backed off right away, but Kat had been wary of Theo after that, looking at him differently. We'd parted ways for the night, and I hadn't called her since, except when I'd told her Theo was missing, presumed dead. She hadn't called me either. If we both got through this, maybe our friendship was over. She wouldn't be grateful to me for involving her in this mess.

My legs were cramping, and I tried to flex them without making noise. I waited a few more minutes. Where was Terian? Theo would have killed everyone by now, had both Kat and I safe in the car, and been on the way back to Danial's.

I sighed. Terian was here now, not Theo. He didn't enjoy killing unless there was no other way. Not the most decisive man to have as your protector. In addition, to my knowledge, anyway, this was Terian's first time in a real situation against humans. He was likely doing the best he could. I probably should cut him some slack. However, if he got me hurt, I was not going to be happy.

I adjusted my legs again. I waited a few more minutes and then peeked over the counter. I saw nothing. Where was everyone? Why wasn't there more shooting? I checked my watch and decided to wait another ten minutes. When they were up, I was going to move, at least farther into the back room.

Ten minutes ticked by slowly. I stepped backwards, still crouching, until I was in the back room and then shut the door. I stood up and moved quickly into the motel hallway. Which room to try? Did I dare call her name? What if the bad guys heard me instead of her? What if some guest startled me, and I shot him by mistake?

I walked down the hallway, listening closely. There was no sound. I walked back down the hallway and put my back to the wall near the door. I waited there for another twenty minutes. Just as I was about to open the door to go find Terian, a shotgun blast splintered the door, spraying wood pieces everywhere. Covering my eyes with my arm, I waited in silence. A man kicked the door fragments, clearing an opening. He walked through it right into my bullet.

I looked down at the twitching corpse. He'd been trying to kill me with that blast. He'd known I was in here. I began to shake and bit my lip, telling myself to pull it together.

I waited a minute, but no one else stepped through the door. I opened it and stepped through, quickly looking in all corners at all views. No one was there.

I walked out to the parking lot, but didn't see anyone. Where had Terian gone? I got back in the SUV we'd came in and settled into the seat with relief. I had my gun. I'd be safe...

I heard a click, the sound of a safety being drawn back right next to my ear. SHIT.

"Sarelle," a man's voice said. "Put down the gun and get out of the vehicle."

I did what he'd said, kicking myself. I'd been stupid not to check the back seat.

"I didn't expect you to be hot," the man said, eyeing me appreciatively.

"Fuck off," I said politely, my eyes averted.

"No, but I might fuck you," he said, leering.

"Whatever," I said dismissively.

He fired a shot at my feet, and I jumped, my eyes wide.

"I can hurt you before I kill you," he said. "If you want it that way, keep acting like you are. Look at me when I talk to you."

I looked at him and stayed silent.

"That's better. Now get moving," he said, nudging me with the barrel of his gun.

"Where?" I said, unmoving.

"Back into the hotel. Room twelve," he said snidely.

I did as he asked. We got to the room and entered it. There was no one there.

"Where is Kat?" I said, glaring at him.

"Wherever she lives," he said. "You might be hot, but you're still a dumb blonde."

"What?" I said angrily.

"We hired a woman to call you, to say she was Kat. I can't believe you fell for it, Sarelle." He laughed at me.

Neither could I. I'd assumed Kat had been distraught and drove around for a while after her fight with her husband. Now the odd sounding voice and her being out here in the sticks made a hell of a lot more sense. At least I wouldn't be losing her friendship over this, assuming I still had it in the first place.

"Get undressed and get on the bed," the man said.

Stall for time. "No," I said. "If you want ransom, Danial will be glad to pay—"

He shoved me down on the bed and held me there. I struggled and tried to get the gun from him, but he managed to grip both it and me. He began licking my neck.

"With those scars, you must go in for pain, ," he said roughly. "Good." He bit me gently. He wasn't even a vampire.

Yuck. "Get off me!"

The hotel door burst open. Terian fired at him, hitting him in the side. The man fell onto his back, and I rolled away, to give Terian a better shot. Terian didn't shoot him.

"Terian, kill him," I yelled, huddled on the side of the bed. "Now."

"I'm out of ammo. C'mon, let's go," Terian said, extending his hand. Abruptly he yelled and dropped the gun, his hand bleeding. Three men stormed into the room, all holding guns. Terian backed away, staying between them and me.

"You okay, Bobby?" one of the men called to the man Terian had shot.

Bobby got up then, miraculously not bleeding. "Yeah."

He'd had on a bulletproof vest. "Why didn't you bring the better gun?" I said to Terian in exasperation.

"We were here to pick up your friend, not to fight a war."

Theo would've had the gun with explosive bullets, plus a few others. I hadn't brought a gun, either. Neither of those facts would help us now.

Bobby, the man Terian had shot, stripped off his vest and then his shirt. He was pissed.

"I got shot, so I get her first. Then you guys can take turns. Then we do them both and get out of here."

He went to reach for me and Terian blocked him with his body. "No."

"Do him first."

One of the men loosed a clip into Terian's head. Terian fell like a deadweight to sprawl on the floor. Bobby turned to me.

"Sarelle, get on the bed and take off your clothes, or I'll do worse to you than just fuck you on your way out."

"You could have a million easy, if you'd just let me make a call—"

"You're going to die," he said with a shrug. "We've been paid already. We don't break our contracts. It's bad for business."

His easy tone scared the shit out of me. "Why me?" I said softly. "I'm no one important. Danial is the one—"

"Got that right," Bobby said loudly. "You aren't important and shortly you'll be no one. Now shut up. Whoever your boyfriend is isn't important, either."

Bobby grabbed my arm and wrestled me onto the bed. He began pulling off my clothes, even as I fought him. Soon I was down to my underwear.

Bobby stopped for a minute, considering. "I almost forgot, Sarelle. I'm supposed to tell you, before you die and now is as good a time as any." He paused dramatically. "Alphonse sends his regards."

I looked back at him blankly. "Who the hell is Alphonse?" I said slowly and deliberately.

"Someone you insulted," he said. "He said you'd remember."

"I don't know any Alphonse!" I shouted. "You have the wrong person! Stop this!"

"Hold her," Bobby said to his men, undoing his pants. "I've had enough of her thrashing."

I let out a scream and blackness seeped into me, curling up from the floor. Terian was standing again, his eyes glowing red.

"Get off her now," he rasped hatefully. "I won't ask again."

"Bobby, look at the joker. He doesn't even have a weapon." One of the men laughed.

"Kill him already," Bobby commanded, pulling at my underwear. "I'm busy."

"I don't need a gun," Terian said coldly.

He reached toward Bobby and pulled his arm back, grasping something, grinding his fingers together, shouting words that were more like sounds. Bobby screamed, and his body convulsed, blood running out of his mouth. He looked at me with wide shocked eyes and abruptly collapsed on me. The other three had already started firing at Terian, but he took the bullets, staggering at each one. He reached to each of them in turn, pulling and rending with his fingers, shouting the sounds. Each one screamed and convulsed, blood running from their mouths. They stood for a moment, swaying, and then collapsed to the floor, still twitching.

Terian reached to help me up. "C'mon. We've got to go, Sar."

I pulled on my blood-spattered clothes and hurried to the SUV. I huddled there, smelling the blood on me and trying not to be sick.

Terian went back to stand in front of the motel. He stood there, saying something and holding his hand up, with the palm open as if waiting for a gift from someone directly to his left.

Slowly, a ball of fire took form in his hand. First it was white, then red, then orange, then yellow, and finally blue. It didn't burn him, but hovered there in his hand. He looked at it for a moment, then heaved it at the hotel. The fireball hit the building and exploded, blue fire becoming white, red and yellow as it spread like it had been fanned by a huge wind. Within seconds the entire place was burning, even the metal and brick.

Terian strode back to the SUV, started the engine, and peeled out of the parking lot. We rode in silence most of the way home. I was trying not to think of how close I'd come to being raped and killed and how bad he'd been about preventing it. Bitterly, I told myself Theo would never have let it get so far. Then a little voice inside reminded me Devlin could have raped or killed me last spring when he stormed my house. The expert Theo had failed me that night.

I told the voice to shut up and sat sullenly, looking into the graying dawn.

We finally got back to Danial's as the sun was rising.

I raced inside, Terian following. Danial met us in the mudroom. He came toward me with a smile. His expression changed to worry when my face crumpled. He hugged me quickly, as I began to cry.

"What happened?" he said to Terian, his eyes red. "Where is Kat?"

"Sar's friend Kat wasn't there. It was a trap set by a man named Alphonse, specifically for Sar. They were to kill her and were also planning to rape her," Terian said. "This wasn't about her connection to you. The men didn't know who you were."

"Are they all dead?" Danial said angrily. "They had better be, unless you brought one home to torture."

"Yes, they're all dead. I crushed their hearts," Terian said. "I'm sorry, I should've brought one back to find out more about this Alphonse person. Sar says she doesn't know anyone by that name."

"Was she in danger?" Danial said softly.

"Yes," Terian said.

"You overreacted," Danial said, relieved, "but that's okay, Terian. Sar's safety is your first priority. Information can wait. Are you hurt? I smell your blood."

"I took at least ten bullets, but they were regular ones, Danial. I'll be fine."

"Rest today then and tomorrow," Danial said. "Get one of the foxes to cover for you."

"Okay," Terian said.

"Did you cover your tracks?" Danial asked next.

"The motel is ashes by now," Terian said. "I hit it with a blue fireball. Everything, even the bodies and the metal, was burned utterly."

"Again overkill," Danial said. "Next time, just burn the motel or building with regular fire. Wipe down anything with your prints on it if possible. Take the guns, all of them."

Terian said nothing.

Danial stepped to him, still holding me. "Terian, you saved Sar. You did an excellent job, especially as none of us saw this as anything other than a friend in need. I don't know an Alphonse, either. There was no reason to suspect anyone was after Sar. If you both weren't sure of this, I'd think it had to be a mistake."

"It was no mistake," I said, scared. "They were after me."

Terian looked at Danial, his eyes sad. "Theo would have known," he said softly. "He would never have walked into a trap like this. I should've known."

"When Devlin came for Sar almost a year ago now, Theo had forgotten all about him. He wasn't there to help Sar, and he would have been killed if he had been. I expect you to do your best, Terian, which was what you did. Second-guessing yourself now is a waste of time. "

I looked up at Terian guiltily. "Danial is right, Terian. You saved me. That's what matters."

"I hesitated to kill," he replied. "I shouldn't have."

"You're new at it," I said, shrugging. "It gets easier when it's them or you."

Terian looked at me uneasily, then looked away.

"Go rest," Danial said, putting his hand on Terian's shoulder. "You did fine for the first time out."

Terian left, shutting the door behind him. Danial turned to me. "Do you want to take a shower, or a bath?"

"A shower, please," I said, beginning to undress.

"Do you want me to stay or do you want to be alone?" he said quietly.

"Please just wait outside for me, Danial."

I took a long hot shower, washing away all of the night's nastiness along with the blood. When I emerged, Danial was waiting.

"Elle is up eating breakfast. Cia is taking care of her. Come to bed, darling."

Exhausted, I was asleep almost instantly.

My dreams were nightmares, where Terian did not stop Bobby in time, where Bobby became a shadowy figure called Alphonse, where Theo was alive, but when he came to save me he got shot instead and died in front of me on the hotel room floor as I was raped. I woke up screaming each time. Each time, Danial held and soothed me.

Sometime around noon, Elle woke me knocking on the door, asking why I hadn't made her lunch.

Danial let her in. "Speak softly, Elle. Mom's still in bed."

"Mom, what's wrong?" she cried and ran to hug me.

I hugged her back. "I'm okay, Elle. I just had a bad scare last night."

"Are you going to be okay?" she said anxiously.

"I'll be okay," I assured her. "I've got you and Danial."

Danial gave me a soft look and put his hand on my face. "Stay here," he said softly. "I'll be back." He turned to Elle, taking her hand. "Come, Elle. I'll make you lunch today."

After they left, I crept back under the covers and fell asleep. Some time later, Danial returned to gather me into his arms again. I slept again and dreamed no dreams.

As soon as I woke up, last night came flooding back. I turned to Danial and grabbed him tightly.

He hugged me back. "Are you feeling better?"

"Much better," I said, giving him a grateful smile.

"Tell me what happened to you. All of it."

I relayed the story. When I finished, Danial was as puzzled as I was. "This man, Bobby, he said Alphonse was insulted by you?"

"Yes," I said, "but I don't remember insulting anyone, not purposely."

"It's odd this man could be so offended and yet you have no memory of the event. Think hard, Sar. Did someone ask you for a date and you told him you were already taken, already in love?"

"I've thought it over, but can't place anyone. If someone comes on to me, usually they gave me a name to go with the proposal." I gave him a self-effacing smile. "It happens rarely enough anymore so I'd have remembered."

"That's something I'm pleased about," Danial assured me quickly, kissing my cheek. "No one should approach you with intent, not with a diamond on your ring finger and the choker about your throat. You say they didn't know who I was?"

"No."

"You were only single, so to speak, for those months last spring when you stayed alone at your farm. No one asked you for a date then?"

Unbidden, the man who'd scared the hell out of me that night by my barn came to my mind. I pushed the thought away, repressing a shudder. "No one asked me out." I colored suddenly, realizing I was lying.

"Who?" Danial demanded.

"Terian," I said sheepishly. "It's irrelevant, as he's obviously not this Alphonse."

"You're right. I'd forgotten that,. I'll check into any known Alphonses locally," Danial assured me. "As for Terian, he will get more comfortable in his new role. This kind of job isn't a textbook one and experience is the best teaching tool."

"He wasn't shooting to kill," I said grumpily.

"You can't compare him to Theo," Danial retorted evenly. "He has neither the experience nor the ruthlessness, not yet. That comes with time."

"You're saying Theo used to be squeamish too?"

"Theo didn't even want to kill the man who made him were, Sar. He did it for his parents," Danial said. "He first worked for me as the other foxes do now, mostly guarding, mostly non-fighting, non-killing work. He hated killing."

"What happened to make him change his mind?"

"A few times when we were attacked, he hesitated. Once it cost him a bullet that would have put his eye out if it were an inch more to the left. Once it cost him a finger, which took him a year to regrow." Danial paused. "Finally, one attempt on my life killed a woman I was with who was feeding me. She took a bullet in her head."

"I'm sorry," I said, horrified.

"I didn't feel about her like I do about you," he assured me quickly. "She was a good friend, someone I'd known for years. It was one of the last times she was donating to me. She had a fiancé and was graduating college. Her whole life ahead was a good one, and I was happy for her. Theo knew her well; they were friends. They joked and laughed together like you used to do. Her death made him ruthless. Remembering how he could've saved her, if he hadn't hesitated, preyed o him."

My heart ached for Theo. When I'd first met him, he'd been a killing machine with one purpose: to protect Danial at all costs. After I'd gotten to know him, finding out how tender and loving he could be, I'd always wondered about his more ruthless side. It seemed so at odds with the woodcarver who only carved forest life. Now it all made sense.

"If you've rested enough, you should eat something," Danial handed me a robe.

I went in and fixed myself a quick dinner. As I was finishing, Elle came in with Danial in tow.

"We've come to say goodnight," Danial said.

I hugged her. "Did you have a good day?"

"Yes," she said with a wide smile. "It will be spring soon."

I gave her a kiss. "Sleep well."

Danial led her to bed. I stayed where I was for a moment and then picked up the phone to call Kat.

She was surprised to hear from me after all this time, but we picked up where we'd left off after a few awkward moments. I told her about Theo's death and then about Elle, making it seem she had been born a few years ago, and been in Europe with her mother until now.

"I can't wait to meet her. We should meet at the park sometime to take a walk together."

"Are you free this weekend coming?"

"Sure. It's a plan."

Might as well go all the way. "I'm also back with Danial," I said hesitantly. "Don't be surprised if I announce a bundle of joy soon. We're trying."

"I'm very happy for you," she said with relief. "I've got to go. See you this weekend."

As I hung up the phone, I wondered if she was relieved I was back with Danial, because he was a less dangerous person than Theo had been. Pushing the odd thought aside, I turned to find Danial standing there.

"Do you want to go out tonight?" he offered. "I'd love to escort you."

"I could use a movie," I said eagerly. "If you don't mind some badly done horror flick."

"Of course not. Let's get going," he said, heading back into the bedroom.

* * * *

By the time we got there, the movie was sold out. Rather than settle for another, we walked around the mall for a while and eventually ended up in a bookstore. He bought some new bestselling paperbacks, and I bought a few Audubon guides for Elle on North American mammals and birds. She was trying hard to get down the names of various birds and to tell the difference between the similar animal tracks we would come across on our forest walks. I wanted to encourage that interest. I wanted her to know about the kind of life that shared her world, both as a cougar and as a human, but more important, I hoped to ease her sadness over Nineva.

He'd healed up most of the scars he had had from the dogs he'd fought and would be leaving America soon. Horribly, at least twenty thin white lines of scar tissue remained on his back in lion form. Though he didn't say so, I assumed those were from a whip. It spoke to the severity of the beating he'd had that layers of skin were still damaged so far down inside him.

Elle had mastered changing now, and she and he often went out together to walk the forest in lion form. He was teaching her to hunt with success. She had caught rabbits and a deer so far, though Nineva had helped her with the deer, and she admitted it had already been lame.

Later that night, Nineva had spoken to me privately. "She's smart. Don't worry. When the time comes, she'll remember what to do."

"Thank you for all you've done, Nineva."

"I'm sorry I couldn't do more," he'd said sadly…

"Sar," Danial said loudly, breaking into my thoughts. "They're closing. Do you want to buy those books?"

"Sorry, yes," I said, heading toward him quickly. "My mind was elsewhere."

* * * *

Saturday morning, I took Elle and the dogs to the park to meet Kat. Elle liked Kat at first sight and spent much of the walk talking to her while I held onto Ghost and Darkness. They were not too happy to be leashed after more than year of walking without constraints.

"You be good," I said sternly to them. "Stop pulling."

"They're beautiful," a passing man remarked as he walked by with a poodle.

"Thanks," I said pleasantly. "Your dog is cute, too—"

"That's my mother," Elle broke in loudly, glaring at the man. She turned to me. "Come on, Mom, we've got to go look at that silver maple."

I nodded to her, casting a wave to the bemused man who was already striding away.

"You don't need to announce Sar's your mom," Kat said quizzically. "The man was just being friendly."

"Sorry," Elle said, shooting me a look. "I just didn't like the look of him."

Kat and I chuckled, and we resumed walking.

Though I enjoyed the outing and Kat's company, Elle's odd behavior worried me, especially when it was repeated several times throughout the walk. Elle did not want any man she didn't know within reach of me. If a solitary man walked toward us, she moved so she was between him and me. If a man looked at me, and I looked back at him, and he didn't look away when I did, she would stare at him until he noticed her and dropped his gaze.

I chalked up her overprotectiveness to her losing Theo as a baby and didn't mention it to Danial. That was something I came to rue one day.

Chapter Eight

On the first of May, Danial came home after a late night meeting carrying a dozen red roses... I had been reading on the couch with Jessica and Cavity, waiting for him. Elle was in bed, long since asleep. Danial had kissed her goodnight before heading out to his meeting

"For you," Danial said with a smile. He handed the roses to me.

My face lit up. "Danial, they're beautiful," I said with unadulterated happiness. I smelled them, and they were fragrant, the way roses should be and most often were not.

"I wasn't sure if you liked flowers," he said hesitantly.

"I love flowers," I said, giving him a wide smile and hurried to the kitchen to get them some water. "Especially roses."

I arranged them in a large vase and put in the flower food packet. I stood back to admire them for a moment, then took them into our bedroom, and setting them on the nightstand. I knew if I left them out in the great room, Jessica or Cavity would knock them over by morning.

"You really like them that much?" Danial said happily, hugging me from behind.

"Yes," I said, kissing him.

"Why have you never asked me for some?" he said, surprised.

"Because it means more to me you thought of them yourself."

"That sounds nice, but it doesn't sound like you," Danial said, chuckling.

"Okay," I admitted. "I thought it would be kind of tacky to ask you to bring me flowers. You give me so much already."

He held me close. "It is because I am finally ready to give you something that I brought them for you, Sar."

I went still at his words. Fear was sliding up my spine like ice water. "I'm ready," I said quickly.

He held me closer to him. "You're trembling."

I was. There were tiny tremors all through my body. "I'm afraid," I said honestly.

"About what happened last time?" he said.

"Yes. Also about not having it happen at all." I swallowed hard, and turned to face him. "I'm no virgin, Danial, but this…I've never done this before."

"Shh," he said gently. He drew off my clothes slowly, carefully. Soon I was naked before him. I made as if to lie down, but he stopped me. I stood naked before him as he slid off his jeans and unbuttoned his shirt, watching me with his dark eyes growing steadily darker, drinking in the sight of me. Then he stood before me, naked, his body I knew so well.

"Come to me, Sar," he said.

I went to him, still trembling, even though I wanted him. Danial kissed me softly, moving closer to me so our bodies were pressed together. I felt he was ready to make love, but he didn't hurry me. He just kissed me softly, his tongue tasting me, opening my mouth to him. He held me in his arms, but loosely, running his hands over my arms and my back.

I began to grow warm. He kissed my neck and then my breasts, squeezing me gently, rubbing me until I moaned. Then he reached down with his hand and slid his fingers inside me. I jerked against him, but he held me still, his arm tightening around me, still kissing me. His kisses were more insistent now, deeper, his tongue drawing mine into his mouth. He pushed me gently down on the bed and rested his body on mine, still kissing me, still touching me.

I wanted him badly, but still he didn't move from where he was.

The more he kissed me, the more aroused I became. Soon, I was panting, straining against his arms holding me down. Then, in an instant, he stopped holding me down and moved onto me, easing himself inside. My back arched against him, and he began to move, slowly. He was so warm.

I groaned, and he kissed me again. He was slow and tender, taking his time. I slowly felt the orgasm build, until it broke over me in a wave. I cried out and clutched him to me, thrusting up to take him all in. He held me tightly until the feeling faded and then started moving inside me again. I writhed under him and soon, I came again. He again held still, and when I'd finished, he'd resume his gentle movement.

I hadn't known Danial could do this repeatedly. Yet as much as I liked it, it was too gentle. I wanted more. I wanted him to take me utterly.

I kissed him hard, sliding my tongue deep inside his mouth. The dam he'd been holding back burst. He thrust faster, and I threw my head back, expecting him to bite me. He did, but just gently, as a human lover would. I felt his fangs in his kiss, but he didn't use them. Then he was crying out his release. He lay there, still inside me, breathing hard. I kissed him with passion, and he kissed me back with enough love to make me swoon a little.

"That was wonderful," I said, touching his face gently. "You were amazing—"

"I'm not done with you," he said, grinning above me. I jerked, feeling him flex inside me.

I looked at him in shock. "Terian gave you something," I said with a knowing look.

He gave me a sly smile. "Maybe," he said with a kiss. Then he started moving again, and I lost myself in the sensation.

Danial made love to me for a solid two hours. After, we lay exhausted in each other's arms. There was no maybe; Terian had given him something. He'd never been able to do this before. I'd have to thank Terian profusely the next time I saw him.

"Do you think we did it?" I said in a small voice, resting next to him.

"I'd be surprised if we did," he said gently. "It might take months, years even."

I looked at him, considering.

"Will that be a problem?" he said, looking at me with lowered eyes.

"Not for me," I said to him in a low voice and drew him down for another kiss.

* * * *

The spring passed quickly. I asked Danial if he would move back into my house with Elle and me for the summer, at least for this one. He said he would, though some of the foxes would have to come with us, and he didn't know if he would want to every year. I said that was understandable, but I wanted to try it, to see how it would be.

It was a disaster from the start. Suri and Demetri had stayed there the last winter and kept the pipes from freezing and the fire burning. Still, everything needed a thorough cleaning, and there were some repairs to be made. That took me a week with Elle's grudging help. She hated housecleaning and repair, though she enjoyed the break from her schooling. After that, I had Ivan till the garden for me, and I put in some vegetable plants. Elle, like Theo before her, was amazed something so small could become the vegetables she was not overly fond of eating. To make matters worse, just as the plants were sprouting, rabbits got in through a hole in the garden fence and ate the tops off everything. We had to re-till and replant.

"So much for our cats," Danial said that night as we relaxed on my deck.

"Cavity and Jessica are getting too old to chase rabbits," I said defensively. "Anyway, we should be all set now. I fixed the fence, and Ivan did the hard work. Elle helped me replant."

"I'm all set up in the basement," Danial agreed, slipping his arm around me.

"I'll help with the email tomorrow," I said quickly.

"Enjoy yourself," Danial encouraged. "You're supposed to be relaxing a little."

"Is Terian coming by later?"

"Yes. I'll be leaving with him for overnights most weeks, but nothing will keep us away longer than that."

"I'll be fine here," I assured him. "I'm sure Alphonse realized he targeted the wrong girl. I'm just upset for her, whoever she is."

"I'm inclined to agree, but I'm still not leaving you alone overnight or all day without one of us until a few more months have passed," Danial retorted and smiled. "No arguments. You'd think you didn't want me around."

"That's not it," I said grumpily. "I just feel like there's so much to do and not enough time."

"If you need help, just ask the foxes, Sar. They'd be glad to help you most days."

"I just have too many interests," I said, shrugging.

"You're upset about your sewing stuff being left behind," Danial said suddenly.

"No," I said reluctantly, "but Elle's upset she's in the old sewing room, because it's so much smaller than her room at your house."

"I wish you'd call it our house," Danial said softly. "I understand. You wanted her to enjoy being here. She's resisting that and missing home instead."

"I wanted us to be happy."

"We are," Danial assured me. "I've got my business office downstairs, and you've put up the blackout curtains in your old bedroom behind the forest ones. I'm content."

I didn't reply. My thoughts were in turmoil. It had been hard at first; waking up with Danial in the bed I'd shared with Theo. I'd felt sad and cheated, thinking about how little time we'd had.

Danial nuzzled me. "I don't want you to work so hard. You'll need to take it easy if you conceive."

My angst rose a notch. Despite Danial and I trying now almost every night for months, I was still not pregnant. I'd worried when I'd asked Danial about having a baby that it had been too soon. I'd worried I wasn't ready. Now I was glad I hadn't waited. I'd turn thirty-two this summer. Danial had been right. It might take us years.

"Don't be upset," he murmured, hugging me. "I'm a patient man, Sar. I've patience enough for both of us."

"I'm okay," I said finally. "I've been focusing on the bad things, but there are a lot of good things, too. All the bulbs I planted last spring came up."

Danial didn't reply.

"Does it bother you to mention that time in my life?" I asked quietly. "We never have, since I decided to come live with you."

"I am not bothered, just sad," Danial said, releasing me. "I'm in love with you and was then. He was my best friend. The reality is I had to lose him to gain you."

"I'm sorry," I said softly.

"Let's not speak of it for now," Danial said, taking my hand. "Come inside. It's late."

* * * *

Weeks passed and spring became summer.

I spent a lot of time with Elle, teaching her skills. I made her help with the firewood, and she fought me every step of the way. She looked about eight now. Though Danial and I had forbidden her to change outside while we lived at my house, I suspected she slept in cougar form whenever she could. She was aging much too fast for a regular child. She had outgrown all her clothes at least twice already, and Danial had bought her all new clothes each time. With her new growth came a disdainful attitude.

"I hate this. I don't understand why I have to do it. Why don't the people living here in winter do it?"

"We don't need other people doing work we're capable of doing ourselves," I said firmly. "I want you to know how to do the skills I'm teaching you, like felling trees or operating the machinery here. You won't have to do it next summer if you don't want to."

"I don't mind the work. I don't like getting dirty."

I remembered Theo's irritation at getting dirty and laughed. "Let's have you practice driving the tractor into the barn and then quit for today."

Elle started the tractor fine, put it into gear, and slowly drove toward the barn with me walking behind. Just as she went to turn in, she forgot the front-end loader's length and didn't give the door enough clearance. With a squeal of metal, the loader ripped off part of the barn's steel sliding door, breaking off a two by four in the process, and cracking several more.

Elle slammed on the brake and then scrabbled with the gear, putting it into park. She looked at me and burst into tears.

Looking at the damage, I was annoyed with her. If she'd been paying attention, she'd have done fine. We now had an hour's work in front of us. Elle already knew that, and yelling wouldn't put the door back together again.

"Stop crying," I said loudly over the diesel engine, climbing up beside her and hugging her. "It's okay."

"I broke it," she cried.

"I can see that. The important thing is not to panic. Cry if you have to, until you can calm down long enough to understand what to do," I said, calm and reassuring.

She looked at me with surprise, then wiped her tears away. "I'm calm," she said, taking a deep breath. "What do we do?"

"You and I will hammer the two by four back together and put in some extra screws. It will work fine in no time. C'mon."

I backed the tractor up out of the way, and we got to work. It didn't take long to fix the door with Elle's strength and mine. The sun was almost down when we finished.

Elle smiled in relief as we put the tools back. "I'm glad we fixed it. I'm ready to go in."

"You need to park the tractor first, Elle," I said gently.

"No," she said quickly. "I don't want to drive it anymore."

"Elle," I said sternly and firmly. "You can do this. Get back on the tractor and do it."

"What if I hit the door again?" she said worriedly as she bit her lip, tears threatening in her eyes.

"This time be careful and give the loader a little more clearance," I said, putting a hand on her shoulder. "Remember, you've already hit the door. That's the worst that could happen, and it's already happened." Technically, there were worse things, but I was trying to make a point. "The world didn't end. I'm not angry with you. We fixed what was broken."

She looked at me, a glimmer of understanding in her eyes. "It can't be worse than it was."

I nodded. "You don't have to be afraid—"

"Because the worst has happened, and I'm okay," she finished.

"You got it," I said encouragingly, hugging her. "Now get up there."

Elle got back on the tractor and this time she parked it right.

"Perfect. Let's go in," I said.

Following her inside, my eyes glanced at the fireplace mantle. I'd brought the carved cougar with me, and it was back in its place there, looking out and down from its rocky perch.

"Go get cleaned up for dinner," I said absently to Elle.

After she went to her room, I sat on the couch, taking a clandestine moment. I was getting to where I was able to remember Theo these days and not be sad. He'd been so wonderful. He'd made me so happy, made me feel so loved.

The basement door opened. "Sar, are you done for the day? Would you and Elle like to take a walk as soon as the sun sets? We could bring Ghost and Darkness."

Danial made me feel just as loved. He was trying his damnedest to make me happy. I put Theo from my mind.

"Yes," I called back, getting to my feet. "That sounds wonderful."

* * * *

Summer passed, as July became August. To celebrate our birthdays, Danial planned an expensive dinner out followed by a marathon shopping spree at a nearby mall. Though I appreciated his largesse and was looking forward to it, I wanted to do something simpler for Elle and myself, something just for us. So that afternoon, before beginning more work, I took her down to get an ice cream to celebrate.

As we waited for our order, I heard my name from behind me. It was my neighbor, Ken.

"Hi, Sar," he said, patting me on the arm. "I'll take three dishes of vanilla, please."

"Ken," I said excitedly. "I haven't seen you for months." I gave him a hug.

"Not since meeting your fella," he said jovially. "How're you doing?"

He'd met Theo one day back last summer. Not wanting to go into all that, I just nodded. "I'm doing good. This is Elle, Theo's daughter. Elle, this is our neighbor, Ken."

Elle glared at him. Ken smiled at her, then visibly recoiled at her open hostility.

"I didn't know Theo had children."

"Theo met Elle's mother in Europe," I said quickly. "She lives with me now. I'm sorry to tell you Theo's dead."

"I'm sorry," Ken said, nodding. "He was a good man."

"I've got a father," Elle said defiantly. "Danial is good to Mom."

"I'm happy for you," Ken said uncomfortably to me, glancing at Elle. "No one should be alone. I'm dating a widow myself. Grandma Flora introduced us right before she died."

"I'm glad to hear that," I said earnestly. "I miss Flora very much. I wish she'd lived to see me happy again and to meet Danial and Elle. She had a huge effect on my life."

"We're happy," Elle said flatly, a trace of growl in her voice. "Danial, Mom, and me."

"I'm here getting my dogs some ice cream," Ken said uncomfortably again. "I'd better go, before it melts." He collected his trays from the counter. "See you later, Sar."

"You had no right to be so nasty to him," I admonished Elle.

I got our ice cream, and we left, Elle giving Ken one last look of hostility. She didn't speak on the drive home, as we ate our cones.

"Mom, why did you hug that man?" Elle said suddenly, as we pulled into our driveway.

"Ken?" I said, eating the last of mine. "He's a friend, and I hadn't seen him in a long time. His grandmother was a dear friend—"

"Won't that make Danial jealous, like before?" she said, glaring at me.

Whoa there. "Elle, Ken is a friend. Danial knows there is nothing between Ken and me. He is not going to be jealous."

"Maybe that's what he thought about Theo until you left with him," she said.

I was shocked, to put it mildly. "Elle, that's enough."

She just looked at me and then away.

I tried to understand where she was coming from, saying these things. "I'm not going to leave Danial, Elle. If it will make you feel better…we're trying to have a baby."

Elle gasped. "Dad didn't tell me that."

"I promised not to mention it to you because we aren't sure we can," I said meaningfully. "I'm telling you now so you'll stop overreacting to strange men. I'm not about to run off with some stranger."

"I'm sorry," Elle said softly. "I'm just happy. I don't want Danial to leave like Theo did."

"He won't," I said, hugging her tight. "You can trust in that."

"I don't want you to leave either."

"I'm not going anywhere," I said emotionally. "Trust me."

* * * *

Shooting lessons also continued that summer. Terian came to my house now every week to practice with Elle and me. Sometimes Danial would join us, though that was rare.

When we finished one afternoon and Elle had gone inside to play, I pulled him aside and asked him to take a walk with me.

"Is something wrong?" he said quickly, blackness coiling out of him.

"No," I said quickly. "Danial and I are fine."

"I'm glad you asked me out here," Terian said with an exhalation of breath. "I've been thinking a lot about what happened back in the spring. You were right, I should never let it get as far as it did with those men. I should've killed them."

"You did kill them," I said, repressing a shudder at the memory.

"I didn't mean to bring back bad memories," he said regretfully. "I just wanted to apologize."

I forced a smile. "You have nothing to apologize for."

He smiled back, and his hand touched my face. "Thanks. Now what did you need?"

I took a deep breath. "If I'd had a baby with Theo, would it have been okay?"

151

Terian gaped at me. "What?"

"I'm asking hypothetically," I added quickly.

"I have no idea," Terian said, shrugging.

"Could you find out?" I asked. "Please?"

"Why does it matter now?" Terian said, looking at me like I'd grown a tail. "He's dead."

"I don't know," I said, shrugging. "I can't seem to let this go. I know it's bizarre to be still thinking about this with Theo dead. My best guess is guilt over wanting a baby now." I met Terian's eyes. "I was going to refuse if Theo asked me to have kids, Terian. I didn't want to end up like Tawny. Yet I asked Danial. He didn't ask me."

"I'll do some research," Terian said, nodding. "I'll let you know when I find out definitively."

"Thanks," I said, giving him a hug.

* * * *

Danial informed me late one night in mid-August Devlin had been asking about the child we were trying for. "I let it slip, Sar. I'm sorry."

"What did you tell him?" I said, wary.

"That you aren't pregnant yet. That's all," he said, hugging me.

"How is your deal going with him, by the way?"

"So far, so good," Danial said, pleased. "He is handling everything well and not making too much of a mess or letting the killing get out of hand. The clients I've sent to him have been happy, all of them."

Danial had been worried about refusing some of those contracts. His old business partners Tony and Thane had been none too pleased when he had not accepted their last two hits. Devlin had taken care of both.

"That's great," I said to him warmly.

"It's more than great, it's a miracle," Danial said, relieved. "This was important, and he came through for me. It's almost as if the rift between us is finally closing." His voice dropped lower. "He still knows not to come here, Sar. You don't have to worry about that."

I nodded, relieved. "Good."

* * * *

The end of that summer was a peaceful one. Danial and I took long romantic walks in the dark, and Elle and I took long walks in the day, working on naming the plants and birds we saw. She was excellent now at it. The dogs enjoyed the quiet relaxed summer days, sitting on the deck as Elle and I read or did art. She, like her father, had artistic skill. I could do watercolors with a lot of effort, but she could do them easily and make them look almost as good as photographs. Elle could also sketch. She was shy about her work, as Theo had been about his wood carving ability. When I showed Danial some of her work with some of my old supplies, he bought her oil paints, canvases, bound books of paper, and special pencils for drawing. She created masterpieces, some of which I framed, and hung on the walls of our home. Most were forest scenes, but she did a few of me and a few of Danial.

One she did of us together. I had been wearing the red dress, the choker, and the fox earrings. Danial had been in his red shirt, and black leather pants. He had been taking me out for dancing and up to visit Tatiana. Elle had made us sit for an hour while she got the lighting right and sketched in the details. The delay had made us late, so much so we'd gotten back just in time to get inside before dawn. The resulting painting had been worth it. We looked supernaturally good in the picture, like something out of a fable. Danial had it framed and put in our bedroom at his house.

Finally, on September first, early winter hit. We had a killing frost that took out many of the local farmers' crops, though my gardens were covered. Though sunshine persisted in the following days, the temperature stayed abnormally cold. Admitting defeat, I gathered the last of the edibles up and left the rest for wildlife. It had been a bad harvest because a lot of the plants needed another few weeks to develop.

That night, Danial watched me put up the last vegetables. "It's time to go home, Sar."

"Yes," I said sadly. "We've been running the woodstove nonstop this week."

"I'll pack up tonight," Danial said. "Elle is already packed. We can leave tonight, if you've no objections."

"You both go ahead," I said. "I need to shut off everything, including the water. It'll be easier to do when I'm not tired like I am now."

"You're sure you don't want me to hire a housesitter?"

"Yes. The wood will keep 'till next year. Ken has promised to check the place once a week and call us if there are any problems. You've set up Henry to plow the drive for us."

"Are you okay with being alone here tonight?"

"You don't mean alone. You mean without you and Elle," I corrected gently. "Yes, I'll be fine. I'll be able to come home faster tomorrow if you take her with you tonight. The pets will be hard enough to transport tomorrow, even with Suri's help."

Danial nodded. "All right. I'll leave most of the foxes here with you and take Terian with me." He went back downstairs.

I sat down and began making a list. The reason for closing the house up this year was because Suri had broken up with Demetri over the summer. She was now dating Ivan and sleeping with him, A vicious triangle was threatening to send at least one person to another job. Danial said he was tired of the bickering and jealously. Demetri had tried to start a fight with Ivan twice already. I'd tried to keep them logy with baked goods, but it seemed to have no effect.

Danial strode in. "Elle's already in the SUV. Are you sure you won't come?"

"Go ahead," I said firmly. "Take Demetri with you. I don't want a fight with you not here."

"I told the three of them to settle it one way or another. There are to be no more fights. I pay them to guard you, Elle, and me. If they want to hook up, that's okay, but when it interferes with their job, it's not okay. Demetri will likely take a few weeks off. He's got vacation coming."

"What's the problem, really? Too few females and too many males?"

"Some of it is the close quarters of the compound. It's like a college dorm. Most of the foxes are young, only in their early twenties. They aren't thinking about settling down yet. They want to have fun. This bed hopping and resulting fighting isn't unusual."

"You're probably right."

"Take care," Danial said, kissing me lightly. "I'll call you before dawn."

I hugged him goodbye and then returned to my list. Finally, it was complete, and I collapsed into bed.

Late the following morning, after everything was done, I went back through the house for one last check, to make sure nothing had been forgotten. I walked through the house, grabbing a few forgotten items, like my hairbrush from the shower and my new black velvet robe from the back of the door. Lastly, I went to Theo's drawers and took out a few of his shirts. I smelled them, inhaling his scent. It was so faint now as to be almost nonexistent. The smell of cedar from my scented drawer woodchips had almost replaced it completely.

I put his clothes back in the drawer, moving aside the diamond ring he had bought me in its box, wrapped in my blue velvet robe. The potion Terian had given me to recreate the dream was also there, wrapped in bubble wrap to protect it. There it would stay for the winter.

Driving back, I debated if it was time to let go. The past summer had been such a disaster. Ghost and Darkness had liked the summer there as had the cats, but Danial and Elle were happier at Danial's house. It was time to face facts: Theo had been gone over a year. He was not coming back, not ever. I had a new life now, one with Danial and Elle. Sooner or later, I was going to have to cut the old life loose.

I wasn't ready yet. I couldn't do it now.

Chapter Nine

I'd envisioned coming to Danial all summer, letting him know with some kind of quip or meaningful words I was going to have our baby. I'd hoped for it to be on my birthday or Elle's, but those had passed. Though we'd celebrated often in the summer with parties and good times, I was beginning to feel disheartened, wondering if we would ever succeed.

As was usual for me, the actual moment was nothing like I had imagined.

I woke up one evening in the second week of September feeling awful. My first thought was what had I eaten to make me feel this bad? In the next moment, I was dashing for the bathroom. I made it just in time and heaved until there was nothing left inside me to come up. Danial saw me rush out and made as if to come in and help me.

"Get out," I yelled at him from the floor. He backed up and shut the door with a sharp click.

"Sar, are you okay in there?" he said.

"No," I said, worried. I stayed there a few minutes more, just breathing. I was scared. I almost never threw up, so I knew what was probably happening: I was finally pregnant.

I got up from the floor, brushed my teeth, used some mouthwash, and washed my face. When I finally opened the bathroom door, Danial was waiting for me, leaning against the wall, dressed.

"Get dressed, Sar," he said, trying to make it sound like a gentle prod.

"I want to go back to bed," I said, moving past him slowly.

"No. You are going to get dressed. Now."

Well, all pretenses at asking had gone right out the window.

I looked over at him defiantly. It had been a long time since he'd ordered me to do something. He just looked at me, watching me with dark eyes that dared me to say something.

I went back to bed, covering myself up and drawing my legs up to my chest. The next thing I knew, Danial was rolling the sheets around me and picking me up. My stomach heaved again.

"Please, put me back in bed," I pleaded with him.

"No, you're going to see Stephen now. I am taking you there dressed or wrapped in our bed linens. You and I both suspect why you threw up, but I need to make sure this is what I am hoping it is." He carried me out toward the front door.

"Okay," I said reluctantly. "Let me get dressed."

"No," Danial said firmly, opening the door. "We are going now."

Terian was on the other side, waiting. He ran to the SUV and opened the back door for Danial to help me inside. "Excited?" he said to me with a smile.

I looked at him with tired eyes. "You have got to be kidding."

"Get going, Terian," Danial commanded.

Terian rolled his eyes, frowned and then got in the driver's seat.

We made it in record time to the doctor's office, mostly from Terian's affinity for seventy-five mph. Terian again opened the door, and Danial helped me out of the backseat, again picking me up. He took me inside, walking quickly over the pavement wet from a recent rain and glittering blackly in the streetlights, Terian following.

Dr. Camlyn gave me a urine test and a blood test. Neither one was conclusive.

"That might be due to the baby being part vampire. I'll have to physically look."

I rolled my eyes, assuming the stirrup position. A few minutes later, Stephen moved back, gently shutting my legs.

"Your cervix is sealed up tight. Congratulations."

"You're sure?" Danial said anxiously.

"As sure as I can be without fluid testing. Sar, when was your last period?"

"Almost two months," I said, thinking back. "I've been late before."

"I'll do additional tests on your blood and some swabs I took," Stephen said. "I would act as if you're pregnant from this moment on. You most likely are."

Danial hugged me gently, and Terian was beaming as well. I just still felt sick.

"When is she due?" Danial asked. "Nine months would be sometime in early March?"

"I'd say more like April or May, probably."

Danial thanked him profusely and then hugged Terian. Instead of acting surprised or standoffish, Terian hugged Danial back hard enough to crack his back.

"Thank you," Danial said softly, tears in his eyes. "This wouldn't have been possible without you."

"I was glad to help," Terian said softly, nodding.

"Hey, I'm the one having the baby and feeling sick," I said irritably. "I'd like to go home now."

Danial picked me up in his strong arms while Terian collected some prescriptions for vitamins.

"Danial," Stephen said warningly, "Don't take any of Sar's blood. She's going to need it all."

"Understood," Danial said, nodding once. "Thank you again, Doctor."

As we were driving home, reality set in. This was it. I was pregnant.

I didn't feel any different, except for being nauseous. My apprehension grew the closer we got to home. Danial had me now. I'd promised him control of me until I delivered.

Despite my worry, I knew he'd take good care of me. He wanted this child badly enough to do anything to keep us both safe. Still questions flooded my mind, questions that would need answering.

What would I say to my mother now? How would my baby feel knowing I wasn't married to its father? Would he or she care? What if having the baby killed me? What if I miscarried again? Would Danial want to try yet again if that happened? Would I? Worse, what would Theo think to come back now and find me not only living with Danial, but pregnant with his child?

What had I done?

Harshly, I beat down my guilt. It had been more than a year since Theo had gone missing. He was not coming back. For the first time that meant relief.

"I'll cancel my meetings for today and tomorrow," Danial said to Terian. "We need to work out a schedule of keeping watch over Sar. She is to go nowhere outside the house without one of us there from now on, not for any reason. Is that clear?"

"Of course," Terian said, "but that's going to mean a lot of conference calls."

"Not necessarily. Sar agreed to abide by my rules. She'll just be under house arrest." Danial gave me a smile. "I'll have to lay in a supply of books for you."

Claustrophobia engulfed me at his words. As soon as Terian pulled up in front of Danial's house, I opened my SUV door and raced inside. Heading straight to the kitchen, I poured myself a huge glass of wine and drank half of it down immediately. In a few seconds, the alcohol hit me and I stopped caring so much, because everything was good. Thank God for the over-sizing of American glassware.

Danial came through the front door, calling for me. I hurriedly drank half of the remainder, having a hunch he would not approve my self-indulgence. Quickly, I fled to Elle's room and shut the door. Turning on her TV, I happened on the very end of the Sci-Fi parody, *Spaceballs*. Either because of the large amount of wine or the movie, I began laughing uproariously, rolling on the bed. Too soon, the credits began to scroll across the screen. Abruptly, the TV clicked off. I looked up to find Danial glowering down at me.

"What exactly do you think you're doing?" he growled at me.

"Dealing," I said bluntly and reached for the wineglass.

"You are not having any more, Sar, is that clear?" He took the wine out of my reach.

I rolled my eyes and made a face at him. He shook his head slightly and then picked me up.

"Where are you taking me?" I said getting the words out slowly.

"You are going back to bed, my drunken darling," he said, kissing my forehead. He carried me through the new addition to our bedroom. "You need your rest."

"I want to watch TV," I said stubbornly. "I want to relax. I need to relax."

"I will stay with you," he said consolingly. "You can relax."

"You don't relax me," I said defiantly.

"Don't I?" he said, kissing my neck. "I could try a little harder—"

Something uncurled itself within me that had been sleeping and opened its eyes wide. It was so hungry, so full of craving. AAHHHH.

"No, you don't," I said softly, then lunged for him. I began kissing him hard, my passion so forceful he took a step backward.

"Sar," he said worriedly, breaking away from me. "What's gotten into you?"

"Nothing yet," I said, sultry and rough, "but maybe you can help me with that?"

Danial blinked at me, and his mouth fell open.

"I want you, Danial." I unbuttoned his pants with a yank, undoing his belt, and throwing it to one side. I stroked him with my hand, feeling him stiffen. "That's right, get it up."

"Stop it—"

"Take me now, Vampire, or by God, I'll find someone else who will," I snarled.

He bared his fangs and hissed, anger flooding his eyes to red. Then he was on me. Without preamble, he shoved me against the wall, yanked down his pants, and pushed inside, thrusting so hard it hurt. I lolled back my head against the wall as he hammered himself into me.

I looked down at him through half lidded eyes, drinking in his lust. I wanted what was happening with everything I was. I was slippery with arousal. Yet strangely, the desire raging through me didn't want release. What it wanted was his release.

Abruptly, Danial came, crushing my body against his. As he finished, the desire faded, leaving me weak and shaky.

"You didn't seem to enjoy it," Danial panted angrily. "Why not?"

"I'm so sorry," I whispered, tears in my eyes. "I didn't mean it, Danial—"

"You meant it," he groaned, pulling out of me. "Stay there. You're bleeding."

He moved for the bathroom, pulling up his pants. Scared, I slid down the wall slowly to sit on the floor.

Danial returned with a wet washcloth. He carefully helped me clean off the slight blood smears, then helped me to the bed.

"Don't worry," he said, taking me in his arms. "The blood is minimal. You have a couple tears in your skin, from me being so rough. The baby is fine."

"I am so sorry," I whispered. "I don't know what came over me."

"Shh, Sar, it's not your fault. This is likely a side effect of having my child."

"Being wanton?" I said, incredulous. "Wanting to be hurt?"

"You didn't want to be hurt, you wanted sex. I think my desire for blood is manifesting itself in you. Our baby is half vampire. It makes sense it would feel the same desire."

"How do you conclude my wanting sex has anything to do with the baby needing blood?"

"It's not logical, when you put it that way. I'm only saying you may have odd urges because of our child's dual nature. Most pregnant women have them with human children. Your urges may be slightly more...aberrant."

"How do you know this?" I said softly. "Stephen never said anything—"

"Terian mentioned because baby would be half vampire, some of its vampire nature might cause you to do odd things as it was developing. He also reminded me of the transformative power of demon blood. He said he didn't know how either might manifest in you or if it would do so at all. We are all operating blind, Sar. No vampire has ever done this in my lifetime."

"I didn't know that." I hugged him tighter. "Terian told me dhamphirs were rare."

"They are. None currently exist," Danial said gently. "Don't be afraid. Whatever you need me to do, whatever you ask, I'll do it, Sar. You're okay. I'm here."

"I'm so afraid," I said in a small voice.

"I'll take care of you. Don't worry, darling," Danial said softly. "I'm here."

We lay together for a long time in silence. Finally, I fell asleep.

* * * *

The next few months brought repeat performances. I'd be doing something normal, like working outside, reading, or showering and suddenly I'd be overcome with desire, what Danial and I began to call "The Lust." The mood was all encompassing, complete and total, and until it passed, I was helplessly in its grip. Within days, it quickly became clear the surest way to break the Lust's hold over me was through sex, primarily fierce sex. Often, sex involved bloodletting.

My complete loss of control while under The Lust, coupled with its provocative sluttish behavior, mortified me. I had never been a prude, but my demands went beyond the familiar realm of loving sensuality to base carnality, almost sadism. Even worse was my constant worry if Danial wasn't nearby, I'd try to find someone else to sate me. Worst of all was my fear The Lust wouldn't end until the baby was born.

True to his word, Danial was always there to take it from me by sex and bloodshed. He had me on Elle's bed, in the kitchen, on the dining room table, on the great room couch, on his desk in his office, outside on the lawn, and even on the stairs. It was always the same. We coupled in varying fashions. I drank in his desire for me and then came back to myself, often bruised and sometimes bleeding. The blood was always mine, usually from bites I asked for in the heat of passion.

When I was again myself, Danial usually healed the bites either with a little blood or with gentle kisses. We both worried about me turning so he used blood to heal only the worst ones to the point I wasn't in pain. Some of the bites were deep, in places where I regretted asking for them when The Lust had left me.

By luck and a lot of planning, we were able to keep my condition from Elle. Helpfully, The Lust—save for the first occurrence—manifested itself only between dusk and dawn. Oddly, it came in intervals that while not regular did form a kind of pattern, so over time Danial and I could make reasonable guesses of when I'd likely be affected and when I'd probably be okay. Though not perfect, the analysis gave me a handle on an otherwise untenable situation.

I saw my mother briefly a few times, trying to reconnect with her. I didn't tell her I was pregnant, knowing how she still felt about Danial. Though Danial was nearby, waiting in the car, those visits went off without incident or embarrassment. Other than that, I stayed indoors, secluded, emerging only for nighttime walks with the dogs and Danial as often as possible.

Suddenly one night, without warning, our carefully worked out analysis fell apart. I'd recovered from an episode with Danial in the early evening and, thinking myself safe, had gone with Cia to the werefox compound to see Aran Jr. In the midst of our visit, The Lust possessed me again. It was only by luck Danial was nearby when it happened, target practicing in the indoor range beneath us, and I headed in the direction of the faint shots. Needless to say, I missed the Hallows party the next week as a result. Unable to secure chemically-induced unconsciousness in my pregnant state, I stayed up for almost twenty-four hours before to ensure I would sleep the whole time Danial was gone. Happily, it worked. Yet when I awoke, I reached for him, The Lust again in control.

After that, The Lust again fell into a kind of pattern for a few days, then abruptly stopped. I breathed a sigh of relief when a week had gone by with no recurrence.

"I think it's over," I said confidently that night as we lay together in bed.

"I agree," Danial said with relief. "You've never gone even half this long without symptoms since it started."

"It scares me, though," I murmured. "What other weirdness can I expect? I've still got at least five more months."

"We'll solve it like we did this," Danial assured me. "I'm not leaving town again until you deliver." He kissed my forehead. "What are you going to do tomorrow? Elle has an outing planned, I believe."

"She's visiting the local nature preserve with Bill and Janice. Her interest in tracking and wildlife is still going strong. I'm not going, of course."

"I concluded that. What are you going to do?"

"I need to weed and cover the flower gardens one last time. There's snow predicted by the weekend. The roses you had planted for me need to be pruned back for next spring. The job's way overdue as it is."

"Fine, but don't overdo it," Danial cautioned. "You're not as strong as you should be."

"I'm fine," I said grumpily. "I've been gaining weight steadily."

"Not enough," he amended. "Your morning sickness stopped you eating fruit—"

"I'll be fine if I can get a good night's sleep," I said crankily, turning off the light.

Danial hugged me gently and didn't reply.

* * * *

The next morning started perfectly. I enjoyed working with the roses, singing to myself. The sky was blue, and the air was fragrant, if a little chilly.

Suddenly, The Lust hit me like a physical force. I took a ragged breath, and then looked around me. No male was near. The nearest was Danial, inside sleeping.

I got up, tossing aside my gardening gloves and my trowel, and headed inside. Slamming the front door, I stalked in, then grabbed the large mirror off the mudroom wall and smashed it on the floor. Stepping on shards, I headed toward the bedroom deliberately slowly, breaking every picture on the walls along the way. My one consuming thought was to wake Danial, to make him furious, to bring him to me, red-eyed and wrathful. To my disappointment, despite the crashes of shattering glass, he didn't emerge before I reached his door.

I would not go to him like some simpering wench with no power or pride. That son of a bitch was coming out here to me.

I stalked to the far end of the great room, my desire heating up with the flames of anger. Grabbing the huge framed topographical map of Colorado in both hands, I began to pull it down off the wall. Breaking this would bring him out of his dreams, if I could just tear loose the screws…

A noise came from behind me in the kitchen.

I turned slowly, inclining my head and then glided toward it. Terian was there in front of the open fridge, his back to me. He was dressed in a loose shirt and some stained and dirty torn jeans. The scent of blood, pine, and earth was suddenly strong in my nose. The Lust loosened its control over me, peculiarly hesitant. I gripped the doorframe with one hand and leaned heavily against it as I shook my head slightly, trying to clear it.

"Hi, Sar," he said, not turning. "Want a sandwich?"

"You have blood on you," I whispered.

"I've been practicing how to dive and roll while shooting," he replied. "It's harder than it looks, but no worries, I'm already healed." He rubbed his thigh slightly, mud and specks of dried blood flaking off. "I've just got to find a spell to get rid of pine pitch."

Swiftly the three scents became overpowering. The Lust roared up within me, screaming to be fed.

I grabbed Terian by the hips, pulling him back hard against me. "Fuck me."

He jumped and then turned in my arms. "Sar? What the hell—?"

I kissed him, my tongue sliding fast between his parted lips.

Terian kissed me back and grabbed me in his arms, heat radiating from his skin. He ran into the great room, getting hotter by the second. Bursting through Danial's door, he dropped me on the bed in a tangle. Danial sat up with a start, blinking his eyes.

"Help her," Terian said, backing away. "It's The Lust—"

He turned and went for the door. Before he got a step, I grabbed him by his belt loops, yanking him backwards. His weight knocked us sprawling, pushing Danial out of bed and onto the floor.

I crawled on top of Terian before he could stop me. "You want me, I can feel it," I said, my lips parted, my eyes dark forest green. I moved my hips on his. "Don't be shy now."

"No, Sar," he gasped.

"Yes," I said, reaching for his belt.

"No," he yelled, the blackness seeping out of him, winding out to curl around me.

I drank it in with an amorous sigh and smiled. "Yes," I cried with glee, unbuckling his belt and reaching inside eagerly.

"Stop!" he shouted.

I suddenly couldn't move my limbs. I tried with all my will, but managed only to twitch.

Terian moved carefully from under me and retreated to the door, watching me with fear and distaste. I couldn't go after him so I leered instead, letting my lust show itself on my face.

Danial pulled me back against him on the bed. "Get out of here, Terian."

Terian slammed the door. Suddenly I could move again.

"Let me go. I don't want you, I want him," I said, sneering.

"You want to be fucked," Danial said coarsely, pulling off my pants. "Cooperate."

I shoved Danial away and tried to get up. "Not by you, you bastard."

Danial grabbed me by the neck and threw me down on the bed, suddenly enraged. I struggled furiously, but he turned me over on my stomach roughly, tearing me as he thrust into me. I let out a yelp, then relaxed, the pain and motion of his body on mine stilling me.

Danial did not relax his death grip, his panting loud in my ears. The sex was hard, rapid, and devoid of emotion, desire without love, care, or conscience. I drank it in, wallowing in it.

Danial came, screaming utter release. I shifted beneath him, beginning to regain my will. The instant I moved he sank his fangs into my shoulder, bringing a scream from my throat. The pain was instantaneous. In that act, whatever had been fueling my urges finally let go of me, and I fainted.

* * * *

I woke up sometime later in Danial's arms. He quickly tightened his arms around me.

"Sar, are you back?"

"Yes," I said wearily. "Thanks for healing me. You must have, because nothing hurts."

"Of course, sweetheart. Now what happened?"

I related being possessed by The Lust and finding Terian in the kitchen. "I'm sorry I broke your pictures."

"Terian has already gathered them and the glass has been cleaned up. I'm more concerned about you."

I began to cry, gripping him tightly and sobbing. He hugged me back, whispering soothing words.

"No one blames you for what happened. Don't cry. This can't last forever."

"I feel like I'm losing my mind," I whispered, drying my tears on my sleeve. "I can't take much more of this."

"You'll sleep days with me and be up at night," Danial said tiredly. "I'll stay near you at all times and you'll go back to being confined to the house when I'm not with you. We should probably have done this from the beginning—"

"What about Elle?" I said, panicked. "Someone has to get her up and make breakfast—"

"Cia can do that—"

"Until when?" I said hysterically. "I'm not due for another six months."

"I can't have you assaulting the bodyguards either," Danial said loudly.

I cringed at his words. "I'll stay in the house," I whispered, ashamed.

"Do not be ashamed," he said firmly. "I'm not judging you, and you must not judge yourself. No one here thinks badly of you." He kissed my cheek. "Let's try my suggestion, okay?"

I nodded, burrowing into his chest.

* * * *

For the next few weeks, I did as Danial asked, but The Lust did not reappear once. Two weeks from the last occurrence of The Lust, a new symptom emerged; hot flashes. Soon that built into a general feeling of overheating so much I sweated almost constantly, despite the steadily cooling weather.

Stephen had no answer. "I'm sorry, but the baby you're having is outside my realm of expertise. I don't know of a single dhamphir outside of novels and myth. I can't help you."

"What should I do, Stephen? I'm dehydrating from all the sweat, no matter if its sixty degrees or forty."

"If you're hot, use ice to cool yourself. That's all you can do," he said. "Just watch your temperature doesn't fall too rapidly."

"I'll watch over her," Danial assured him. "Thank you, doctor."

Ice became my close friend for the next few months. The heating problem increased to the point where I'd sit in cold bath water laced with ice, sweating. Surprisingly, that not only helped with the heat, it also helped my aching back, a result of my advancing pregnancy

One night as I was cooling myself, Danial came in and sat by my side, his face expressionless. From experience, that meant something was wrong.

"Danial, what is it?" I said, clasping his hand and luxuriating in its coolness.

"Samuel called a little while ago. He said he has evidence Theo escaped from the sadist who bought him."

Chills not from the cold water surrounding me ran up my spine. "What proof?"

"An American cougar was on board a ship that arrived in Alexandria, Egypt. It was bound for a sheik's palace somewhere in Ishafan, Iran."

Hope rose in my heart. "Did Samuel find Theo?"

"Samuel sent some of his people to check out the situation. They paid off a guard for information, trying to find the best way to attempt a rescue. To their surprise, they discovered the cougar never made it to the sheik's palace. It escaped."

I breathed a sigh of relief. "I'm happy for that, but there is no proof it was Theo, or even male. It could have been a female for all we know."

"I know, after Nineva I'm afraid to hope either—"

"It's not Theo. He's dead, Danial." I turned to face him. "We've been here before. Each time, we hear some more clues about what might have happened and get our hopes up. What do we have to show for it? Ghosts and rumors."

"I agree. The last sighting we have we're certain of was Nineva's. Theo would never stay away this long, but I didn't think it fair to keep the information from you."

I stood up with effort as Danial helped me from the tub. I looked into his eyes, asking him to understand. "Danial, I can't keep hoping anymore. Every time we get more information that turns out to be nothing, I'm torn apart all over again."

"I know, Sweetheart." He wrapped me in a large towel and hugged me gently. "I'd ordered a headstone almost a year ago and had it inscribed, before we found out the body wasn't Theo's. The empty grave was filled in, after we exhumed Will's body. I'd like to hold a service next week, if you're willing. We never held a proper funeral. I would like to now."

"Yes," I said, nodding. "It's time to say goodbye."

"Will you be going to your parent's home for Christmas?" Danial said neutrally, changing the subject.

"No. I'm visibly pregnant, and I don't want them to know. I'll make some excuse."

"You've not seen your friend Kat lately either," he said softly. "Is it because it's mine?"

"Some of it," I admitted, moving away from him. "We aren't married, and my mom will give me shit just for that. She doesn't know what this child means to you."

"You mean the same to me," Danial replied. "I don't mean to push, but—"

"Then don't," I said sharply.

"I love you," he said sharply back, his eyes tinting red. "It bothers you you're in what you see as an illicit situation, enough for you to shun your friends and family. I'm merely telling you the situation is of your own choosing."

"You told me once, you didn't want to marry me," I said bluntly, feelings of sadness and anger roiling together.

"I told you I'd prefer to be Oathed," Danial countered. "I still feel the same. You've seen marriage isn't respected by most non-humans, as the choker is."

"I'm already wearing the choker," I said with a sigh.

"I know, darling," he murmured, taking me in his arms. "I'm just asking you if you'd feel better wearing a ring."

I was silent a moment. Danial was offering to marry me. Part of me wanted to because it would immediately make my pregnancy more kosher to everyone, including myself. Was that really the best decision for me in the long run? Would I feel the same way about being married or Oathed to him when I wasn't pregnant anymore? It wasn't fair to Danial to say yes now, and reconsider later. Unfeeling as that possibility was, I knew I couldn't promise forever now, not if I wasn't sure I could give him that.

"I'll marry you, if you want me to," Danial continued gently. "Just say the word."

"No," I said gently back. "I know you're committed to me and to our baby. I don't need another symbol of that commitment."

"As you wish," he said with a sigh. "Come, let's get you to bed."

* * * *

Christmas was peaceful that year. Again, I set the tree up at night with Danial and Elle's help. This year, more than my memories graced the tree. The spiders we had made last year hung in its branches along with ornaments Elle had made of clay, wood, and paper.

Christmas Eve came without interruption, and we exchanged gifts. I had sewn Elle a ballerina outfit, and she tried it on, dancing for us.

"I want dance lessons," she said sweetly, lunging around the great room.

"Your mother and I have agreed on private ones," Danial replied, "provided you are on your best behavior. Children are often more perceptive than adults." He handed her a package. "However, you must leave time for learning."

"Is it the new telescope?" she said excitedly, grabbing it.

Danial nodded. "Yes. I'll take you out later tonight if you like. The night's clear and cold, perfect for stargazing."

"Here is another treat for you," I said, handing Ghost and Darkness their third Cheweez of the evening. They took them happily, retreating to their beds to chew.

Elle handed us some drawings she had made of us walking together on a moonlit night. "These are for you and Dad."

"Thank you." I was astounded at her level of skill. "We'll have to frame them. These are wonderful, Elle."

"Thank you," she said shyly, taking off her outfit. "Can we go look at the stars, Dad?"

"Yes," Danial said, "Get your coat."

Elle ran to the mudroom, and Danial turned to me. "Would you like to come?"

"No," I said, taking his proffered hand. "I'm oddly chilled. I'm going in to bed."

"I'll see you in a bit, then," Danial said, leaving me at the bedroom door. "I started a fire, so you should be warm."

I gave him a kiss. "I'll be fine. Go on."

Danial left, and I went to the woodstove, throwing on another log. Jesse and Cavity were in front of it, lying in happy, blissful warmth. I petted them and then went to bed.

Lying on my pillow was a small box of Godiva Chocolate. I picked up the card beside it.

"To my Love, on our third Christmas, Danial."

I put the chocolates beside my bed, resisting the urge to eat one. The next thing I knew, it was Christmas afternoon.

Danial was gone when I awoke, the rumpled bed the only testament he'd come to bed. Worried he was up, I wrapped a robe around me and went looking for him. Opening the bedroom door, I stepped into flowers.

There were vases everywhere with roses of all colors—red, white, yellow, blue, pink, and multi-colored. The sweet fresh scent of roses wakened my senses. I took a deep breath.

"Here's another one," Terian said with a grin, handing me a bucket filled with water and more roses. "We've run out of vases."

I took it from him, taking a deep breath in the silky petals. "How many did he order?"

"One for each day we have spent together," said Danial from above me.

I looked up to the loft, meeting Danial's eyes. "Danial, that is over five hundred flowers!" I said, shocked.

"Five hundred, thirty-three," he replied with a loving smile. "I've been listening for you to get up for hours, hoping you'd delay long enough to get them in position. There are four hundred and eighty here so far, so it was pretty close."

"I can't believe you did this," I said slowly, looking around me in wonder.

"This Christmas called for more than a box of chocolate," he said, leaning over the railing, his dark hair falling forward. "I know you like flowers."

"I love them," I said, burying my face again in soft fresh petals.

"Here's another," Elle said, carrying in an armful. "There are no more containers."

"I'll get another bucket," Terian said, rolling his eyes, and we all broke into laughter.

* * * *

The roses ruled the great room for a week. They overpowered the pine tree and everything else. I loved seeing them all together and watching them open more each day. Cavity and Jessica had a field day, knocking them over almost faster than I could right and refill the vases. I took to locking them inside the pet room with their litter box when I couldn't be there watching them. They couldn't go outside anyway, and I knew the roses wouldn't last long. I wanted to enjoy them.

Too soon, they began to die. By the end of two weeks, I was down to one large vase of around fifty.

"So you want a boy?" I said to Danial late one night, as I removed the dying roses from the vase.

"I'd like any child of ours, you know that," he said, kissing me, "but I would like a son. We have a daughter we love."

"I'll see what I can do," I said softly, kissing him.

"There's more," he said, pulling away. "We were right in our suspicions. Elle has been changing at night and sleeping in cougar form to speed up her development."

"She looks about eight now, though she's only about one and a half years old. How did you get her to admit it? She denied it when I asked her."

"I asked her to stop changing at night. She cried and said she would."

"Did she give a reason why?"

"Because there aren't any kids to play with here. She thought if she looked older, she would be allowed to do more. I told her she'd have a sister or a brother soon to play with."

"She just said okay?" I said in disbelief.

"I told her the baby wouldn't have anyone to play with except Aran Jr. and would need her not to be too old. She agreed to change only once a week from now on."

"Good," I said, relieved. "That was what Nineva had recommended for Elle before leaving for Africa."

"Are they still corresponding?" Danial asked. "I worried he would lose interest after the first letter or not want to continue because it might bring back bad memories of his suffering."

"Elle still gets letters from him about once a month asking her how everything is. I'm surprised too, but grateful he's her friend. We don't know any other werelions."

"They're rare in the United States," Danial said, after a moment. "There are some cougars out west, but not an abundance of them. Most werelions reside in Africa and some in South America, but they are the African lion, not cougars." He took my hand. "Are you ready for bed?"

"Yes. Please start a fire."

"Are you cold again?" he said worriedly.

"It's normal for me to be cold in winter," I said nonchalantly. "It's wonderful to not be too hot."

I went to sleep easily and slept well. The next morning I awoke feeling chilled again. This time it was deeper than a draft, like I'd been in a strong wind that had driven cold into my bones. Danial started a fire, and I sat down before it, telling him and myself I was fine. Yet as the morning wore on, despite the fire, I got colder and colder. Finally, my teeth began chattering.

I called Terian on the cell with shaking fingers. "I need you. Come to me."

"What do you need?" Terian said apprehensively.

"Your body heat," I said, trying not to sound seductive. "I'm so cold, I feel like I'm going to freeze. Something's wrong."

"I'll be right there," he said and hung up.

As I waited, I wondered if Terian would bring someone with him to chaperone. I'd apologized for what had happened during The Lust, but he'd stayed at least ten feet from me ever since. I'd let him get his own gift under the tree this Christmas rather than see him back away yet again when I moved toward him.

The memory brought a smile to my face. I'd gotten him a collar and tag for Asher that had her name on it and his.

Terian had protested at once. "Sar, she's really yours—"

"Let's face it, she's always liked you better. She's your cat now and everyone knows it. It's time we made it official."

He thanked me, though I noticed he didn't get any closer to me. "Your gift is in the lower tree branches, near the sparkly unicorn ornament."

I found it easily. It was another tiny vial with a few ounces of something in the bottom.

"What is it?"

"My blood mostly, mixed with a few other things."

Ick. I tried not to let my distaste show. "Why are you giving me your blood?" I said, trying to be smooth about it.

"Remember when you thanked me for what I gave Danial that one night?" Terian said.

I gave him a blank look and then remembered and flushed down to my toes.

He laughed. "That's right, Sar. My blood was what let him behave the way he did."

"How was that discovered?" I said smirking. "Someone thought what the hell, we've tried everything else, let's try demon's blood?"

"Likely an accident," Terian said, frowning. "Some barbarian supernatural being killed a demon and swallowed a tiny bit of blood, then saw a cute peasant woman nearby—"

"Enough," I said, holding up my hands. "I just never thought demon blood could be used so many ways."

"I'm not that unique, really. All of the more potent spells contain demon blood, but older vampires and other supernatural beings also have powerful blood that can be sometimes be substituted or used in spells. Still, demon blood is the most transformative. The demon part of me is where all my power comes from. The human side is basically powerless, in comparison."

"Thank you," I said warmly, pocketing the vial. "I'll put it to good use."

"I know you will," he said suggestively.

Terian knocked at the door, snapping me out of my memory. "Sar?"

"Come in."

"What do you need me to do?" he said cautiously, coming inside.

Okay, say this casually. "I need you to hold me and to let your temperature go back to what it was before you learned to control it. I need you to be hot for me."

"You aren't going to try anything?" he said, looking at me out of the corner of his eye.

"No," I said with a smile. "I haven't felt The Lust in months."

He picked me up easily, moving fast. "Then we should be under blankets." He brought me to the bed and laid me down, then carefully climbed in beside me. Pulling me close, he covered us both with blankets, wrapping his hands in the sheets.

"Tell me if you're too hot," Terian said. "Your clothes and mine should act as a barrier to protect your skin, but be careful of your face and hands."

I nodded. "Go ahead."

Terian's body began to generate heat like an oven. My body absorbed the heat, and I stretched against him, basking in it.

"Better?" he said softly. "I can go hotter."

"This is great," I sighed.

* * * *

Someone was saying my name softly. I opened my eyes to Danial kneeling beside me.

"Now I see why Terian turned his cell off," he said, bemused.

"Danial, I—" Terian began.

"Terian, it's fine. Sar needed you. There's nothing you need to explain," Danial said, caressing my face gently with his hand. "She's still cool, though I can feel your heat from here."

"I was so cold," I said sleepily, rubbing my face on his hand. "Like ice—"

"Stay there and keep warm, darling," Danial said fondly. "I'll watch over us tonight. Call me if her condition changes or she needs something. I'll be outside in the great room—"

I fell back asleep before Danial finished his sentence.

* * * *

After that night, though I still had chills occasionally, I never again got to the point Terian had to warm me. Most of those chills I attributed to Danial going off the potion. Though neither of has spoken of it, he'd continued to take it, remaining warm through mid-January.

As I entered my third trimester, he abruptly stopped taking it, going from warm to cool within a few days. Despite that, I was relieved he was no longer worried about a miscarriage. Getting used to the coolness of his naked body next to mine again at night took some time.

Danial noticed, of course. "Am I making you too cold?"

"No," I said hesitantly. "I'm okay."

Danial stroked my back and kissed up my neck with cool lips. "Good."

"Do you miss it?" I said suddenly.

"Being warm? I admit it felt very uncomfortable—"

"No, sex."

"Of course," Danial replied, moving his hips suggestively against my bottom. "It's been three months almost, but I'm not going to risk you having any trouble for a night's pleasure."

I didn't reply.

"I loved the card," he said softly. "I didn't expect one, especially not from my son-to-be."

I congratulated myself again on my brilliance. "He'll be here soon. I'm glad the nursery is finished. Elle and I put the finishing touches on it this week. Luckily there was room for everything stored there in the basement."

"I'm glad you liked the chocolates," he said happily. "I got the biggest box Godiva offered." He paused. "I was worried, I admit. Last year you asked me not to get you anything for Valentine's Day, to just get something for Elle."

Last year I'd been mourning Theo and had not wanted to celebrate the holiday. "I ate more than I should've," I said lightly, "but I thought, why not indulge? This year at least, I can blame it on being pregnant."

Danial didn't reply. The silence stretched.

"What is it?" I said, turning toward him with difficulty.

"I wanted to reply, but was worried to speak my heart," he said finally.

"Just say it."

"You can eat as much as you like, always," he said gently. "Go to sleep."

I fell quiet instantly, disquieting thoughts taking shape. Danial hadn't been worried about telling me I could get fat. He'd been going to say something to the effect I could use the excuse of being pregnant again in years to come.

I felt a surge of happiness. It was wonderful to be loved as much as he loved me, to know he wanted our child so much. It was even more moving he was willing to go through what we'd endured during this pregnancy again, that he wanted to.

Yet the old problem was still there, marring my joy. Danial would not age. I would. Last time I had left to deal with that and come back with no real answer.

I snuggled closer to him. Fuck it, I didn't need an answer.

Where had all my plans ever got me? All of them had combusted, the ones involving men rather spectacularly. I had a man who was committed to our child and me. That was enough for now. I'd figure out the rest as I went along.

* * * *

The months passed, as February became March. I wasn't freezing, burning up, or trying to grab anyone. The only trouble was I was really big now and uncomfortable all the time in my body. Danial and I went to see Dr. Camlyn weekly now, at Danial's insistence.

"Everything looks fine. The baby is developing normally."

"She looks as if she'll deliver at any moment," Danial said worriedly. "Are you sure the pregnancy isn't further along that you originally thought?"

"May is still the due date, but it might be sooner. You're right. The baby is big. Too big for how many months he is supposed to be."

"Is something wrong?" I was scared.

"Don't worry, Sarelle," Stephen assured me. "This is not outside the norm, even for a human baby. Danial is a tall man. It's normal his child would have his bone structure. He's also right, it's possible you became pregnant earlier than I originally suspected."

"Do you have the results of the test?" Danial said eagerly.

"Yes," Stephen said, giving us a wide smile. "It's indeed a boy."

Danial kissed my hand fiercely, murmuring words I didn't understand.

"Was that Spanish," I asked later, as Terian was driving us home.

"Yes," Danial said, gripping my hand. "I was saying a prayer to God for your safety and giving thanks."

"You once told me you didn't believe in God."

"You've made me believe in many things I'd lost faith in," Danial said lovingly. He gave me a soft kiss.

That night, I lay on my side in bed, propped up on pillows. Danial lay behind me, spooning against me, one arm under my head, and the other resting possessively on my belly. Sometimes the baby kicked for him, and he would stop all movement, waiting again to feel it reaching out, the expression on his face pure joy.

"You're sure of the name? I thought once it was a boy, you'd want to call him Danial Jr."

"No," he said. "We'll call him Theoron after my uncle. We'll call him Theo for short."

Chapter Ten

Despite Stephen's predictions about an early delivery, March passed and became April. As the weeks passed, I grew absolutely miserable. I was too hot, too big, my back too uncomfortable.

I saw Stephen the last week in April.

"Is everything still okay?" Danial asked.

"Yes."

"No, the answer is that everything isn't okay," I said irritably. "It won't be okay until I deliver. Can't you induce labor?"

"Sarelle, most women feel this way, but we don't induce labor unless there's a problem."

"There is a problem," I said crossly. "I need this baby out of me. Now."

"Sorry. The baby isn't ready yet to come out of you yet. Come back in a week for your checkup."

I glared at him and left with Danial.

"We'll stop for Chinese food," Danial said soothingly as we drove home. "You'll like that."

"What I want is some space to myself," I said crankily.

Danial did not leave my side now, afraid he would somehow leave me, and come back to find out he had missed the birth or something had happened to me. This of course had caused some tension.

"You can rest when we get home," he said pleasantly.

"I don't want to rest! I need to go for a walk, Danial."

"Then we'll go for a short walk when we get home," he said stubbornly.

"No," I said, just as stubbornly. "I'm going with Terian."

"No," he said. "You're going with me and Terian."

Nothing I could do would persuade him to give me some time alone. I couldn't sneak out past him in the daytime, either. He woke up once when I'd

174

nearly made it to the front door and brought me back to bed.

"You are staying here," he said with mild anger. "Don't try that again, Sar. I worry too much about you."

"I'm okay," I replied, getting up again. "I just want to sit on the front porch in the sun. I have my cell. I promise I'll call at the first sign of trouble."

"You are staying here if I have to tie you to the bed," he replied angrily. "Now lie down and rest, please."

"I need some time to myself. Alone."

"Too bad, Sar. You gave me your word, and I'm holding you to it. Now lay down."

I lay down fuming and didn't speak to him the rest of the day.

* * * *

A few more days passed this way. Then one evening, I awoke in terrible pain.

"Danial" I gasped. "Something's wrong."

He was awake immediately. "You're ready to deliver. Hold still." He picked me up in his arms, carrying me towards the door. "Terian."

Terian ran up. "What is it?"

"Call Dr. Camlyn and tell him the baby's coming early. I'll get her shoes and coat. Meet me outside in one minute."

Terian dashed for the front door, dialing his cell phone. Cia came from the kitchen as we entered the mudroom.

"Danial, is everything okay?"

Danial slipped on my shoes and put my coat on. "Yes. Watch over Elle. We'll be back soon."

"Good luck," Cia said, squeezing my hand.

Danial carried me out the front door. The Expedition roared up, Terian braking hard, the wheels sliding on the wet pavement to a screeching stop. Danial got into the back seat with me.

"Go."

Terian hit the gas. Danial clutched me tightly as the SUV lurched forward.

As fast as Terian drove, I was sure I'd deliver before we made it there. Every moment was pain and pressure.

"Hold on, we're almost there," Danial said excitedly.

Terian stopped before the door, and Danial helped me out, quickly carrying me inside. Stephen was there waiting for us. He helped me up on the table, put my feet in the stirrups, and checked me over.

"The baby is coming," he said, preparing instruments. "Sar, just breathe and lie still."

"Give me some drugs and give me them now," I said loudly.

"Here," Stephen said, giving me an injection. "Breathe."

Although the pain didn't go away completely, it was now bearable.

"How far apart are your contractions?"

"They're contracting over and over again, trying to push the baby out, but nothing's happening," I said in frustration. "Why isn't anything happening?"

"Don't worry," Stephen soothed. "This is normal. Try to relax."

Angrily, I lay there for a while, feeling my muscles moving, but waiting for something to happen. Danial was on one side of me, and Terian was on the other, looking so excited I wanted to strangle both of them.

"I'm glad we hurried to get here," I said nastily. "Since—"

The first real contraction hit me, and I screamed, feeling as if I was being torn open. Terian and Danial moved as one, grasping my hands. Another one hit, making me gasp.

My water broke and came out of me in a drenching wave. Terian's eyes were huge. Danial was anxious, but calm. Something suddenly moved inside me, raking my insides with what felt like knives.

"Get it out of me!" I screamed.

"Push, Sar," Danial said, stroking my forehead.

"Bear down and push," Stephen said.

"I am pushing," I yelled at them. I bore down and pushed as hard as I could.

"I see the head," Stephen cried out.

"Push again, Sar," Danial said, excited.

I pushed again and felt something tear. I screamed again. "Something is clawing me."

"Once more," Stephen said with trepidation.

I stopped pushing, the note in his voice scaring me deeply.

"Once more, Sar," Danial said urgently, squeezing my hand.

I pushed and something slid out of me. I went limp with relief.

A soft, unnatural noise filled the air, somewhere between a reptile's hiss and a creaking door.

Stephen cut the cord and wrapped the baby in a blanket. "He's okay. Danial, I need you over here."

Again, there was something wrong with his voice. What sort of monster had I given birth to would make him sound like that?

Danial kissed me joyfully and let go of my hand. "Terian, watch over her." He went over to see his son, stepping close to look at him on the table where Stephen was cleaning him off.

He took a sharp intake of breath. "Is Sar okay?" he said at last.

"We have to stop the bleeding," Stephen replied. "Take over for me here. Sar should be fine if we—"

"Why the hell is it you think I can't hear you both," I yelled at them.

"What did it do to me? What's wrong? I felt it claw me up"

"I've got this," Danial said, nodding. "Take care of Sar."

Stephen moved back between my legs and began to clean me up. "Hold still, Sar. I need to see where the blood's coming from."

Danial handed him to Terian. "Watch over him."

Terian recoiled a little, but took Theoron over to stand in the corner.

Danial went to Stephen. "Do you need some of my blood?"

"No, the bleeding is slowing. Sar, don't move until I tell you to."

"Tell me please," I half screamed, half pleaded.

Danial came over and took my hand. "Theo is fine, but he was born with his vampire-half present, not the human-half. He has inch long claws, red eyes, and fangs like mine."

"How am I supposed to nurse him?" I said, upset.

"You can't nurse him," Stephen said. "In fact, you shouldn't even hold him."

I looked down at him, aghast. "Not hold my own child?"

"He's tasted your blood, Sar. It's obvious he wants more. He was trying to bite me as I cleaned him."

"How long until I can?" I whispered.

"Until he's old enough not to attack you. In his current state, he'll need blood, not milk anyway."

I cried then, great racking sobs. Danial held me the best he could while Stephen continued to check me over.

Finally, Stephen stood. "The bleeding has stopped. You should stay in bed for the next week. Only get up to go to the bathroom. Call if you start bleeding again or have pain."

"I'll make sure she does," Danial said. "What about the baby? In your opinion should I arrange for donors, or buy fresh blood?"

"Animal blood? I thought most vampires—"

"Human blood," Danial corrected. "I have some connections now I'm Lord."

Stephen turned to Danial. "Danial, the child is not going to know not to attack to get blood, and he's too young to teach. Keep him away from humans, for now. Sar should not feed him, though she can watch from a safe distance. I can give you powdered blood to mix as a formula for him, we keep some on hand for badly injured vampires. That should feed him okay. I don't want to know any more about your connections."

"Thank you, doctor," Danial said cordially. "May I take her home?"

"Yes. Have her come back in a week for me to check how she's healing. Congratulations to you both."

Danial helped me out, as Terian came after us, carrying Theoron and the bags of powdered blood.

Danial put me in the back and then took the formula from Terian, putting it in the back too.

Terian yelped. "He bit me," he said, sucking his finger.

Danial shut the trunk, then took the baby back from Terian. "He bit you?" he said in surprise. "In that short amount of time?"

"He's hungry," Terian said, laughing.

"He won't bite me," Danial said confidently. "At least more than once," he said a few seconds later.

Terian drove us home. When we arrived, Danial took the baby and formula inside. "I'll feed him. Please put Sar to bed, Terian. I'll be in shortly, darling."

I nodded, exhausted.

Terian carried me inside to the bed, laying me down gently. "Sar, I know it wasn't easy, but believe me, Theoron is beautiful. He has Danial's dark hair already."

"I'm glad," I said, worn out and happy it was all over.

He kissed me on the forehead. "Get some rest, Mom."

I gave him a tired smile. "Thanks."

Danial came in sometime later, waking me. "Sar, are you awake?"

"Yes," I said, yawning. "You knew I was. You've told me you can tell by my breathing when I'm asleep or not. How's Theo?"

"He's so beautiful." He held me gently and sighed. "I can't believe how lucky I am, that after so many centuries, I finally fell in love again and have a son. After everything that's happened between us, you were willing to do this for me, and by some miracle the potion worked for us."

"Are you happy, Danial?"

"I couldn't be happier. This is more than I hoped for." He kissed me. "Cia is feeding him, Sar. I told her you can't do it, and she volunteered to take care of him until he goes back to human form, if not longer. She wanted to take off time anyway to spend with Aran Jr. He's about two now, in terms of maturity."

We had started talking "in terms of maturity" in the past year, because of Elle. What else was there to do when someone seemed nine years old, but was really barely two?

Danial held me to hi. "Sar, I love you more than anything. If there comes a time when you want to give me your oath, or get married, or whatever, just say the word, and we'll do it. I don't ever want to be without you."

I lay in Danial's arms, sighing inside. I wanted to say yes, because it would make him so happy. I wanted to tell him he wouldn't ever be without me. Yet I didn't know that, not for certain. Promising what I wasn't sure I could give in the heat of the moment was the worst thing to do.

"If I ever decide to, Danial, you'll be the first to know," I said, kissing him softly. "It's enough to just be here with you, to know you love me, and that I love you. That we've made a child together. Tell me you love me again."

"I love you."

* * * *

The next week passed slowly. It was icky, not being able to take a shower or bath. I cleaned myself as best I could and tried to sleep as much as possible. There was one good thing: I felt more comfortable already in my own skin. Some of the weight I'd gained was already coming off. I could tell by how my clothes fit.

The bleeding didn't start again, but my insides ached dully where I'd felt the claws rake me. As the days passed the discomfort persisted enough so I finally told Danial about the pain one night.

"The cuts are shallow according to my sense of smell," he said, "Lie back and hold still."

I did as he asked. He spread my legs, bit into his finger, then gently inserted it into my vagina. He moved his finger slowly a few times. The aching disappeared.

"Thanks," I said awkwardly.

He slipped his finger out. "Don't be embarrassed. Is the pain gone?"

"Yes," I said, relieved.

"That's what matters," he said, hugging me. "I just hope Camlyn tells you tomorrow you're able to get out of bed. Everyone wants to see you."

"And I want to see them," I said happily. "It will be good to rejoin the world."

* * * *

The next evening, I waited grumpily in the stirrups as Dr. Camlyn checked me over.

"Did Danial give you his blood to heal, Sarelle?" he said, strangely upset.

"Yes," I said defensively. "I'm glad he did."

He looked grim, but didn't say whatever was on his mind.

"Are we done?" Danial said impatiently. "Sar hasn't seen Theoron all week. I'd really like to get her home."

"Theoron had claws when he was born," Stephen said. "I think he may have clawed you up inside, Sarelle. I need to look. There may be some pain."

"Go ahead," I said grumpily. "You already took five vials of blood. How much worse could whatever you're going to do be?"

"Do you want Danial to be here when I do the procedure?" he said.

Danial gave him an odd look, his eyes tinting red momentarily.

"Of course," I said quickly.

Danial took my hand. "What is bothering you? Is she okay?"

"Let me look, and I'll tell you," Stephen said coolly. "You'll be able to see everything I see on the monitor to your right."

He slowly inserted the device inside me. I flinched, feeling a little pain. Danial held my hand, telling me it would be over soon.

Stephen turned on the monitor, focused the lens and gasped.

I tried to get up immediately.

Danial held me there. "Stephen, what's wrong?"

Stephen didn't answer, panning the lens around at the walls of my uterus. Watching the monitor, I thought they looked okay, but never having seen them before, who was I to know?

"Stephen, speak," Danial said. Anger was heavy in his tone mixed with a little fear.

Stephen looked at us and pursed his lips. "Danial, I need a sample of your blood."

Danial began rolling up his shirtsleeve. Stephen quickly took the blood sample and then set it near one of mine. "I need to check a few things. You two sit tight." He left, taking our two samples with him.

"What is it?" I looked at Danial. "I'm afraid."

"Don't worry," he soothed me. "Theoron and you are healthy and that's all that matters. The worst thing I can surmise is you're anemic, from losing so much blood during the delivery."

"What if it's something worse?"

"Then I'll help you through it," he said staunchly, kissing my hand. "You're going to be fine."

The minutes passed, but Stephen didn't return.

"What is taking him so long?" I said angrily. "This is unbelievable!"

"He wants to be sure of something," Danial said calmly. "We want him to be sure, Sar, especially if it's something important. It's only been a half hour. Have patience."

I was not five years old and resented his talking down to me. "Easy for you to say."

"On the contrary, it's not easy at all," Danial said flatly. "Us bickering won't help."

I looked away, knowing he was right.

After a few more minutes, Stephen finally came back and sat down heavily in front of us. "I'm sorry, but I have bad news for you both."

"Tell us," Danial said, his hand squeezing mine.

"Sar, you were badly clawed up by Theoron. There are scars running all across the inside of your uterus."

"What's that mean?" I said.

Danial echoed my question.

"It's unlikely you'll ever have another child," Stephen said. "I'm sorry."

I took a shaky breath, and Danial hugged me.

"Why?" I managed.

"There is too much scar tissue on the sides of your womb. A baby won't be able to adhere so it can grow. If you get pregnant, you'll most likely lose the baby, probably before you even know you're pregnant."

By Stephen's tone, he thought he was delivering crushing news, but I wasn't devastated. I'd had one child with a man I loved. That would have to be enough.

"There must be something you can suggest," Danial demanded. "Sar has made my dream come true. I will not accept her cost for that was to lose one of her own."

I turned to him in surprise. He was more upset than I'd ever seen him, tears in his eyes.

"Danial, it's okay," I said gently. "I don't blame you."

"I blame myself," he said, anguished.

"You must accept it," Stephen said. "Whatever you intended, that's what happened."

"Isn't there anything we can do?" Danial said desperately, looking hopefully at Stephen. "There must be something you know we can try."

"Sar has healed as well as she was able." Stephen looked at Danial angrily. "She has healed too well, in fact."

I looked at Stephen in confusion. "What?"

"What are you saying?" Danial said slowly.

"Sarelle can take off her collar, can't she?" Stephen said.

"Yes," Danial replied. "We discovered she could do so right when Elle was born, a few years ago—"

"A few years ago?" Stephen yelled. "You never thought to mention that to me?"

"Talk plainly," Danial rasped, his eyes completely red. "What are you getting at?"

"Didn't you ever wonder why she could?" Stephen said, exasperated.

"We thought it was his blood, the blood he took from me, and the blood he'd given me to heal the wounds," I said.

"It was his blood," Stephen said, glancing at me. "That's why you can take off the collar. There was a reason I asked him not to take your blood while you were pregnant."

"Will you say it already, before I shake it out of you?" Danial growled.

"Danial, you have been with Sar for a year and a half now. You are taking her blood regularly and giving her yours to heal her. You were having sex, too. What did you think was going to happen?"

Danial's face went white. "She hasn't had enough," he whispered. "I was careful to space out our times together. I have given her my blood only a very few times, just to heal her worst wounds and drunk none of hers for the past year—"

"That doesn't matter. Your other bodily fluids are getting into her systems on a regular basis. That is all it takes, given enough time."

"Will you both tell me what you're talking about?" I said loudly.

Stephen looked at me, resigned. "He's turning you, Sar."

Chapter Eleven

"What?" I screamed, suddenly panicked.

"He's turning you into a vampire. That's the only reason you didn't bleed to death having Theoron. The scratches he inflicted healed a lot faster than a normal human could heal them. I suspected that when you delivered, but the blood test confirmed it."

"Can it be reversed?" I said, scared.

"You aren't a vampire yet, but you're really close, according to your blood levels of the virus. That is why the choker responds to you so well. Moreover, it's his choker and he would be your sire."

"That isn't true," Danial protested. "My brother has turned women. Even as vampire, they are unable to unfasten their collars themselves."

"He's turned women wearing other vampire's chokers at those vampire's requests," Stephen retorted. "To my knowledge he's never turned a woman wearing his own. Sar's tainted blood has a very similar arrangement your choker recognizes, because the virus in her all came from you."

"If you're right, what can we do?" Danial said.

"I don't want to be a vampire," I said desperately

"Then no more biting her, or unprotected sex. Especially no more giving her your blood, Danial, not for any reason," Stephen said, putting emphasis on the word "any".

So basically, no more being with Danial. I shot him an anguished look.

"If we don't stop," Danial said brokenly, "how long would we have?"

"A couple of weeks," Stephen said flatly. "Maybe more or less."

Danial sighed. "What do you suggest?"

"Sarelle needs to get away from you, Danial. Frankly, if you live together and sleep in the same bed, you are going to want to be together. At this point, all it will take is a couple more times of being with each other for her to turn."

"For how long?" Danial asked quickly.

"At least a few months, if not more. Time enough to see if her blood will go back to normal or not."

"What if it doesn't?" Danial growled, suddenly furious. "What if we spend months apart and she's still partly turned? I don't want to be without her for one day, much less months."

"Do you want to take the chance you'll turn her accidentally?" Stephen said quietly.

"No." Danial closed his eyes and kissed my hand. "No, I don't."

I found my voice. "Why did this happen now?" I yelled at Stephen. "We were intimate every night for months the first time we were together. He took my blood and gave me his—"

"That was before he drank Devlin's blood," Stephen said. "Devlin's blood was powerful. It made Danial's blood more potent. He could make vampires where he couldn't before. That's the difference."

I closed my eyes. Finally, when we were happy and things were going okay, this had to happen.

Danial gathered me to him and hugged me. "Can Sar get up and walk around now, or do you still suggest bed rest?"

"She's healed. She should take it easy, but normal activity, like walking is fine."

"Thank you," Danial said, pushing Stephen from the room. He turned to me. "Sar, please get dressed." Then he left.

Hurriedly, I dressed. When I emerged from the room, Terian was waiting for me.

"Danial said you were healed," he said, curious, "but he was very upset. What's the matter?"

"Nothing," I lied. "Stephen said I'd probably have no more children."

"I'm so sorry," Terian said, clearly horrified.

"Don't be," I said, shrugging. "I've got two kids and that's enough. I'd really like to go home."

Terian nodded and followed me out. Danial was waiting behind the wheel. Terian gave him an odd look, but didn't say anything as he got into the passenger seat in front. I slipped into the back seat.

No one spoke on the trip home. I barely noticed the trip because I was so consumed by my thoughts.

Danial and I could be together and not exchange blood. We'd done it the entire time we'd been trying for Theoron and more than half of the time that I'd been pregnant. We'd had a lot of unprotected sex then, and now we would have to use condoms. Maybe it was the sex and not the blood that brought me to the edge of the precipice upon which I found myself standing.

Maybe this was why there were no dhamphirs before now. There had been no way around the Lust, no way of stopping it besides the biting and bloodletting. How many vampires could have been near a woman behaving as I had and acted with Danial's restraint? Something told me the number was low. How much more blood would Danial and I have needed to share to turn me? By Stephen's tone, not very much.

"Sar, we're home," Terian said.

I come back to myself. Terian was holding the door open for me. Danial was nowhere in sight.

"Female vampires are sterile, too, right?"

Terian gave me a curious look. "Yes, of course. Something in the vampire virus causes sterility."

If I'd turned, I would have lost the baby when I changed. "Can female vampires take the potion?"

"No," Terian said, giving me an odd look. "From what I've read, their entire reproductive system shuts down, outside of menstruation. There's no potion existing capable of restarting it because it's so much more complex than a man's or that can keep it going for the nine months necessary to grow a child."

I had walked a fine line having Theoron. I hadn't realized how fine it had been until now.

"Danial went inside," Terian added. "He said he'd be right back."

Terian's previous words sank in. "Female vampires have their periods forever?"

He nodded. "If they're turned before menopause, yes."

I shuddered at the thought and got out of the car. "It's probably good I don't know any, then. They've got to be miserable."

Terian laughed as we walked to the door. "Some of them have surgery to remove their reproductive organs. It wasn't an option until a few decades ago, but it can be done now."

I didn't reply.

"I'm glad you're home," Suri said, giving me a hug. "Do you want something to eat?"

Home, but would it be for much longer?

"Sar?"

"No, thanks," I said quickly. "I'm heading in to shower."

"Do it fast," Suri replied. "Everyone will be here in another hour for your celebration. Cia is getting Elle and Theoron ready right now."

I nodded, not really listening and went into the bedroom. I started the water and took off my clothes, then stepped under the spray.

It was the first week of May now and summer was coming. I could always go back to my house for the summer. I'd be alone, but what other option was there?

I quickly washed my hair, loving the feeling of being clean. A bad snarl made me grimace, and I spent the next few minutes working out the tangled mass.

It was as long now as it had been when I oathed to Danial, down to my hips. I was all for being sexy, but there was a limit to how much time every day I was willing to devote to my hair. Maybe it was time to go short again…

Danial's arms went around me. "Are you okay?" he said softly.

"No," I said honestly. "I'm afraid of you turning me. I'm afraid of having to leave you. I don't know what to do. I'm pissed off we finally seem to be making it work and now this had to happen."

"I'm sorry for the part I played in this, Sar. You know I didn't do this on purpose, right?"

I turned in his arms and hugged him. "Of course," I said, putting my arms around his neck and kissing him.

The kiss deepened and in a moment, he had me against the shower wall, kissing me hard, his tongue sliding into my mouth. His erection pressed to my belly. It had been almost six months of no sex. Now I was healed, it was just him and me, and I remembered with vivid clarity just how good he could be.

"I want you," I whispered urgently.

He helped me out of the shower quickly. "Dry off. I'll meet you in bed."

I dried sporadically, put some conditioner in my hair quickly, then ran into the bedroom. Danial was waiting for me on the bed, a condom already in place. A second later, he was on me, easing inside. He felt wonderful, and I shifted my hips to help him. Inflamed with passion, we sought each other's flesh with abandon, cries of eagerness permeating the air. Before long, our orgasms broke over us, and we came screaming together.

He squeezed my body close to his, holding it tightly. "I don't want you to go, Sar," he said, breathing rapidly. "I'll do whatever I have to, but say you won't go."

"I won't go," I said softly.

Danial's face relaxed into that soft look of his I loved so much. He rolled off me, threw away the condom, and crawled back beside me.

"I'm so relieved," he whispered. "I was worried—"

Terian knocked on the door.

"What is it?" Danial said, in the voice of a man who was in the middle of something important.

"In case you two forgot, there's a party waiting for you out here."

I blushed red, thinking of all those people outside the door listening to me screaming my head off.

Danial was not embarrassed in the least. "We'll be right out."

We got dressed in a few minutes. I was still too big around the middle to wear my jeans, so I settled for some maternity leggings and a large shirt. I'd just had a baby. I was not going for vixen just yet. Maybe in a few weeks, when I had a chance to do some walking.

Danial took my hand and escorted me out into the great room. The guards were all there, including Aran Jr. Everyone was milling about, drinking and eating.

Aran came up to me. "Hi, Sar." He leaned in close. "Suri has broken up with Ivan, and he and Demetri are friends again. Thought you should know."

"What about Suri?" She hadn't looked upset earlier.

"Suri is taking some time alone, at least, that is the phrase Cia used. She's pulling guard duty tonight, running solo."

"Good. I didn't want to see any of them leave."

Cia came up and hugged me and then proudly showed me her son who was just learning to walk. Aran Jr. was handsome already like his father. He had Cia's blond hair, but Aran's eyes, though they were a little darker than his father's. One by one, the rest of the foxes came up to me, saying they were happy I was better. It was wonderful to feel all the love in the room and to know they all cared so much for me.

Elle ran up to me, looking bigger already than she had the last time I saw her. I hugged her hard, as she practically squeezed the life out of me. "Mom, I missed you. They wouldn't let me see you, because you were sleeping."

"I'm all better now though," I said, hugging her. "I love you, Elle."

"I love you, too," she said, hugging me back. "Thank you for giving me a brother. I love Theo."

When she said those words, all the noise around me seemed to stop. A tremor passed through me. I felt alone suddenly in the midst of the party with Theo's ghost.

"I need some air," I said to Cia. "Keep an eye on Elle?"

"Sure," she said.

I walked out onto the front porch, closing the door on the noise inside. Slowly, I walked from the front to the side of the house and back. For a few moments, I stood there looking into the black trees.

I should have asked Danial to name our baby something else. Theo had been gone almost two years. Yet only I had to hear his name, and I remembered everything he'd been to me.

Danial had done so much for me. We'd had a child together. Yet I was here at the party for our baby, missing my lover of two years ago and not thinking of Danial at all. Guilt overwhelmed me.

It was warm now. It would be time to plant soon. Maybe I should leave because I didn't deserve Danial, Theoron, or this good life.

"Sar, are you okay?"

I turned. Terian was coming toward me.

"No," I admitted. "I miss Theo. I hadn't realized how it would feel to hear his name again."

"Sar, that's normal. You loved him."

I didn't mention the turning scare to him. He'd tell me to leave before I turned, but he hadn't seen Danial's face. "I should just ask everyone to call the baby Theoron."

"Sar," Terian said seriously, then abruptly went quiet.

I looked at him, waiting for him to finish.

Footsteps came up the deck slowly, each footfall deliberately loud. Terian and I both turned.

"It's touching," a cold, sarcastic voice said "You're still good friends after all these years."

Devlin emerged from the shadows, walking closer. He looked as ruthless and gorgeous as he had more than a year ago.

"The party's inside," Terian said, stepping closer to me.

"The hostess is out here," Devlin replied evenly. "Go inside if you want to."

Terian didn't move or reply.

I'd known I'd have to see Devlin eventually. I was just lucky he'd stayed away so long. "Why are you here?"

"To see my nephew, of course," Devlin said with a grin, his golden eyes shining.

"Come in then," I said reluctantly, moving past him.

Devlin reached out and stopped me. "Wait, please."

I braced myself, sure he was going to say something nasty about Theo or me.

"These are for you," he said, handing me two dozen fire and ice roses with a large silver bow.

My jaw hit the floor. "Thanks," I said finally, taking them.

"Sar, I wanted to tell you I'm sorry for what happened before, with you and me."

"For trying to kill me, you mean?" I said charmingly. "For scaring the hell out of me, hurting me, and leaving the scar on my neck I'm wearing right now?"

"For past transgressions en masse," he said politely. "I know what you went through to have this child with my brother. I know what Theoron means to him. It means a great deal to me to have a new immediate relative, much less a nephew, something I thought I'd never live to see if I lasted another thousand years." He went to one knee. "I have been a bastard, but even worse, I've been an utter fool." He lowered his eyes. "Forgive me."

I didn't want to. I didn't want his flowers, beautiful though they might be.

Devlin didn't move from his position. I debated leaving him here and dropping the flowers at his feet. What stopped me was the truth in his words. Theoron was his nephew. Devlin was my baby's uncle, his only living relation on Danial's side. If something happened to Danial and I, who would take care of Theoron until he was grown? Who else would be qualified as Devlin was, who would know firsthand what a vampire needed to live?

"You aren't a thousand," I said softly. "Danial's only four hundred plus."

"True, though some nights it feels that way," Devlin said with a smirk.

"This looks familiar," Terian said scathingly. "You on your knees."

Devlin gave him a faint smile. "Maybe so." He turned back to me. "I do this out of respect for you, not him. Let us heal the animosity between us."

"Why?" I asked warily.

"I'd like to visit with my brother and nephew as often as my schedule permits. Danial forbade me from coming here and said you had to give permission. I ask for that permission now. If you wish not to be present when I visit, I'll do my best to stay out of your sight."

"Don't give in to him," Terian growled, blackness coiling from him.

I shifted the flowers in my arms, and their enticing scent wafted up to my nose. I brought them closer and took a deep breath. They were heavenly.

"Call first, always," I said softly. "Yes, you can visit."

"Danial said you liked flowers," Devlin said hesitantly.

"I do," I gave him a smile that was trying hard not to be a grimace.

"Good," he said, giving me another wide smile. "May I get up now?"

"Yes," I said, breaking into a small smile. "Come inside. Danial will want to see you, and you can see Theoron."

Devlin got to his feet. "Lead on, lady."

The three of us went back inside. All talk hushed when Devlin entered with us. I led him quickly to the bassinet set up in the center of the great room.

Theoron lay with his eyes closed, looking the image of Danial. I saw nothing of me in him until he opened his eyes. They were a dark green like a spruce tree branch.

"He has your eyes," Devlin said to me. "May I hold him?"

"He may bite you," Terian cautioned, obviously hoping for that.

"He's right," I said sadly, resting my hand on the edge of the bassinet.

Theoron immediately sniffed the air and turned to strike at me, his fangs bared.

Devlin grabbed him so fast, he moved as a blur. "No, no."

Theoron turned to him, smelling him. The tiny fangs receded, until his teeth were normal.

"So you know vampire blood won't taste as good as human already?" Devlin murmured. "You're going to be a smart one."

Danial came up and shook hands with Devlin, sliding his arm possessively around me. "I'd wondered when you'd arrive, Dev."

"He's beautiful, Danial," Devlin said lovingly, cradling Theoron in his arms. "He looks just like you."

"Thank you," Danial said modestly.

I smiled. This was almost comical, after all that had happened with the three of us, but all families fought and then made up, right? So long as Devlin behaved himself, I had no problem with him visiting if I didn't have to be there.

The rest of the night went peacefully. Eventually, everyone left. Devlin was the last to go. Danial and I put Elle to bed, and Cia went to put down Theoron for the night.

"She'll be back at dawn to feed him," Danial told me as we let the dogs out. "Janice is taking care of him at night. He wants to eat or, I should say drink, every few hours."

"That's such a relief," I said tiredly. "Can you go let the cats out of the pet room? I locked them in so no one would escape out an open door."

Danial nodded. "I'll meet you in the bedroom."

I called the dogs in, turned off the lights, and went in to Danial. He was waiting for me in bed, under the covers. I took off my clothes and slipped in beside him.

"Here," I said, handing him Terian's vial.

"Is this what I think it is?" Danial asked.

"A present from Terian to us," I said seductively. "If you're in the mood to celebrate, that is. We were interrupted earlier."

He downed it and put the vial on the nightstand. "It's good I laid in a supply of protection," he said. "Come here."

* * * *

The next morning when I got up, Danial was still asleep. I kissed him and went out to have breakfast with Elle. After she left for her lessons, I shared my milk with Cavity and made a list. Now my life was finally mine again, it was time to get back into a routine. First on the list was exercise. I walked for a few miles with the dogs in the woods. Afterwards, I took a good hard look at my body. It really wasn't too bad; I had some fat around my middle, but not too much extra on my hips or thighs. With effort, it shouldn't be too hard to lose.

Next, I walked over to see Cia and Aran.

She looked at me. "Are you going to go back to the house for the summer like last year?"

"I have to talk to Danial about it," I said vaguely. "Is Terian in his lab?"

"Probably," Aran answered. "He spends most of his free time there or in target practice. Makes sense; Danial and he will be going out on jobs again in a few weeks."

"Thanks. See you later."

Terian's lab was empty; all the jars lined up neatly.

I walked out to the woods and listened. Soon enough, single spaced out shots came from the spot we normally used for target practice. I walked into the clearing and was just in time to see him hit the bull's eye of a target lined up about forty feet away.

"That's good for the semiautomatic you're holding." I gave him a round of applause. He smiled and bowed.

"Seriously," I said, eyeing his handiwork on the other targets, "that's really good, Terian."

"How is it you seem to be able to find me no matter where I am?" he said, giving me an odd look.

I was surprised at his emotional tone. It was clear he wanted me to find him, to be able always to find him.

"There are a limited amount of places you could be, Terian," I said lightly. "I just followed the shots."

"Are you out for a walk?" he said, again all business.

"Yes," I said resolutely. "I have weight I want to lose."

"Sarelle, you'll always be beautiful," he said, giving me an appreciative smile.

"Thanks, but I know how I used to look, and I want to look that way again. Soon." I smiled to soften my words.

"Want some company then?" he said. "I'm almost done here."

"Sure."

I helped him gather up the targets and store them in the shed. He holstered his gun, and we walked into the woods.

"Are you happy, Terian?" I said as we walked.

"Yes," he said. "I like being here with everyone. I'm thinking of calling Tatiana and asking her out."

"After all this time?" I said incredulous. "You mean you never called her? She clearly wanted you to. She was interested."

"I'd just broken up with Sundown. I was going to marry her. I don't move that fast from one person to another."

I flushed down to my toes and didn't say anything.

"Sar, I didn't mean—"

"I know what you meant," I said curtly.

"No one thinks—"

"Don't they?" I said softly. "You clearly do."

191

"No, I don't," he said stubbornly.

I dropped it, and we walked for a while leisurely, talking about the weather and the coming summer and my plans for it..

"I'm not sure," I admitted. "Danial and Elle don't want to go back."

"Then why don't you sell the place?" Terian said.

"I might be moving back by myself," I said sadly.

Terian grabbed me by the shoulders. "What the hell are you talking about? Tell me everything!"

"Being with Danial so long and having Theoron…well, it's put me close to becoming vampire," I said heavily. "Camlyn advised me to leave for a while, but I've promised Danial not to—"

"You need to leave," Terian said worriedly, taking me by the shoulders. "Get away before you don't have an option anymore. I know you love him, but—"

"He promised to abide by what Dr. Camlyn said. If he doesn't share bodily fluids with me, then I'll be fine—"

"Sar, if he does it by accident, it's still done. Then he'll have power over you in ways he doesn't now. He'd be your sire, your master. You'll never walk in the sun on a spring day like this with me again."

"Terian, he would never do that—"

"I know a reason he would," Terian said darkly.

"What reason?" I stared at him.

"In order to keep you with him, Sar."

"I'm already with him, Terian. What do you know that I don't?" I said harshly, my hands on my hips.

He looked at me, clearly considering his words.

"What?" I screamed. "What is Danial afraid of? Spit it out."

"Theo's alive," he said roughly.

The End

Coming soon

Taken for his Own, Book 4 of the Promise Me Series

Taken in the Night

Tara Fox Hall

Taken in the Night

www.ingramcontent.com/pod-product-compliance
Lightning Source LLC
Chambersburg PA
CBHW020436180626
46812CB00003B/1266